ℭATFISH

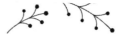

'This thought-provoking debut combines
magical realism and Japanese myths with an
exploration of grief, time and memory.'

The Bookseller

'A powerful voice in YA fiction. I cannot recommend
it highly enough. Myth and mystery, tragedy and time
weave together in an exquisitely crafted story of love,
loss and belonging... I adored it.'

Deirdre Sullivan, author of *Wise Creatures*

'Excellent, evocative and thoughtful with
genuine depth... I feel as if I'm in the hands of
a writer who knows what she's doing.'

**Nicola Yoon, author
of *Everything, Everything***

'Sensational. Breathtakingly
original and beautifully written.'

**Katya Balen, author of
October, October, winner of the
YOTO Carnegie Medal 2022**

CATFISH ROLLING

CLARA KUMAGAI

ZEPHYR
An imprint of Head of Zeus

First published in the UK in 2023 by Zephyr, an imprint of Head of Zeus
This Zephyr paperback edition first published in the UK in 2024
by Head of Zeus, part of Bloomsbury Publishing Plc

9 7 5 3 1 2 4 6 8

A catalogue record for this book is available from the British Library.

ISBN (PB): 9781803288055
ISBN (E): 9781803288024

Typeset and designed
by Ed Pickford and Jessie Price

Printed and bound in Great Britain by
CPI Group (UK) Ltd, Croydon CR0 4YY

Head of Zeus Ltd
5–8 Hardwick Street
London EC1R 4RG

WWW.HEADOFZEUS.COM

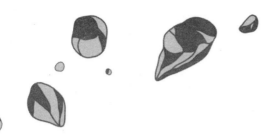

For Ronald, who told me where the wild
things are.

And to all those whose lives were affected
when the catfish rolled.

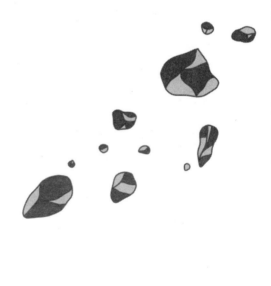

永

ETERNITY

There's a catfish under the islands of Japan. That's what shakes everything up: the catfish twisting and turning in the mud beneath us. It rolls and the ground trembles, water crashes, time cracks and breaks.

I hate that catfish.

When it happened, it was springtime. The cherry blossoms looked like clouds – so pink and fluffy, they might rain sugar. I ate sakura mochi and the saltiness of the leaf surprised me. Ojiichan fed me dango whenever my mother wasn't looking. I was eleven years old.

Me and Dad were in the supermarket. Mom was at home with Ojiichan. She was airing the futons, hanging them out of the wide windows upstairs, laying them along the roof. She had wanted me to help, but I wouldn't. I'd whined until Dad said he would take me with him to get food for dinner and Mom had sighed and given in.

I wandered up and down the aisles, prodding mysterious packets, picking up sweets and bringing them to Dad, usually for them to be rejected. Even though we came to Japan at least once a year, it was still like a wonderland, everything strange and brightly coloured. Dad wheeled the trolley serenely and reminded me of the shopping list, while I sneaked in snacks and desserts.

'Natto,' he said. 'Pickled daikon. Kombu dashi.'

I retrieved them, inspecting the pictures if the writing wasn't within the limited range of the kanji we knew.

'Get something sweet for your mother,' Dad said.

'Sure!' She might still be annoyed that I hadn't stayed at home with her, so I had to choose something good.

I decided on mochi ice cream. It was cold in my hand when the ground began to shake.

Some people paused, others shrugged and continued pushing their trolleys. I wasn't used to earthquakes and I stayed still, waiting for the shiver to end, as if the ground had just become a little chilly. But it got stronger and stronger, and people began to move to the doors, panicked but remaining orderly. Then things started to fall off shelves. I clung to the side of the freezer until I heard Dad shouting my name.

'I'm here, I'm here!' I yelled back.

He ran to me and grabbed my hand. We rushed out, as jars and bottles smashed everywhere. Everyone had gathered in the car park, but now the ground was shaking so hard it was difficult to stand up. I fell down and Dad crouched beside me and put his arms around me. There was a screeching that made me think of the gate at my school back home in Vancouver, which was metal and old and when it dragged over the uneven concrete it sounded the same, but this was a giant version, and if this was a gate then was it being opened or closed? There was a groaning that was probably buildings splintering or glass cracking, but might also have been the earth itself breaking, shrieking as it stretched and tore apart. It was thunder and lightning beneath the ground, it was something alive and twisting deep in the centre of the earth.

I put my hands on the tarmac to hold myself up, or maybe to try to hold the ground down, and I realised that I had run out of the shop with the mochi ice cream now softening and melting. I thought, *I hope Mom doesn't mind.*

'Mom,' I shouted, and when I looked at Dad I could tell that's what he was thinking too.

I tried to stand but Dad pulled me back. 'Wait,' he

told me. 'We have to wait.' His voice was calm but his arms held me so hard that they trembled.

When the shaking finally stopped, the alarms began. The noise of frightened people grew louder and we all began to run to cars, along streets to our homes, clutching phones and calling parents and children.

Dad called home, holding the phone tight to his ear, and the longer he held it there, saying nothing, the faster my heart beat, until the pounding in my ears was like an alarm all of its own. He tapped in another number and then another.

'Where are they?' I asked.

He said, 'I don't know.'

We got in the car even though we weren't supposed to. There were policemen and ambulances and fire engines, but Dad ignored any that tried to wave us down. I stared out of the window and saw roofs of houses slumping and smoke rising and people everywhere. Some were walking or running and some weren't moving at all.

The ice cream was still in my hand. It was almost entirely melted inside the wrapper. *If I put it in the freezer, it will be fine. It will freeze again,* I repeated over and over, as we drove along. *It'll freeze. It'll be fine. It'll freeze.*

Dad slowed the car and swore. The road ahead was blocked with cars, bumper to bumper, not moving. He rolled down the window and waved at a passing policeman, who paused, wiping sweat from his forehead, saying, *No further, no further.* Dad got his phone out again and started tapping and waiting, tapping and waiting, and I sat quietly. People were getting out of their cars. Some were going on ahead, others were turning back.

And then something happened. I didn't know what it was then, only that something had shifted in a way that had never taken place before, like the texture of the air thickened, or the temperature dropped, or the lights went out, except it wasn't any one of those things. It was the sensation of things switching, moving, fracturing. Dad felt it too. He lowered the phone from his ear and everybody around us paused, steadying themselves against each other or cars or the ground. On the radio, there was a sudden silence.

It felt as though the world had stopped, and for a handful of heartbeats we all floated, suspended in space. My ears popped, and then gravity or momentum returned with a *whoosh*, like a huge wave breaking over the land. We were all thrown about – some backwards, some forwards, because it wasn't water or wind that had crashed over us. It was *time*.

I think I fainted then, because it was all black, and when my memory started again, Dad was holding me in his arms, even though I was too big for them, and we were at the roadblock that the police had set up. He was shouting at them, but they wouldn't let him through. From his arms, I stared up at the sky and saw that something was very wrong. The clouds looked like they had been shattered, or cut by some gigantic knife.

Over the buildings, smoke was trailing, but plumes right beside each other were rising faster and then slower, as if they were being tugged by different currents of air.

I felt dizzy and sick and I buried my face in Dad's chest. He was breathing rapidly and I could hear his heart galloping.

He put me on my feet. 'We have to go somewhere safer to wait.'

He held my hand and he walked so fast I had to jog to keep up. We weaved through cars and people and I focused on the ground because I didn't want to see the nightmare sky. I noticed that my other hand was empty; I'd lost the ice cream for Mom. I shouted and Dad turned to me.

'What's wrong?'

I twisted out of his grip and started to run back towards the car, but there were so many people coming towards us, all trying to get away, that I was tangled up in legs and rushing bodies. Dad was yelling at me but I couldn't stop and didn't until I felt his arms grab me and lift me roughly.

'What are you doing?' he shouted. He shook me, hard.

'The ice cream,' I said. 'It's for Mom. I lost it. It's for her.'

Maybe it was the shaking that did it, but my tears came loose and I was crying and Dad hugged me and then, without a word, took my hand again, and we made our way back up the hill with everyone else, trying to escape from whatever had happened behind us.

We had been shaken. Our entire world shook.

春分

VERNAL EQUINOX

1

I didn't want to come to my high school graduation ceremony, but here I am. The chair is hard and I'm hot and uncomfortable in my uniform even though it's only March, and why do so many people have so much to say and for such a long time? There are only so many ways you can say that we should be proud, that we should keep working hard, that the future is waiting for us. None of it applies to me, but my classmates are bright-eyed, faces set with both determination and happiness. I try to arrange my mouth and eyes in the same way, but it makes my face feel weird. I glance at Koki, sitting further down the row with the other boys, but he's staring straight ahead like everyone else.

I try to concentrate on the student president guy who's speaking now. He's tearing up too – funny, because he's always been the serious type who only shows emotion when he gets his grades. I wonder what university he's going to go to, and if he'll cry when he gets there. When he finally finishes, it's time for us to collect our diplomas. There are only two classes in my grade, and mine is called first. We line up neatly, waiting to walk across the stage and receive our nice pieces of paper.

I glance at the rows of families and teachers. Mothers are wiping their eyes, some fathers too. I search for Dad as subtly as possible, through the men in their black and navy suits. He's not there. It's boring, obviously, and I wouldn't have wanted to come either, no way. My heart burns.

It's my turn now. I'm concentrating on not falling over and trying to remember what a normal walk looks like, when there's a shuffle and a murmur at the back of the hall. It's Dad, sidling in and trying to squeeze into the back row of seats. He dips his head and apologises and people move to let him pass. He settles into a chair, pale-faced, blond-grey hair dishevelled, wearing a suit with a wrinkled shirt. Some of the teachers look back, and then at me, and the principal clears his throat. I realise I'm frozen on the stage and I thaw into hot embarrassment. I take my diploma without making eye contact with the principal and then escape to my seat. I stare up at the ceiling, not at the other students or back at Dad, and pretend that I'm gazing into my dazzling future, and not just empty space.

I can't pretend for long. I lower my eyes to my watch. A watch is a beautiful thing. It holds time right there, strapped to your wrist, pinned on a disc the size of a five-hundred-yen coin. I wear my mother's watch, always. It's ugly. The silvery steel is tarnished around the edges, and the hands are thick and decisive as they move around the hours and minutes, marked in black on a white face. It's never failed me.

I'm told I check the time too often. It annoys teachers, makes me appear rude, like I'm bored or waiting for the conversation to end. But I need to know what time it is, and that it's still running at the right pace, that it's running at all.

Everyone has their diplomas now, but the principal starts droning on about perseverance, and I count the seconds that I won't ever get back. There are some people in my town who've stopped caring about polite punctuality; who've thrown their watches away, put all the clocks in the house in the bin, who've set the oven or rice cooker to 0:00. Maybe they got tired of measuring time and never knowing if it was right. Or they simply didn't want to be reminded of it.

The class is smaller than when I joined it seven years ago. A lot of people moved away, to the places where you don't have to think about the time except when you're rushing for the bus, or when your egg is boiling, or when you have to tell your kids that it's past their bedtime. A few people became obsessed with time, like me. Like Dad.

'Why is time doing that, Sora-chan?' he asks me. 'How? And why?'

I have no answer. He doesn't really expect me to have one, but he always wants me to try. He never asks me why I check the time because he knows; he's the one who taught me that experiments need to be monitored.

I look over at Koki again, and he gives me a sidelong glance. I roll my eyes and he flicks his gaze forward, trying not to smile. I don't feel like smiling.

I met Koki in a time zone, back when kids used to dare each other over the boundary lines. Even then, not many would do it. It was after school one day, just before the summer break, everyone giddy at the prospect of a holiday. That was why I'd tagged along with a group of kids from the class instead of going home alone, like I almost always did. We traipsed through fields, into the thin woods that ran beside a section of the boundary fence that wasn't patrolled. Some of the other kids said they had been there before. We gathered at a point where the fence had been pulled apart, a gap wide enough for a thirteen-year-old to fit through and cross over into places where time ran faster.

We all stood around. I hovered at the back of the group, interested to see what would happen; the kids in my class were way better behaved than the ones in my old Vancouver school. The boys who'd led the way pushed each other and laughed, but suddenly nobody wanted to volunteer.

'Go get something from one of the houses and bring it back!' one said to the other. 'So we can see what it looks like.'

'You do it!'

'I don't wanna come back all wrinkled and old!'

'I heard you go insane if you spend a while in there, like those gaijin doing experiments,' a girl added.

There was a pause, and I felt everybody not looking at me. My face was hot.

They watched me, maybe waiting for me to tell them that none of those rumours were true. I didn't know they *weren't* true. I just hadn't seen them yet.

Nobody else spoke, so it was up to me to say, inevitably, 'I'll do it.'

The boys who'd been arguing looked at me and then at each other.

'Really?' one said.

I nodded. I hadn't searched this area yet. I figured I could do it now. I squeezed through the fence.

'Bring something back!' a girl called.

I turned and waved and then I started walking.

This side of the fence, the trees thinned out but the grass was longer. It was quieter. There were houses close by. I wanted to run but made myself walk. I looked over my shoulder and could see them clustered at the fence, watching me in a way that made me wonder for a minute which side was the safe one, and which I actually wanted to be on.

I reached the first house, which had been white, once. The front door was locked, or stuck. The next house was open. I stood on the doorstep and peered in. It was very dark. I had been in the houses before, a few times, but the other kids had put the creepiness into my head and now I felt a prickle down the back of my neck.

I stepped inside and the dark settled into the ordinary inside shade of a house. My foot hovered over the floor but it was too dirty for me to take my shoes off.

'Excuse me,' I mumbled, and winced as I walked down the hallway.

The air was hot and thick. I went to the kitchen, which was generally the best room to go to because it is the most familiar and the most used to people. There wasn't much there; the house was close enough to the boundary that it had probably been properly cleared out. The family might have even been able to come back for their things, if they had been here before the fence was put up. The cupboards were empty. I could hardly bring back a chair, though it would have been funny to see everyone's expressions if I hauled back something really stupid like that. The other downstairs rooms were empty too, aside from the big furniture. I didn't go upstairs.

I returned to the sunlight, which glared so harshly that it was a relief to duck into the next house, but it was as hollow as the last, and the next was the same. It should have made me feel better to find these houses empty, if it was because people had been able to take their lives with them. But somehow the empty houses felt worse, as if they'd never had anything or anyone living inside them and hadn't ever been used for what they had been built for.

There weren't many more buildings ahead; a small house and a big shed and then fields. I don't know why I went to the shed first. Maybe because it was a change from the houses. The doors were hard to open. When I finally did it, light leaked in, and it was a nightmare of bones.

The tales of people's flesh falling off them while they were still alive, turning into skeletons that walked before they collapsed into dust on the ground – no, they weren't true, this couldn't be that! I took a breath to calm myself and gagged at the trace of decay in the air. My head cleared. The shed was separated by bars into small sections. Pens. The bones were animal bones. The long skulls – cattle.

I walked in. Some bones were in heaps, where cows had lain down or collapsed. Other skulls rested outside the pens, near dry buckets and dusty troughs. Had they died because of the time zone, or had these been deaths from starvation, thirst? Everyone had had to evacuate, and the cows were left behind. Of course, because nobody could have taken all of them. And hadn't they been raised to be slaughtered, anyway? But the poor things.

I kneeled by a skull and touched my fingertips to it. 'Sorry,' I said. 'I'm sorry.'

There was the faint sound of cattle lowing, mournful, layering and echoing.

I stood up very slowly. There was nothing to see. The noise faded. It could have been the wind, the trees, anything really. I began to back away. I'd shut the doors and never return here. But – that's what had happened before. I forced myself forward, to the first pen. The bolts were dry and rusty, scraping as though they were in pain as I dragged them back. I opened the pens wide. I took a bucket and went outside to find a tap, and when I twisted it water sputtered out miraculously.

'Hey.'

I clapped a hand over my mouth to stop my scream. There was a boy, wearing a school uniform. I knew his face but couldn't remember his name.

'Sorry,' he said. 'We got worried.'

'I'm fine. I just...' The bucket of water overflowed.

He turned the tap off. 'What are you doing?' His eyes landed on the shed. 'You went in there?'

I nodded.

'There were cows...' he said.

'How did you know that? You've been here before?'

After a moment, he said, 'Yeah.'

'Why?'

He stuck his hands in his pockets.

'Did you live near here?' I asked.

He shook his head and kicked at another dry bucket. 'Used to be my uncle's farm. My brother worked here. Kinda weird part-time job. He wanted to be a farmer too.'

'You shouldn't go in there. It's only cows,' I added quickly. 'But—'

'Yeah, I know. That's why I never did. It's bad?'

I nodded.

He looked down at the spilled water instead of me. 'What were you doing?'

I cleared my throat. 'I thought I would clean it.'

He walked away suddenly. I watched him pause before the shed door, take a breath, and go in. He came out a minute later, rubbing a hand across his face. I looked down, stared at my reflection trapped in the bucket.

He didn't say anything, just picked up the other bucket and filled it. We went to the shed. Inside, we sprinkled water over the bones, the way you wash a gravestone. Neither of us spoke but the silence was full of words, like there was a conversation happening in spite of ourselves. It was him saying that his brother was gone, and me saying that I understood, and that I had lost somebody too, and him saying that it was shit, and me saying, yeah, it was, it was the shittiest thing in the world, and I came here too, looking too, for anything that I could find. And this is what we had found.

When we finished, we returned to the battering sunshine. I began to push the doors closed.

He shook his head. 'I don't want to close them.'

We wedged the shed doors open and paused. We bowed and clapped and bowed. We washed our hands. Then we left, and perhaps the ghosts of the cows did too.

As we passed a house nearby, I said, 'They told me to bring something back.' I went inside, and he came with me.

It seemed more like a workspace than a home, but there was a small kitchen. I opened a cupboard and found a dull silver metal bento box with a faded sticker on the lid. 'This would be okay, right?'

He came closer. 'Let me see it,' he demanded. He

examined it as though he was searching for evidence. 'Let's take it.'

We left and walked in silence until we came to a lone, dutiful vending machine. I wiped the dust from it with my sleeve. 'I'm thirsty. You think it's okay to drink a Pocari Sweat?'

'Yeah. That stuff lasts for years.'

I dug around in my pocket and fished out a hundred-yen coin. I put it in the slot and hit the button. Nothing happened. The machine was dead, obviously. I kicked it. I turned around, but the boy wasn't there.

'Hey?' I hadn't heard him go. 'Where are you?'

There was a crash of heavy things falling and then he appeared from around the corner, holding a narrow length of metal in his hands. I didn't move or speak because I was calculating whether to run away or to leap at him.

But he went to the vending machine. 'Watch out.' He hefted the metal in his hands like a baseball bat, and then he swung it against the vending machine.

I expected a smash, but there was just a thud.

'Let me try.' I grabbed the metal from him. I stepped up and pretended I was at the home plate and that the vending machine was some kind of huge baseball, and I swung. There was a crack and the vending machine door creaked open.

The boy pulled the metal from my hand and then reached in and grabbed a Pocari Sweat. He handed it to me and took one himself. He tapped his bottle to mine. 'Kanpai.'

I laughed and we drank. I choked and spat it out and heard him exclaim in disgust.

'Yuck!' I spat again. It was sour and warm and tasted like poison.

The boy scrubbed his sleeve across his mouth. 'That better not make us sick. Didn't think it could've gone bad so fast.'

I checked the expiry date on the cap. 'It should be okay for two more years, but here…' I poured my drink on to the ground, hoping it wouldn't murder the plants that drank it.

'We should go.' He walked over to the vending machine again. 'But you should get your money back.' He levered and wrestled at the machine until the money drawer opened.

We counted it.

'Two thousand yen!' he said triumphantly. 'Twenty bottles of Pocari Sweat.'

'I feel bad.'

'Who else is going to use it?'

We divided it up. It weighed down my skirt pocket, the metal clinking and jingling. We didn't say anything much on the way back.

'How long were we in there?' he asked.

'It felt like I was in there for an hour. And time goes fast in there, right? If the Pocari went off… Maybe it's twice as fast. We've been gone about thirty minutes, maybe.'

'Maybe?' he said, but it didn't sound like he was making fun of me.

We waded through the grass.

'What's your name?' I said.

'Koki.'

'Right. I'd forgotten.'

'You're Sora.'

'Yeah.'

The small group of kids were waiting in the shade of the trees. When we reached the fence, one of the boys held it back to let us through.

They all talked at the same time.

'What did you see?'

'Was it strange?'

'What did you do?'

'We drank a Pocari Sweat,' Koki said, 'but it had gone bad. It was disgusting.'

'Did you bring any back?'

Koki shook his head. 'It was too horrible.'

I remembered the bento box. 'Oh, wait.' I pulled it out of my bag.

Everyone gathered in close.

'Looks normal,' one of the girls said.

'Open it!'

I unclipped the stiff clasps on the lid and opened it. We all leaned forward in fear and excitement, but there was only dust inside, and a pair of wooden chopsticks. Everybody sagged with disappointment, or relief.

I picked up the chopsticks carefully. They were completely normal, pale cheap wood. A breeze blew and my fingers tingled. The chopsticks lightened in my hand

and then disintegrated into ash, like a spell breaking, like a sped-up time lapse of decay. I dropped the bento box, and when it hit the ground it began to corrode, rust redness blistering over one side of it. Everybody jumped and yelled at once.

'Did you see—'

'Turned to dust—'

'Rusted—'

'Gone—'

We were shaken, but revived too; it would be an excellent story to exaggerate in school next day. There was some debate on whether to bring the bento box or not, but it had stopped aging and now just looked like any dirty old thing. One of the girls poked it with her shoe. Nobody wanted to touch it.

'Is your hand okay?' Koki said.

I hadn't noticed I was rubbing it against my skirt. 'Yeah,' I muttered.

'I'm thirsty,' he said.

There was a general murmur of agreement.

'How long were we gone for?' I asked suddenly.

'I timed you,' one of the boys said. 'Thirty-one and a half minutes.'

Both of Koki's eyebrows rose and I tried not to be too smug, but I probably didn't succeed because he snorted a laugh.

One of the girls glanced from his face to mine. 'So you two—' she began.

Koki had already turned away and was walking with

the other boys, and I fell behind everybody, like I usually did. The heat slumped into evening. I remembered the coins in my pocket; when I pulled them out to look at them, they had tarnished and dulled. Money, of course, is made to last.

Later, in the conbini, Koki bought two bottles of Pocari Sweat and handed me one. I tapped my bottle to his, but we didn't say anything. We drank and it was so cold and fresh that I felt like I was waking from the strangest dream.

雀始巣

SPARROWS START TO NEST

2

The ceremony is finally over.

'Congratulations,' Koki says into my ear.

'Why are you whispering?'

He's standing very close to me. He bites his lip and I know what he's thinking. I shake my head and grin.

'Stop it.'

He leans forward and hugs me quickly and tightly, and for a second I think he might kiss me, which even I couldn't do here, in front of everybody. He lets me go.

I hope my face isn't as red as it feels, and I bow deeply to hide it. 'Thank you very much.'

He laughs. '*Too* formal! Or you're never formal enough.'

'I'll never get it right, will I?'

'I didn't mean—' Koki's indignant at the annoyance in my voice.

'I was joking.' I touch his hand. 'Obviously I would never be so respectful to you.'

Koki smiles again and it's all okay.

I survey the crowd to avoid his face. 'That was boring.'

In front of the school, people are smiling, laughing, taking photos with their families. It's not so warm outside, but the sun is hard and bright and the sky is so smoothly the same colour blue that it looks flat. Good for pictures.

I look back at Koki and our eyes meet, and all of a sudden we're in a pause so full of expectation that it could pop.

'I should tell you—' Koki begins.

Something inside me clenches with excitement, or trepidation. I'm not sure what I want him to tell me.

But then the moment is saved, or ruined, because Koki's mom and dad appear, both of them wet-eyed in a loving parent sort of way. I mumble thanks to both of them as they congratulate me.

'Sora-chan—'

It's Dad, standing patiently, surrounded by a slight distance that's subtle enough not to be noticeable unless you're used to feeling it.

'I apologise,' he says. He bows to me.

'Stop that,' I say in English.

'I lost track of time.' He half-smiles, because it's a half-joke.

I shrug.

He pulls me to him in an awkward hug. 'I'm proud of you.'

I rest my head against him for a moment. 'Thanks,' I say into his shoulder.

'Shall I take a photo of you?' Koki's mother offers.

I like her. Right now, I wish she would go away.

'Oh, no—' I begin, in Japanese.

'Yes, thank you so much, Fujiwara-san.' Dad switches to Japanese too. 'Sora-chan, can we use your phone? It's better than mine.'

'Of course.' I hand it to Koki's mom. 'Thank you.'

Dad puts his arm around me awkwardly.

'Chee-*zu*!' Koki calls merrily.

'Very nice,' Fujiwara-san says. Her husband peers at the screen and nods agreement.

'Thank you, thank you,' Dad says. He takes the phone but his gaze skips away from the photo. He passes it to me quickly.

I stare at the photo. Me and Dad look similar after a moment, but at first glance you might think we're not related. He's white and fair and blue-eyed, and I'm dark-haired, brown-eyed, skin a handful of shades darker. Mom is the missing piece, the Japanese part that makes the puzzle of me understandable. I know Dad felt that empty space as well, because of the anguish in his eyes and the shadow that flitted over his face.

You can't see any missing pieces with Koki and his parents, at first.

'Sora-chan, will you miss school?' Koki's mother asks me.

'Not so much. I'll be working,' I say vaguely. This is an intention more than a plan.

'You're so intelligent, university isn't really necessary, I think,' she says.

This would sound sarcastic coming from anybody

else, but I'm pretty sure Fujiwara-san means it. Still, I can see Koki shoot her a *please-stop-talking* glare.

I smile at her to counteract this. 'At least Koki won't be going too far.' He's going to commute to the university in the closest city, and I can't admit to him how grateful I am for that.

'You young people have so much energy! Tokyo seems far to me, but I'm an old man now,' Koki's father says in a jolly way.

'Tokyo?' I say. 'Tokyo.'

Koki's biting his lip. Now Fujiwara-san is giving her husband a death glare. Koki must have inherited it from her.

'Off to Tokyo for university, that's wonderful,' Dad says into this void.

Koki says quietly, 'They gave me a scholarship. I'm very lucky.'

'Congratulations. You should be proud,' Dad says.

Koki and his parents all murmur the obligatory, *no, no, thank you, thank you.*

'Great. It's really so good,' I whisper.

Koki's face is caught between pain and embarrassment and something else. Happiness. His eyes search for mine but I can't meet them.

'Would you like to get any more pictures with people?' Dad asks me.

Other students are taking photos together, with best friends and with members of their clubs. I'm not in any clubs.

'No,' I say.

'All right. Well, let's eat a nice lunch.' He bows to the Fujiwaras. 'Good to see you all. Have a good day. Congratulations, again.'

I echo this and turn away from Koki. I start walking blindly.

'Your choice of lunch.' Dad takes my arm and steers me to the school gate.

'Curry.'

'No, it should be something special! This is a special day, Sora-chan.'

'It can be an expensive curry,' I say, as generously as I can manage.

'Fine. Is there anything else you need to do here?'

I look at the crowd of classmates and families, the sun shining and their faces beaming back, and there's so much light that it hurts my eyes and makes them water.

'No.' I check my watch but I can't read the time because for some reason the numbers are blurred and the hands seem to waver. 'Let's go.'

﹀

The first clock I made was a stick in the sand on a sunny day. Me and Dad were at the beach, and I asked him what time dinner was.

'Six p.m.,' he said.

'What time is it now?' I asked.

Dad found a straight thin piece of driftwood and dug

it into the wet sand, then pointed out the shadow cast by the sun.

'A sundial,' I said.

'Exactly.'

'You have a watch.'

'No fun. When it's noon, there's almost no shadow. Watch how it moves. If you're good, you can tell the hour. Observe,' he commanded.

I did. I sat in the sand beside it and watched the sun twirl that shadow out and around. Dad kept asking if I wanted to swim, or walk with him, but I was hypnotised, that such a simple thing could measure time, that it could be caught and read like this.

I sat until the tide came in and knocked the stick over and pulled it away from me.

'Hmmm,' Dad said. 'That was a flaw. I didn't think to check whether the tide was coming in or out.'

'It's 4.45 p.m.,' I guessed at random.

Dad looked at his watch. 'Nope, it's 4.17 p.m. Next time...'

Dad always thinks about what can be improved for next time, because testing and experimenting can be done better and better, even if it fails again and again. He says that there are better ways to fail, and if you just keep getting better at failing then someday you might find that you've succeeded. Yeah, right. Getting better at failing just means failing faster.

But I went back to the beach next day, and the day after that. It was the summer holiday so the heat and the sun made the time easy to tell. I stood sticks in the sand all over the beach and monitored them, drawing lines, testing and measuring, guessing time and checking it, seeing how close I could get. My experiments spread like a little forest that had lost its leaves.

After a week, I brought Dad to the beach to present my findings. He *hmmmed* when he saw the stick sundials scattered about.

'Extensive research,' he said. 'And why are some of them marked?' He pointed to the sticks at the outer points. I'd tied red ribbons around a few of them.

'I'll show you.'

I'd marked the intervals of time around different sticks, some by hour, some by minute, and then by second. I guessed the time from each and let him check and I got it right over and over again.

'Very thorough.'

I glowed, because it was one of the highest compliments he would give a scientist. I led him to the red-ribboned sticks. 'The time,' I said, 'runs slower here.'

We sat side by side, backs to the ocean, and watched the time. On the left, the shadows moved obediently to the same time as Dad's watch and phone. On the right, the red ribbons rippled in the salt air, and the shadows lagged, not by much, maybe not noticeable to anybody else, but I had marked out the seconds so they could be counted. They were two or three seconds behind what everything else said was correct.

We sat and stared until the clouds hid the sun and took the time away.

●

Dad and I leave the school and go to one of the few nice restaurants in town. It's busy because of graduation but we don't have to wait long for a table because everybody else is waiting for tables with more seats. We sit down and discuss the menu and order. Then we sit in silence.

This has been happening more lately. There have always been moments of quiet between us, but the friendly, calm kind that help you think. This silence makes me think too, but in the frantic, *what-can-I-say?* way that blocks out everything else.

'How do you feel?' Dad says.

'Um. Hungry?'

'No, I mean, today. Graduation and ... everything.'

'Oh.' I don't really know how to feel about it. 'The same.'

'Which is?' He's watching me seriously, as if he's really listening to me.

'I don't feel grown up and I don't know what I'm doing. The same as I've felt all this year.'

Dad doesn't seem pleased with my honest answer. 'Well, think about what you're doing next, what your plans are. We should talk about that.'

'We already did. I'm going to stay here and find a job.'

'We talked about this? I don't recall...' Dad mumbles.

'Yeah.' It had been a short conversation. Argument. 'Maybe I'll apply to some Canadian universities next year.'

The food arrives. Mine's a soup curry, and the vegetables are colourful and tasty, steaming spice. Dad has karaage and rice, more of a side dish than a main. He stares down at it as if he's counting the number of rice grains in the bowl.

'Have you really forgotten this?' I ask. '*I* haven't.' I can see him trying to decide whether to admit he can't remember, or pretend he does and stick with whatever it was he told me.

He takes a bite of his chicken. 'I want you to do whatever will make you happy,' he says.

'I don't know what that is. That's why I'm going to think about it for a while. You told me that was fine.' I spoon up my curry and it burns my tongue but I don't say anything. I swallow hard and feel it burn all the way down.

'It is. It's only because Japan doesn't really do gap years – I suppose it looks a little strange,' Dad says.

'When have I ever not been strange here?' I ask.

'Everything is strange here,' Dad says, in an almost-whisper. 'We fit right in.'

I appreciate the *we* in this blatant lie.

We eat for a while – or rather, I eat and Dad takes slow small mouthfuls. I've almost finished my curry when he says, 'So, Koki...'

I grip my spoon. 'Off to Tokyo, apparently. Glad I found out before he left.'

'It really is a fantastic opportunity.'

'I *know*.'

'Do you?' Dad's gaze is suddenly focused and sceptical.

'He should have told me.'

Dad watches me bite aggressively into a chunk of potato. 'It's probably for the best if you kill him now, or better yet, be angry and refuse to speak to him for the time he has left here before he moves.'

'But it's so hard to decide *how* to kill him.'

'A good tactic might be to offer him the choice of two and then carry out whatever he *doesn't* choose,' Dad says wisely.

I can't stop a smile. 'I'll message Koki and ask.'

'Good. Make sure you inform me of your decision so I can prepare an alibi.' He puts his chopsticks down. 'I know it's hard to see people go, but often it's for the best. For them. Try to be happy for him.'

I want to yell, *What about being happy for myself?* 'I'll try.'

'It won't be so bad, Sora. And maybe you can go there—'

'Maybe,' I say shortly.

'You don't have to break up,' Dad says hesitantly.

'We're not really *together*,' I snap, and then I concentrate on my plate until it's clean.

Dad clears his throat, but thankfully gives up trying

to say anything more on the subject. Instead, he gazes between me and the window, not eating.

'Are you finished already?' I ask.

'I'm not so hungry.'

'Really?' His plate is more than half-full.

Dad calls for the bill.

We go home.

I take off my shoes and head straight to my room. 'I'm going to lie down. I really didn't get enough sleep during those speeches.'

Dad follows me to my bedroom door. 'Sora-chan.' He hugs me, a real hug that makes me feel like a kid, that makes me feel safe. 'I truly am proud of you. And your mother would be too.' He lets me go.

'Thanks, Dad.' I swallow hard.

He clears his throat. We smile at each other tightly.

I step into my room and close the door. I wait until I can hear Dad is in his study. I open my wardrobe and pull my hanging clothes to one side. There, on a little shelf, is a photo of Mom. My little makeshift shrine for her.

'Would you be proud of me, Mom?' I whisper. If I ever find her, is that what she will say?

Try to be happy. I'm trying, but I can't feel anything.

My mother was careless with time. *I'll be there in ten!* when we waited hungry outside a restaurant; *Just five more seconds*, when I felt I was getting too old for hugs at the school gate but she wouldn't let me go; *One week more*, when she postponed our return flights from Japan back home to Canada; *Two hundred or five hundred or one thousand years ago*, when she told me stories. For some stories she would sometimes say, *It doesn't matter* when *this happened, but it definitely, one hundred per cent, absolutely happened.*

I used to be like that, in some ways. Early for food, a bit tardy for everything else. But moving to Japan taught me the ten-minutes-early-or-you're-late rule, and living near the time zones taught me not to ask more of time, because it could never give you what you really wanted.

Mom wanted everything, in the best way. She wanted to see more of the world, wanted to meet new people, wanted me to learn the piano, wanted my father to make a vegetable patch in the back garden. When she was still a teenager, she left Japan to study botany at a Canadian university; she met many more kinds of people than she could have in her coastal hometown in north-eastern Japan; when I gave up on the piano, she learned it herself; when Dad was too busy at work to make a vegetable patch, she dug earth and planted seeds with her own two hands.

So impatient, he used to say in varying tones of irritation, or amusement, or frustration, but mostly with love.

She would laugh or shrug or say, *Why should I wait?*
But I'm waiting and waiting and waiting.

I wake up in darkness, still fully dressed. I squint at my watch: 10.43 p.m. I fumble for my phone and see that Koki has messaged me.

hey
sorry about earlier
i was about to tell you but then all the parents arrived
i hope you're not too mad?

I pull off my wrinkled uniform and leave it in a pile on the floor. I'd burn it but there's enough pollution in the atmosphere as it is. I put on sweatpants and a T-shirt and go to the sitting room, where Dad is watching an over-dramatic drama on the TV.

'Hey there,' he says.

'I fell asleep.'

'You had a big day.'

There's a beer bottle and a glass on the table. I top Dad up and then take the bottle for myself. I half-want Dad to take it away from me so I can argue with him, but he's not stupid. On the screen, a young woman in a kimono is sobbing as a man in a topknot solemnly raises a sword.

'Didn't feel that big.' It had made me feel small.

Dad gets up and returns with another glass. He fills it with beer and then pushes it across the table to me.

I pick it up and drink without saying anything. Dad is liberally Canadian but maybe he's now forgetting how old I am. Sometimes I hate that and other times it makes me glad. This is one of the glad times.

I look at Koki's messages. I'll leave him on read. A power move.

Ten seconds later, I write, *so you were actually planning to tell me on our graduation day?*

I watch the young woman swoon while the man says stuff about respect.

i had no plan, Koki replies.

The woman puts her hands on the man's face and says she loves him.

'Don't do that!' Dad says suddenly.

'Huh?'

Dad's staring at the TV. 'That guy is worthless.' He reaches for his glass and misses, knocking it over. 'Oops!'

He's drunk and I hadn't noticed. 'I'll clean it.' I go to the kitchen to get paper and see the line of bottles beside the sink. Shit. I return and mop up the beer. I grab my glass out of Dad's reach. 'That's mine.'

'Sorry. Would you mind getting me another?'

I bring Dad a glass with water.

He stares at it and then at me. 'Yes, I suppose that's a better choice of liquid.'

'You should go to bed,' I say. 'That's where I'm going.'

'It's early,' he protests. 'I thought we could celebrate a little more—'

'You were celebrating without me,' I point out.

Dad huffs.

i was just surprised you didn't tell me, I write to Koki. *but it's amazing. you deserve it,* I add.

On the TV, the woman plucks Topknot's sword out of his hand and slices his head off with an elegant swing.

'That's more like it,' Dad says. 'I'll rest easy now.' He

pushes himself up and knocks over his glass again. At least this time it's empty.

We both go to pick it up. Our hands bump and a spark of static leaps from his hand to mine.

I flinch. 'Did you feel that?'

Dad blinks at me, sleepy and drunk. 'Hmm?'

'Like an electric shock.'

Dad shakes his head. 'Nope.'

'Weird.' I take the glass into the kitchen.

When I return to the sitting room, Dad's head is nodding on his chest.

'Night, Dad,' I say pointedly.

He rouses himself. 'Night, Sora.'

I watch him as he walks down the corridor. He pauses to steady himself against the wall, then disappears into his bedroom.

thank you. can we talk about this tomorrow? come over to mine, Koki writes.

okay, I reply.

you're an important person to me, Koki writes.

I stare at my phone. I want him to tell me how, exactly, I'm important to him. Tell me why. Except now he's leaving, so what would the point of that be?

hope that'll get me in a VIP area in a Tokyo club, I write quickly, as if I'd ever been to one. *going to sleep now, see you tomorrow*

Koki sends an emoji of a rabbit giving a thumbs up.

The woman on the TV has been surrounded by a bunch of topknot men. She ties back her kimono sleeves.

She raises the sword above her head. It's only her, against all of them.

I turn off the TV because I don't want to see how it ends.

●

The Shake was seven years ago, back when we were only visiting Japan, when our real home was still in Vancouver, when my family was three and not two. Pits opened. Hills rose. The ocean deepened and shallowed.

The planet moved on its axis, just the tiniest, most minuscule fraction. The world spun differently. Faster. The year got shorter, almost unnoticeably. This isn't actually new – earthquakes often cause it as well as other natural, terrifying things like volcanoes. The earth moves around all the time, like anything that's alive, so nobody knows why this was different. Because it was very, *very* different.

In Japan, time was shaken up. It changed. In different places, it runs slower or faster. You can step into a different patch of time the same way you can cross the border between countries, the way you stumble when you're walking downstairs and miss a step. But it's more dangerous because you might not be able to tell you've fallen, not until you come out the other side, or back the way you came, and then you could find out that a whole afternoon has passed, or only ten minutes, when it seems like you've been in that other place for an hour. And that's if you could find your way out.

After the tragedy, it was a curiosity. Scientists came from all over the world, and news teams, writers, explorers, charities, photographers, celebrities. Everybody thought it was a glitch, an anomaly of physics, like those roads where a ball rolls uphill, but which are actually optical illusions or something to do with gravity. But it didn't go away. There are places so deep in the zones that nobody dares go there now. Some did, at first; self-defence forces or search and rescue parties, but they didn't return. That's when the government started putting up fences and warning people to stay away. Not that many needed to be told, because people had gone missing, hundreds of them, and nobody knows where they went. A lot of people died in the Shake, when houses fell and fires started and the sea came and rolled over everything, but those others have never really been explained.

We've never found Mom, or Ojiichan. Time had taken them, swept them away, and even though I've never stopped searching, they're still lost between the seconds and minutes and hours that are invisible and shape everything we do in the world.

And we got lost, Dad and me. We might have fallen away from everything even more if we hadn't kept such a tight grip of each other, because now there's a new sort of fear; that one of us might get caught between the hands of a clock and never be seen again. But it feels like Dad is slipping, and my hands aren't strong enough to hold him.

桜始開

FIRST CHERRY BLOSSOMS BLOOM

3

I wake up in the darkness before dawn, thinking of Mom. If I'd dreamed about her, I can't remember the dream, but she's so vivid in my mind I know I won't be able to go back to sleep. I lift an old Japanese history book from the shelf and take my maps from the space I've hollowed inside. I spread them out and examine them in the beam of my phone's flashlight, looking at the places I haven't marked off yet. The closest is in a slow zone not far from here. I dress quietly and leave through the window.

My bike light flickers white in the grey air and the chill against my face brushes any sleepiness away. The roads are empty because people don't like driving this close to the boundary fence, and when the sun begins to rise above the hills in front of me, I stop to watch it. Its pale brightness reaches up and out, resolving into golden light as the sky blushes blue around it. I start cycling again, and a little further on I get off my bike and wheel it behind a thicket of bamboo to the gap I've made in the fence. It's stiffer and rustier since I came here last, and I have to heave to open it wide enough to push my bike through. On the other side, I check my map and start cycling again.

As I go further in the light recedes to grey once more, because this is the slow zone and the sun hasn't risen here yet. I cycle more carefully now. Even though the roads are in better condition than in the fast zone, they're still cracked and overgrown. As I reach the new area, I feel the seconds and minutes drag at me, thickening the tiniest amount as they shift into even slower time. My speed slackens. I pull a whistle out of my pocket and start blowing into it softly. There are a few houses ahead, and when I'm among them I stop and lean my bike against a wall.

I whistle louder now, clear my throat and call, 'Is anybody here?'

The door of the first house is hanging open, the hallway thick with dirt. I don't bother going inside. The second house has smashed windows. The glass edges are still crisp and sharp but the lace curtains inside are startlingly white and untorn. In the slow zone, things can be preserved, sometimes long after they should have been. I whistle louder.

Behind this house is a garden, plants still more or less growing in the straight lines they were planted in. Among tall stalks, a figure. A shadow, cast by nobody, or cast by somebody at some other time. I freeze.

'Hello,' I whisper.

Does it turn in my direction?

I raise my voice a little. 'Are you... Can you hear me?'

The shadow fades, dissipating into the air like the after-image burned by a camera flash. I lunge forward but there is nothing, nothing.

'Hello?' I cry out. 'Is there anyone here? I'm looking for – for people. I won't hurt you!'

There is only silence. The shadows have never made a sound. Perhaps voices can't be caught or carried by time in the same way light and shade seems to be.

I jog around, watching and yelling and whistling until I lose my breath. I pause to catch it, steadying myself against a faded *Stop* sign.

I let myself call, just once, 'Mom?'

But I know I'm alone. The shadow does not return; they hardly ever do. They simply appear and disappear. There are shadows imprinted on the streets of Hiroshima, but these are not exactly the same. They are some stutter of time, I think. The remembrance of someone who had been there, perhaps when the Shake happened, or maybe some time before or after. They could be flashbulb memories of a place, or the imprints that are left on eyelids when a light comes on suddenly. This is not proven research; it's hardly even a rumour. It's what I've seen, again and again. What I haven't seen is what I want to see the most: my mother.

I know it's stupid and wishful and almost impossible. *Almost.* There is a chance the missing people are there, somewhere, caught in a time or place and trying to return. We know hardly anything about the zones, still. Who's to say it could never happen?

Dad, for one. He doesn't want me searching and hoping. He's given up looking for people, says he's only looking for answers. Not that they've been much easier to find.

Before me are the same hills, and beyond them the sun is rising. I watch it come up a second time, and it's as lovely, as bright as the first. I feel sick. I return to my bike, mark this place on my map as *searched,* and go back the way I came.

On the other side of the boundary fence, in normal time, the sun is strong and high in the sky. The roads home are still empty. I climb through my window and hide my maps. I'm about to get back into bed when I hear noise from the kitchen and know immediately that Dad isn't good.

Plates are crashing and pots clanging around and it's not just that; I can hear his voice. He's not on the phone – who would be calling us? – because there're no pauses where the person on the other end of the line would be speaking.

I haul myself to the kitchen and watch him from the doorway.

He's searching through the cupboards, muttering, 'Where is it, where is it?' He's speaking Japanese.

'Dad.' I speak in Japanese too, because it's better to stay in the same language as him.

He jerks around, as startled as some wild animal

caught in headlights. He hesitates for a fraction too long before he says, 'Sora-chan.' He switches to English. 'Where's the red kettle?'

'We don't have a red kettle,' I tell him.

'We do, we've had it for years and years.'

I remember. We left it behind in Vancouver.

'It ... broke,' I say carefully.

'When?' Dad's brow crinkles.

'Last week,' I invent. 'I broke it. I didn't want to tell you. I'm sorry.'

'You should have told me! Where is it?' Dad's getting angry.

'I'm trying to fix it! You were busy, I couldn't ask you...' I can't help adding in some guilt to my lie.

'Sora...'

'What's that?' A searing smell is a helpful distraction. A pan on the stove is smoking, and I rush to turn the gas off. There are blackened circles crisped to ash around the edges. 'Dad, what's this?'

He stares over my shoulder. 'I put those on a second ago. How did they burn?'

'What *are* they?'

'Pancakes. I thought I'd make your favourite, seeing as it's Sunday.'

It's Tuesday.

'I wonder if the stove is broken. It's dangerous, with the gas.' Dad twiddles with the gas knob, snapping it on and off.

I watch him and squeeze my nails into my palms.

He notices. 'I'm sorry I yelled at you about the kettle. And about the pancakes. I just thought I'd make you a nice breakfast.'

'I kinda feel like a Japanese breakfast, anyway. We can make it together,' I say.

Dad smiles at me and it feels like his pancakes used to taste: sweet and warm and comforting in a way that reminds me of weekend afternoons and maple syrup sticky on my fingers.

'I'll do the rice,' Dad says. He swills the rice with water, rinses it, does this again and then a third time. His movements are practised. I'm beginning to see that your body can remember things your brain forgets. 'Too hungry to let it soak,' he says, and turns the rice cooker on.

I go to the fridge and open it, sticking in my head and pretending to check what's inside, but it's hard to see. I rub my sleeve across my eyes and take out eggs, pickles, tofu.

He scrubs the pan and I chop up salad and cook the small piece of fish that we somehow have. We don't talk and we do everything unhurriedly so that we're only just finished when the rice is ready. We carry the plates to the table and settle ourselves there.

'Itadakimasu,' Dad says. He takes a bite of the fish and, with his mouth full, says, 'Delicious. This is nice, Sora-chan. We haven't done this for a while.'

I don't know whether he's still confused or not, because either way he's right; we haven't. I smile back, feeling love and fear, and this is why I can't leave; this is

49

the real reason. I swallow the feelings with my food. We chat about nothing and Dad eats almost everything. We finish and wash up.

'I'm going to work,' he says.

I follow him to the genkan and watch as he puts his shoes on. Even with his suit jacket on, his back is narrower than I remember. He's losing weight.

'You're working inside, aren't you?' I ask.

'Yes, all this week. What a pity, with the weather so lovely.' He sighs.

I'm not sorry at all. 'Don't forget to eat lunch.'

'You should start making me cute bentos. Can you make the little sausages into octopi?' He makes what I know he thinks are puppy dog eyes. It makes him more like a depressed clown.

'Is that what you think a woman at home should be doing? Not very progressive, Dad.'

'So you *can't* make the octopus-sausages.'

'You're not a kid.'

'You're not doing anything else,' he shoots back.

'I'm job hunting.' Well, I've almost started hunting.

'Good. Great. You can—'

The ground trembles. Dad steadies himself against the door. I flatten myself against the wall. We automatically check our watches. One, two, three seconds, I count another second in my head but the hand of the watch doesn't move. There's stillness. The watch resumes time.

Dad takes his eyes from his watch and lowers his wrist. 'A pause.'

'One second. Back to normal now. It didn't stick,' I tell him, even though he already knows.

'That's good,' he says. He moves his hand from the door to its handle. 'I should go to work and check for any other changes.'

'Be careful,' I can't help but say.

'You too,' he replies. He leaves.

I go to my room and check my wardrobe. The photo of Mom has fallen forward. I stand it upright again. On the shelf are dried flowers, a blue-beaded bracelet, a leaf-patterned cup, a green silk scarf, a red daruma with one eye coloured in. I don't know what Mom had wished for so the other eye will always be empty. It's not a real shrine but it's the best I could do. There's a gravestone with her name on it but there's nothing else there; no ashes or bones because we found none to burn or bury. The only thing that was buried there was Dad's memories of Mom, or at least his desire to ever talk about them, or her. Every now and then he'll refer to her, something she did or a place they had gone together, but it's by accident, as if he forgot what happened. As if a curse he put on himself was lifted for a moment.

So I hide the photo and the keepsakes where Dad can't see them. If he did, he'd be upset. Or worse, he'd take them away like he's taken away everything that was Mom's, anything that reminds him of her. I work hard to remember everything, going over and over memories, trying to recall every little detail so that they'll be ingrained in my brain. I won't forget.

After the Shake, Dad switched from his physics studies and began researching time almost immediately. He became one of the most active field researchers in the zones. Other scientists consulted him, and for a while he got all the funding and equipment and assistants he wanted. He went the furthest and stayed out the longest. He was obsessed with the *how* and the *why*.

But Dad's lab ran out of funding a couple of years ago. Most of the other scientists left. Or *had* to leave. I thought some would return, like Soo-Jin, the researcher I had loved the most. They never did. Dad wouldn't give up, so as soon as a company offered him a job, he took it. He didn't have much choice; they're one of the only places still working on the time zones around here. They have some private funding from somewhere and I've never been entirely sure what they do. When I asked Dad, he said they were trying to make money, but seeing as that's what every single company wants to do, it wasn't very enlightening. They needed a scientific expert to do research and tests in the zones, and it seemed that's all he needed to know. He's been going out further and further, for longer and longer.

On the beach, years ago, after I'd shown Dad my experiment, he shook my hand firmly. 'You have made a discovery, Sora-chan, and so beautifully too…'

'It was an accident,' I said.

'Many, many of the most famous discoveries in the

world were not made on purpose. Sit under a tree and discover gravity! Talk to a milkmaid and cure a disease!'

He made me laugh, even though I didn't really believe him.

Dad touched the ribbon on one of the sticks. 'And you did it with grace. The best discoveries are made when there's no harm done, nothing hurt in the way of experimentation. As simple and beautiful as a piece of maths—'

'That's never been simple *or* beautiful—'

Dad held up his hand. 'But doesn't it always look beautiful on a blackboard?'

I shrugged. I'd only seen that in movies about geniuses, when they scribble a lot of numbers and letters and everyone gasps when they write whatever it is after the equals sign.

'Grace. You don't get that from me.' He stared at the sea as if he wanted to punch it.

Mom had grace, but not ballet dancer grace – some other kind that I didn't know how to define exactly. Dad turned back and his eyes focused on the sticks and shadows again. 'Let's not stop here!'

'I'm hungry.'

'Just a little longer and then I promise you can eat whatever you want, no limits!'

'Fiiiine.'

Dad rubbed his hands together. 'You found the line where time changes, which is quite unbelievable, really... But how long does this line stretch?'

'I dunno.'

'We'll have to measure it.'

'I don't have enough sticks for that.' I hopped over the boundary line as if it was a skipping rope. Over and back, fast and then slow, until I had to catch my breath.

'What is it?' he asked.

'I think … I can feel it,' I said.

'What does it feel like?' Dad was watching me very attentively.

'It's sort of—' I closed my eyes and moved slowly, and I could feel it *there*, only for a moment. 'You know when you're swimming in the sea and there's a current that you can feel for a minute and then it goes again? And it might be warmer or colder than the rest of the water? It's like that. Or when your ears pop when you're going high up in a lift. Except you don't feel it as strongly as that, it's more like an – invisible pop?' I opened my eyes. 'It doesn't make sense.'

'You're *making* sense right now, because it's likely that nobody has ever had to describe this before.' His eyes were bright.

I moved between that invisible line, over and back and over. Dad followed me, dragging a piece of driftwood, drawing a line in the sand. It became easier and easier to sense.

'I can't really feel it any more.' I swayed back and forth. 'Maybe it's here a bit, but it's not very strong.'

Dad drew an X where I was standing. 'Let's determine whether there's much of a time difference.' He looked around for two suitable sticks and dug them into the sand on either side of X.

I drew out the minutes and seconds as best I could. We sat and we watched, facing the sun dials and the ocean. We'd only come halfway down the beach.

Dad was writing quickly in a notebook and watching the shadows move. 'Why does it stop right here? And not abruptly, it gets fainter...' He was asking himself questions, not me.

'Like a crack, I guess,' I said. 'Like in a wall.'

'That's one way of thinking about it. That's what marks the line ... but the analogy of concrete only goes so far, because it's not as though the material is different on either side of the crack...' He scribbled and muttered.

I stood up and brushed sand off myself, followed the line, moving over and back, trying to figure out the exact moment things changed. It was like looking at a spectrum and trying to find the point where one colour becomes another.

It was stronger the closer I got to the water, and then I was up to my knees in the ocean. That boundary was getting stronger, as if that crack was widening. I swam underwater with my eyes closed, trying to follow the feeling of time changing as if it was a rope or a path. I surfaced, suddenly tired and out of breath. I heard Dad shout from the shore. I splashed back and he handed me a towel.

'Not so far,' he said.

'Yeah ... I'm tired.' I sank into the sand. 'I was trying to see how long I could follow the crack for.'

'You can feel it in the water too?'

'Yeah.'

Dad started writing again.

The shadows cast by the sticks were getting long, all of them. It was getting cool. 'I kinda don't feel good. I'm hungry,' I said.

'Mmm-hmmm.'

I jogged Dad's shoulder. 'You promised.'

He hissed out a breath. 'Let me finish this sentence.'

I watched him finish that sentence and start another, and then another, and then I stood up and walked away. I counted in my head and I'd reached three minutes forty-six seconds when I heard him call my name.

I stopped, but I didn't turn around. I watched his shadow come closer.

'I just had to finish that thought. Otherwise it'll fall right out of my head and I might never catch it again.'

I watched my shadow shrug.

'To dinner. You choose where. I'll follow my research, like any good scientist.'

Koki's apprehensive when he opens the door. Usually we don't go to each other's houses but I guess his parents aren't home. 'So, you've come to take revenge.'

'If I was, I wouldn't knock,' I tell him.

He laughs a bit nervously, which makes me feel better. I follow him to the kitchen.

'Mugicha?' he offers. 'It's cold.'

'Thanks.'

He pours the barley tea into a glass and hands it to me. He sits down beside me.

'Sorry,' I say quickly, to get it over with. 'For making you feel like you couldn't tell me good news.'

'No, I'm sorry. I kept planning to tell you and kept putting it off. I was afraid you'd be—'

'Murderous?'

'No – well, yes. But more sad. Or disappointed.'

'I'm *proud* of you,' I say defensively.

'Disappointed because I wasn't staying here...'

'Because you're leaving?' Leaving *me*. I shrug. 'Everyone's leaving. It makes sense that you're going too. It would be stupid for you to stay here, and – I'm only going to say this once – you're actually not stupid.'

'Sora, you can make a compliment sound like the worst insult. And your happy wishes sound like a curse.'

I open my mouth to protest and he holds up a hand. 'Please, please don't say anything else positive, because it may end me.'

Stupid Koki always makes me smile.

He puts his hand on my cheek. 'You came around faster than I thought you would. Thought I'd have to watch my back for at least another week.'

'We don't have long to – to hang out, though, do we?' I say.

Koki takes his hand away.

'And Dad told me to get over it,' I add.

'Oh, that's it. How is he?'

I shrug. 'Okay.'

'Yeah?'

'Sometimes,' I say. 'Sometimes he's okay. He says it's overwork.'

'Your father does work hard. He's very inspiring to me.'

Koki has always been a little dazzled by Dad. He's attentive and interested in whatever Dad says, no matter how boring the information. 'Are you still going to study science in Tokyo?'

'Yes. The course there is really interesting.'

'You'll have to tell me what they teach you.'

Koki says, 'You should apply. Next year, I guess—'

'Maybe,' I say, before he can launch into one of his enthusiastic Koki plans. 'You can tell me whether it's good or not.'

'I will. I'll tell you everything.' He's so excited.

I watch him and those bad feelings are roiling about again. Koki will tell me, at least at the beginning – the first couple of months, even. But then...

'I should go,' I say.

'One more minute.' He pulls me towards him. 'So you're not angry at me any more?'

'I never said that.' But what was the point in being angry at him now?

'Nothing to lose, then.' He kisses me.

It's good, the kissing. His hands on the back of my neck, mine on his shoulders, our mouths pressing together like we're each other's oxygen. My mind is blank except for a corner that counts a minute, and another, another, another. But I don't stop because Koki's *here,* and has been here for me in a way nobody else has, and I don't want to let that go.

We pause for breath, staring at each other.

'That was … definitely more than a minute.' I lift my hands from him slowly.

'Don't you think we should talk?' Koki asks.

'About… About us?' I answer my own question before he can. 'No.' I get up quickly.

'Do you have something else to do?' he asks, exasperated.

It stings because, no, I don't have anything to do. 'I'm kinda busy,' I say.

Koki sighs. 'Okay. I'll see you…?' He holds on to my hand.

I pull away reluctantly until he can't stretch any further and lets me go. 'Soon.'

Outside, I press my hands against my lips. Can a mouth hold a kiss? Can a kiss hold time?

雷乃発声

THUNDER SOUNDS ITS VOICE

4

It's been almost two weeks since school ended. Dad's fallen asleep at the table once after too many beers; stayed up all night talking to himself in his study three times; asked me yesterday when term started. It's fine. I guess I never noticed these things because I was at school before. I've been to the zones six times since graduation – more than I should – but I have nothing worthwhile to do except follow my maps and search and find … nothing.

I see Koki, and kiss him, and we spend time in ways we don't exactly call dates. He's busy, though, preparing to leave and saying goodbyes. He doesn't bring up the topic of *us* again. I tell myself it's better not to see him too much. I should get used to that sooner rather than later.

I'm cooking more, which is … also fine. I don't hate cooking, but I hate the feeling of slotting into a routine of home and housework. Dad keeps saying he's not hungry, so the best way to make him eat is to guilt him into it, telling him I've spent hours making it, doesn't he want me to learn practical skills, isn't this what he means by *doing something.* So I cook and he eats. But today I'm actually working. It's a tour day.

The man's waiting at the south exit of the station, like I told him to. He's white, middle-aged, bearded, dressed plainly in jeans and a grey T-shirt.

I put a mask on and walk my bike over to him. 'Steve,' I say.

'Erika? Erika-*san.*' He smiles, and his teeth almost blind me. American.

'Erika is fine.' I bring him around the corner, to the other bike I've left there. 'Ready for a cycle?'

'Sure!' He's excited.

I cycle fast to stop him trying to make conversation, away from the town and along deserted roads to the boundary fence. We stash the bikes behind some trees.

'We're going to go in now. But first.' I raise my eyebrows.

He fumbles around his pockets and pulls out a folded envelope. 'The other half.'

I count the bills. Twenty thousand yen, as agreed. I duck through the fence.

He hesitates and points at my mask. 'Should I have one of those?'

'It's for my allergies.' And to hide my face. Along with my freshly straightened hair, it also helps me pass as fully Japanese.

He nods and follows me through the fence. He stands, gazes at the derelict houses and the grass growing wild, and pulls out a big camera.

'No photos,' I say.

'I'm a photographer. That's why I'm here. I'm doing a project about abandonment. It's really interesting in urban places and *here*... It's extreme, isn't it?'

'You can't take *any* photos of me, got it?' I take a hat out of my bag and put it on, pulling the brim down over my eyes. I glare at him, but the hat is probably hiding its impact. I start walking again, faster than before.

He half-jogs to keep up, but then we cross the boundary and he stumbles. 'Whoa.'

I stop. 'You okay? It'll probably pass in a second.'

He swallows and sways, then begins walking again, more cautiously. 'This area has been totally empty since the disaster?'

'Yeah. Everyone was evacuated, then it was fenced off. They're trying to encourage people to move back to places close to the zones but it hasn't really worked so far.'

'What's the plan for the future?'

I shrug. 'Don't think there's any. Nobody can fix it. People can't live here. In Tokyo they have zones anyone can visit, but here's different.'

'Not *live*, but the land could be used. It's a waste. In the States, I bet people would be fighting over it.'

People are always fighting in the States, I don't say. 'Anyway, about ten years have passed here.'

'Wow.' He takes photos of the white cars rusted to red, a tricycle tipped on its side, a bag of rubbish with contents of dust. 'Lovely,' he murmurs.

I roll my eyes. 'You want to walk around by yourself

for a while? I'll stay close by. Don't touch anything. Remember, you can't take anything from here back to normal time.' He nods quickly. He's nervous, which is good. I watch him wander away, clicking and sighing.

I've been doing this for about two years. One day, a foreigner on the street asked me for directions, and when he found out I spoke English, he asked me, straight out, if I knew a way to take him through. I hesitated, and then he offered me ten thousand yen. It was a fortune to me then, so I took him, and it was probably the stupidest thing I have ever done. But it had been more than a year since I'd been in the zones with Dad, and maybe I wanted the company too. The guy wasn't frightened enough, far from it. But I managed to bring him through and back again and made him swear never to tell anyone. Since then, I've been more selective and raised my prices. I've brought dozens of people in, foreigners from around the world, all ages, all genders.

I climb the narrow stairs of a building I've visited before, up to the third floor to a room lined with bookshelves. From the window, I can see Steve and the ocean. It sparkles and throws out blue, defying the dull day.

There's the faintest noise behind me – or not even a noise, but the trace of the air moving. I turn around slowly in order not to scare anything or let anything think I'm scared. The back of the room is divided by a shoji screen, stained and ripped in places, and for an instant a shadow behind it looks like the slender silhouette of a person. I catch my breath before I see that it has tall, pointed ears.

The light dims. A cloud in front of the sun. Everything falls into shade.

I force my breath even. The edges of the tatami mats have sprouted shy stalks. Every time I think I know the zones, something odder than before will happen. In the slow zone, there are shadows; in the fast zones I've seen creatures, spirits, things not entirely human.

There's a gasping shout from outside, and I rush down the stairs.

Steve is a couple of doors down, staring between his camera screen and a traditional-style izakaya on the other side of the street.

I run to him. 'What did you see?'

'Nothing ... I took a photo of that doorway.' He points to the izakaya. 'And a statue beside it.'

I follow his finger. No statue.

'It was pretty faded, but it was like a little round guy wearing a hat...?'

'Did he have big testicles?'

This seems to snap Steve out of his shock. 'What? Why would I even—' he splutters.

I cough to cover my laugh. 'It was probably a tanuki statue.'

'Well, now it's gone.' He shows me his camera, a photo with the statue, and the next with none.

The time stamp in the corner, taken a second after the first photo. It could be wrong, of course, but... I stare hard at the photo and see, in that narrow alley, a small shape, a darker smudge in the shadow, two pricks of light that could be eyes. I don't point this out. He'll probably see it later and he can freak out by himself.

'Let's leave.'

He hurries after me. 'But – what do you think happened?'

'I dunno. Maybe it fell apart all of a sudden.'

'What if … it used to be here years ago, and then because *I* was here, it returned, for a moment. Like a memory.' He's clearly impressed by this theory.

I glance behind us. 'Could be you've been in here too long already and your camera's getting messed up. Also,' I say, partly to distract and partly because it's true, 'you don't look so good. Do you feel sick?'

Steve clenches his jaw. He's flushed, clammy, as if he's getting a fever. 'I don't feel great,' he admits.

'Then we should go,' I tell him.

'Fine. I'm pretty sure I've got enough.' He glances at his camera and becomes a bit more cheerful.

Of course he does, because now he's got a creepy story as well as a bunch of photos. But it doesn't matter. Nobody will believe him.

The first time I went into one of the zones by myself, I was just going home. Or at least, the home that had been ours whenever we visited Japan: my ojiichan's house. The house my mother had grown up in. Dad said it was too dangerous to go back. He had bought us new clothes and rented a new house, so that everything we had was unfamiliar and unfeeling.

Ojiichan's house is in one of the slow zones, though back then they hadn't differentiated between the zones. It wasn't hard to sneak in. There were no fences, only barriers across the roads, sometimes guards to keep watch. Not that anybody was trying to get past; there were only rescue workers and surveyors and police going in because they had to.

It was almost summer. I was glad of the birds, because they sang and called to each other and kept the silence at bay. There were cracks in the roads, walls tumbled, cars crumpled. There were houses that I knew were empty because of the loneliness that radiated from them, yet still seemed to have slight movements within them. Now and then my skin tingled. I wondered if it was the wrongness of time that I felt, and what it was doing to me. Not that I cared. If time had taken me apart it would have been a relief.

I suddenly saw the shadow of a person, cast on the wall of a house. When I turned my head to see whose shadow, there was nobody there. A shadow without its person. It stayed, unmoving, for two thumping heartbeats before it vanished.

I ran. When I saw Ojiichan's house, it was unchanged, so comforting and normal that I sprinted to the front door and slid it back without even thinking it might be locked. It wasn't, it was never locked, same as always—

Inside, I stopped. 'Tadaima,' I whispered. 'I'm home.'

Home had been vandalised. The shoes and slippers in the genkan were strewn everywhere, as if a child had had a tantrum. I retrieved two matching slippers and walked through the house, haunting it. It smelled of air that hadn't moved in a long time. Everything was jarred, spilled, knocked over, broken. Had it been cracked by the Shake, or had it been the terrible shift in time?

I hated our new house, but I discovered then that it was worse to see the familiar become strange and frightening and sad. I'd thought that I would take back as much as I could carry, but I couldn't bring myself to touch anything. I moved through the rooms, stepping over broken plates, the shattered glass of the TV, books tipped from the shelves, flowers dead for lack of water and light.

I climbed the stairs to the room me and Mom and Dad stayed in. My suitcase with my old life inside. The futons heaped on the tatami. I slumped beside them.

'I'm sorry I didn't help you with them,' I said to the emptiness, the silence, the ghosts. 'I didn't know.' I choked. 'I should have stayed.' I cried until the pain in my head made me stop.

I stood up dizzily and staggered around. I found a blue bracelet Mom used to wear if she was dressing nicely, a daruma doll she'd bought at the temple we had visited together, a silk scarf the colour of grass. The scarf still smelled like her: mint and lavender and the indefinable scent of Mom. I wrapped it around my neck and put the daruma in my bag. I crept down the stairs, which this time were silent. On the low table of the living room, a leaf-patterned cup tipped on its side caught my eye. Mom had used it since she was little. I added it to my bag and then returned to my shoes. I closed the door softly behind me and tried not to look back.

The sun was setting. The sky was the colour of a ripening peach, too soft for what I was feeling, which was red and blue and black. On the street outside Ojiichan's house, I froze – a shadow stretched across the concrete, as if a person was standing there with their back to the sun. But there was nobody. It was only a shadow, lost, unmoored from its person. Like Peter Pan, I thought, before the shadow moved towards me. Did it miss having a body to follow, or was it all that was left of a body?

I ran and ran, and my hands were on the fence when I felt it: the skin prickling, the sensation of tipping, and then the sky darkened to grey and blue. I was almost too tired to be afraid but not too tired to understand. I felt sick. I retched. I held Mom's scarf to my nose. In the zone, things are preserved. In the slow places, decay can be delayed. Night comes later. Back in normal time, everything readjusts to the correct *now*. Her smell had disappeared. All I had was the memory.

Next day I lie on my bed and flick through a manga, but every time I turn a page I forget what came before. I give up and start watching a show on my laptop about teenagers battling werewolves in their cute English town. They have it so easy. I'd love something as straightforward as a cursed dog-human to punch in the face. Though a better option might be to get bitten and then become a werewolf myself, because then I could really be part of a pack. I stop watching the show.

I can't help it; I open up the homepage of Koki's soon-to-be university. There are photos of the campus, smiling students, Tokyo. The city looks new and clean and modern, totally unlike here. Koki's right to go there – how could he not? After university, he'll get a job and have a life and his future will be new and clean and modern too. I hate being jealous, but that doesn't make the jealousy go away.

I only have to hide it for a little longer because Koki is leaving tomorrow.

And with that thought, my phone lights up.

hi! are you at home?

It's Koki.

yeah, I reply.

are you busy?

really busy. Then: *not.*

can I come over? he writes.

when?

now.

i thought we were meeting later!

i know, i'm sorry. My mom just let slip that the family are coming over for a SURPRISE dinner tonight. He adds three eye-rolling emojis.

fun, I type. *come on over.*

i'm actually already on my way.

I send him a row of upside-down smiley faces.

SORRYYYYYY, he replies.

This isn't how I thought it would go. We were supposed to meet tonight and … I dunno, go for a walk and kiss and say goodbye. It's 3.31 p.m. now, which is not a romantic or memorable time.

I stare into a mirror and try to smooth down my hair, which I unfortunately inherited from Dad, so it's disobedient and frizzy instead of straight and smooth. I put on some face powder. I apply mascara, trying not to blink and making my eyes water. I have enough time to wonder if I look as panicked as I feel before the doorbell chimes.

'Hey,' I say.

'Hey,' says Koki.

'Come in.'

He comes in.

'Sit down wherever.'

He sits down wherever.

'So.'

We stare at each other, and if he looks unhappy, then I probably do too.

He taps his finger on the table. 'I didn't want to change plans. At least Mom is terrible at keeping secrets or I'd have to come over here at seven a.m. tomorrow instead.'

'I'd rather not say goodbye than wake up at that time.'

'That's what I thought!'

'You know me well,' I say.

'You should visit me in Tokyo,' Koki says. 'If you want

to. The next few months will probably be busy, getting started and everything, but in the autumn...'

'Won't you be back during the summer holidays?'

'I plan to, but if I have to get a part-time job, I might not be able to come home for long. I don't know yet. But it would fun for you to come to Tokyo, wouldn't it?' I know how nervous he is by how fast he's babbling.

'I'll try to.'

'Sora, I—'

I stand up. 'I have a going-away gift for you.'

'You didn't need to—'

'Don't worry, it's small. And cheap. It's in my room.' I escape down the hallway and I'm in my room before I realise Koki's followed me. 'Oh – ah, my room's a mess!'

'I thought it would be way worse, actually.' Koki doesn't try to hide his curiosity, his eyes travelling over the photos of old friends in Vancouver, an April White print of a Haida-style orca whale, postcard versions of Monet's waterlilies, Emily Carr's pine trees, ukiyo-e woodblock prints. I take my laptop off the bed and dump it on my desk and he sits down.

I reach behind the curtains and take out the flowerpot I'd hidden there. I didn't want Dad to see it. He doesn't like plants or flowers any more. I unceremoniously thrust it at Koki. 'Here.'

He takes it in surprise. 'Thank you.'

I sit beside him. 'It's a four o'clock flower.' The trumpet-shaped flowers are yellow, white, pink, some a combination of both. I touch one, white with streaks and stripes of yellow. 'The petals open at four p.m. – well, around four p.m. – and stay open until morning.'

'So I know what time it is?' he asks.

'Assuming your room in Tokyo has a window that lets in daylight, yeah.'

'Thank you. It's beautiful. It's a very *you* gift.'

'Good or bad thing?'

'Good,' he says. He places the flowerpot on my desk. He holds my hand. 'Sora, I've been thinking…'

I *knew* that this time we'd have to have a conversation like this, *knew* that it would begin with that line, and yet I still don't know what the right thing to say is.

Koki's hands are sweaty, which reassures me. '…we've been close for a while now, and even though I'm going away, I—'

'I don't want to be your girlfriend,' I say very quickly, before he can finish.

He blinks. 'Ah.' His hands tighten on mine, then release a little. 'That's what I thought. Then it's for the best if we don't, now.'

'You think the same?' I watch him closely, and now I want him to protest.

'Yes… That's what you want too, isn't it?' he asks.

I don't know what I want at all. If Koki wasn't going away, if he was staying at home and commuting to the local university, but now—

'It's for the best,' I repeat. What a stupid useful line that is. He nods. We sit there, nodding at each other like bobble-headed toys.

He breathes in. 'I want you to know that I care for you very much, Sora.'

I almost say that I care for him too, that his friendship has almost defeated the loneliness and sadness I've lived with for so long, that without him I don't know what I'll do. I put my mouth on his to stop myself.

Koki makes a surprised sound, but he doesn't hesitate to return my kiss and smooth his hands against my back. We hold each other close, my hands in his black hair, his resting on the bare skin between my T-shirt and my jeans. I press him back down against the pillows and we catch our breaths and stare at each other.

'Sora—' he says.

'Yes,' I answer to whatever question he was about to ask.

We undress each other carefully. We lay our hands on each other. Eventually, I scrabble in a drawer and retrieve a condom. My cheeks are hot as I hand it to him.

'Prepared,' he says, grinning.

'I'm an optimist. Or a pessimist, depending what your priorities are.' I don't want to tell him I've thought about this moment.

We smile and then laugh. We touch. It's sweet, painful, awkward, good. I want to press myself as close as I can to him; I want him to always hold on to me this tightly. We could have been here before now, but it feels inevitable that it would happen this way, because I hide the things I want until it's too late, until there are only heartbeats left.

清明

SKY BECOMES
CLEAR AND BRIGHT

5

Mom in summer, tending a maple tree in the botanical garden where she worked. Sometimes during the holidays, I'd go with her and play or read or roll in the grass while she pulled weeds or coaxed sick plants back to life or fended off bug infestations. When I was seven, she taught me the Japanese name for a maple: *momiji*.

'In fall it will become glowing orange and flaming red, as if it's burning itself up before winter comes,' she said.

'Then it dies?' I asked.

'It might look like that, but it's only sleeping. It dreams of spring, and when it wakes up it turns the world green.'

'I like fall best, summer second best, and spring third best.' I counted the seasons off on my fingers. 'Winter last. I don't like it.'

'In Japan there are seventy-two seasons,' Mom said. 'One for when the irises bloom, when warm winds blow, when hawks begin to fly... I can't remember them all.'

'That's too many!'

'But the winter seasons are very important. The trees need to rest the way you need to sleep at night.'

'It makes everything ugly.'

'Nature is never ugly,' Mom said. 'In winter you can see the tree's lovely branches. Like your arms in short sleeves.' She lifted my arm up, and then hers, much longer and more graceful. Both our arms were tanned and golden against the green and blue of summer.

'Look: see the ways our arms have straight lines and soft lines.' She touched the tip of each of my fingers in turn. 'Your clever fingers. Very simple and pure. That's what we can admire in the trees in winter. And they're much braver than we are, wearing nothing in the cold!' She walked her fingers up my arm and then tickled under my armpit, making me giggle and scrunch up.

When I caught my breath again, I said, 'We're opposites. We wear lots of clothes in winter when the trees are *naked*, and then in summer we wear shorts and T-shirts when they're all covered up.'

'Yes, maybe. But maybe we're not opposite, only different. Nature has the right time for everything. It knows how to wait. *Some people –* ' she taps my nose – 'don't really know how to do that.'

'Because it's boring.'

Mom tutted at me. 'Trees are patient. Be like a tree.'

I stood up and lifted my arms to the air and made a whooshing noise to show the wind in my invisible leaves. Mom applauded.

'Am I a good tree?' I asked.

'Of course. You're as strong as a tree and as beautiful as a tree, and as helpful and as generous and as kind.'

I hugged her. 'You're a good tree too.'

Koki and I lie quietly together. Our arms are touching, straight lines and soft lines crossing over each other. I study the flowers so I can see them opening their petals to the evening.

'Must be four p.m.,' Koki whispers.

I crane my head to see the clock. 'It's almost five. I guess now we know that they're not entirely accurate.'

'They're still nicer than numbers,' he murmurs.

'That's what I think too.'

This close, I can see that Koki's pupils are dilated against the almost-black of his irises.

'I have to go,' he says.

'I know.' I sit up and start pulling on my clothes. Koki straightens my T-shirt, plants a kiss on the back of my neck. I pat down his hair, which is sticking up everywhere.

He picks up the pot and sniffs. 'They smell really good.'

'They attract hummingbirds, apparently. If there were hummingbirds here.' That's all I can offer to the conversation. My head feels empty.

Then the doorbell rings.

'Delivery guy?' I wonder, going to the door, Koki behind me.

It's not a delivery guy. It's a man in a suit and with him is Dad, looking pale, leaning on his arm, home far too early. Dad sways, and I grab him, lowering him on to the genkan step to help him ease his shoes off.

The man is introducing himself as Dad's co-worker. '...taken ill, perhaps it was something he ate—' the man is saying.

'How kind of you to bring him home.' But this isn't just kindness. It's weird. 'Dad, you couldn't drive? Did you collapse?'

'After he returned, he rested for a little but we thought it best to escort him, just in case...' the co-worker says.

'Returned? From lunch?' I ask.

The co-worker pauses, glances at Dad.

Dad is still alert enough to lie. 'Yes, Sora-chan, perhaps it was a bad lunch set.'

The co-worker says hurriedly, 'Of course, please wait until you have recovered before you return, Campbell-san.'

'I'm certain that I will be better for yesterday.' Dad corrects himself. 'Tomorrow.'

'Please wait until you have recovered,' the man repeats. 'I am sure your daughter will take good care of you.'

He looks slightly sceptical as he says this, and I glare at him.

Koki steps forward. 'She will. Really, she is very good.'

I try to look very good. Dad pushes himself up and bows and I catch his arm again because he is tilting forward a little too much.

Dad and his co-worker thank each other until finally he leaves. I lead Dad inside and he sits heavily at the table. Koki brings him a glass of water, and Dad nods at him and drinks it all down. His colour is coming back, but he's still pale. He looks older than he is, and the thought occurs to me that maybe that isn't my imagination.

'I'm fine,' Dad says.

'No, you're not. What happened?' I ask.

'I felt dizzy. I should have taken a break – I didn't eat, I think. I got sick…' He trails off.

'Where were you?' I ask. 'The office, was it?'

Dad doesn't meet my eyes. 'Slow zone.'

'How did you get back?' I say.

'I brought myself back when I woke up.'

'You passed out?'

'I'm fine,' Dad repeats.

'You need to lie down,' I tell him.

It seems like he's going to protest but thinks better of it and nods.

I glance at Koki. 'Sorry…'

'I should go,' he says.

We look at each other for a long moment. There's nothing we can say.

'Take care,' I tell him. 'Goodbye.'

He bows and puts his shoes on and leaves. I stare at the door, but Dad is pushing himself up so I take him to his room and help him lie down. I don't ask him any more questions because I'm afraid of the answers I might get.

Dad and I mapped out the edges of the time zones, the lines that marked the difference between *now* and *then*. Some of the boundaries were already known and blocked off by gates and fences and warning signs. At some of the gates there would be guards, walking back and forth in their white caps. I wondered what they thought about all day, whether they could feel the time difference too.

Of course we couldn't ask them. Dad said that so far nobody else was able to feel the boundaries between time zones the way I could. That made me feel special. I was getting faster at it all the time. I'd seen a book written in Braille, once, and ran my hands over the sequences of dots and marvelled that fingertips could read a story. Finding the time was the closest I could get to doing something similar, except I didn't always understand what I was reading.

Dad made a map and every time we went out, which was about once a week, he would come back and update it. It was the most time we had spent together in years. It was easier because we were both working, both caught on the same puzzle, out in the world rather than sitting around and trying to make sense of it all. He was excited, which I didn't really understand. Because even though we learned more, we weren't really closer to finding real answers. Or people.

'How *do* they make the boundaries?' I asked.

'They mostly observe how things fall apart, or don't. We have tried to observe animals, but it's much more difficult to see any difference with them. As far as we can tell, they move across the zones more or less normally... So food is often used, though it must be kept in controlled conditions. Milk in containers. Objects that rust or break. Usually they are put at spaced intervals, starting at a place known to be in a different zone. They are observed.'

'And then fenced off... What have they said about our research?' I asked.

'Who?'

'The other scientists.' I knew them only as vague, white-coated figures always staring at stuff intently.

'They haven't said anything.'

'You mean *you* haven't told them yet,' I guessed.

Dad gestured to a boundary we had begun marking. 'Can you check this?'

'What about the stuff they're doing? Have they seen anyone in the zones?' I asked.

'Anyone,' Dad repeated, looking at me.

'Or anything,' I added, because Dad didn't like the theories about people still alive in the zones. I turned away and began feeling for the place where time changed.

Dad watched me. 'I would like to get as many boundaries drawn as possible first. Then I'll explain how it was done.'

'Will I have to go with you to help you explain?' I had an image of myself in front of those white-coated scientists, their intent gazes fixed on me.

'Maybe,' he said eventually.

I poke him. 'Are you going to steal my glory?'

He frowned and shook his head, but not in a way that meant *no*. 'Don't be silly,' he said. 'Let's work together.' He held out his hand formally.

I took his hand, bigger than mine, stained with red from his marker. 'Yes.'

I toss and turn all night, tangled in sheets that smell like Koki. When morning finally arrives, I tap on Dad's door.

'Hey. You awake?'

There's a muffled noise that seems to be a yes.

'Can I come in? I'm coming in.' My eyes adjust to the half-light in the bedroom; the curtains aren't closed fully.

Dad's in bed, crumpled and pale. 'Morning,' he croaks.

'How do you feel? You look horrible.'

'Your kind words cure me,' Dad says.

I smile away the worry. 'It's a gift.'

'I have a bad cold, I think. Perhaps the flu.'

'That lunch set was really terrible, huh.'

Dad closes his eyes. 'Sora.'

'What happened, Dad?'

'I over-exerted myself. But this hasn't happened before ... to me.'

'You collapsed? Out of nowhere?' I press. 'How far into the slow zone were you?'

Dad's eyes stutter open. They somehow seem both glazed and too bright. 'Not far enough. There were silhouettes, outlines, there. Of people. Or where people had been.'

I swallow. 'You saw them? What did they do?'

Dad shuts his eyes again and murmurs a half-question, '…trying to speak…?'

'You heard them say something?' I grab his hand. 'Tell me.'

Dad's eyes are shaken open by me. He gazes at me. 'Nothing, Sora… Maybe they weren't there. I'm very tired. Yes, this must be the flu.'

The flu, or the shadows, or the fox spirits playing tricks… Or—

Dad wheezes and coughs.

I release his hand. 'I'll get you some water, okay? And medicine…'

'Soo-jin says tiger balm is good for the flu,' Dad informs me suddenly.

'Soo-jin…' I haven't heard her name in a long time. She's a Korean-Japanese scientist who had worked with Dad for a few years. She's kind and smart and I loved her. 'Did she say that? Seems unscientific.' Then again, Japanese people seem to be the only East Asians to not trust tiger balm to cure everything.

'She just told me,' Dad says dreamily.

'What? When?' I ask.

'When I couldn't breathe,' he replies.

'You're feverish.' I lean down and lay my hand on his forehead, then jerk back as a jolt snaps through me. 'Ah!' The second hand on my watch twitches forward, then back.

'I must be hot,' Dad says.

'Didn't you feel that?' I stare from Dad to my watch, ticking evenly again.

'I do feel warm.'

I grit my teeth and touch Dad's forehead once more, but there's nothing except the restless warmth of a fever spreading. 'Yeah, you're too hot. I'll get water – electrolytes or ... something...'

'Thank you.'

I leave the room blindly, fumbling through drawers for paracetamol, filling a glass of water, running a cloth under cool water. I press the cloth over my own face. What is happening? Because *something* is happening to Dad. His forgetfulness and tiredness, of course, and they're getting worse and worse. But now ... the strange jolt from his body, the *time* – this is different. And I don't know how or what or why. I want to scream.

Instead, I rinse the cloth out again and take everything to Dad.

'Here, drink this.' I put tablets in one hand, water in the other, and watch him swallow it all down. 'Lie back.' I put the cloth on his forehead gently. 'We don't have any sticky fever patches but I'll go get some.'

'This is fine.' Dad lets out a long breath. He relaxes a little.

I look down at him and panic fizzes through me. Can I call an ambulance, explain this to a doctor? Who can I ask for help? The man who brought Dad home? He was some random guy, though, not a manager ... but the company – someone there must know. Maybe they were even the ones *doing* this to him, somehow. I'll – I'll—

'Sora?' Dad whispers raggedly.

'Yeah. Do you need something?'

'No ... I just wasn't sure if you were here, still.' He doesn't open his eyes to check.

'I'm here.'

'I thought I saw you there too, and her. But it wasn't. Only a memory,' Dad says breathlessly.

I know where *there* means. I could shake Dad awake and interrogate him, but his voice is so weak. And suddenly, I'm afraid.

'It's okay, Dad. We can talk about this when you feel better. Sleep now.'

Dad murmurs agreement and I wait until his breath becomes even and he slips into sleep.

I leave the bedroom door half-open. I go to the kitchen, then the living room, then my room, pacing and pacing. I want to run or cycle away, but I can't. I have to stay. Because the thought comes to me that maybe it's not just the company responsible for whatever Dad is doing. Maybe he is doing it to himself.

I was at the kitchen table, copying out kanji after kanji. My arm ached from wrist to shoulder and I still had another worksheet to do.

'Tadaima,' Dad said, punctuated by the door opening and closing.

'Hi,' I replied in English.

Dad came in and peered at my messy practice. 'I thought you didn't have to do that in high school.'

'Japanese students don't.' I started writing miniku. It meant ugly, or shame.

'You're Japanese,' Dad said.

He was the only person around here who would say that. 'I don't think so. Anyway, I'm behind everyone else in kanji.' The next one was koku; cruel, unjust.

'You're certainly able to catch up. It's very good that you're being proactive and doing this.'

'My teacher gave them to me. I have to do them.' He'd said that my kanji were terrible, that elementary school students were better than me.

'That was good of him, to give you resources and so on.' But his voice was unenthusiastic.

'Yeah.' Would have been even better of him not to give me the sheets in front of the whole class.

Next: kou. Fermentation.

'To give you extra time too,' Dad continued.

'The class is smaller than it used to be.'

Less kids to make fun of me. Lucky.

Sei: awaken.

I shook my hand loose. 'Are you okay?'

'A tad tired.' He rubbed a hand over his face.

'How was your presentation thing?' I asked.

Dad sighed. 'Not terrific.'

'How come? I thought they'd name some theory or law after you.'

'It's not quite that easy.'

'You said nobody else had presented research like it—'

'The board weren't exactly focused on the *results* of the research.' Dad sat down heavily.

I fling my pencil away. 'We've done hours and hours of mapping and recording and measuring stuff.' It had been years of work, at weekends and after school, and months of Dad compiling it all, with me checking and correcting and double-checking. It had been years.

'They were more preoccupied with the methods.'

'Like the kinds of clocks we used? Or they didn't understand that I could feel the borders between zones?' Or maybe they were *too* interested in that.

His eyes moved to his hands, resting flat on the table. 'You know that it's illegal to go into the zones unauthorised—'

'You're allowed—'

'I'm allowed by myself. But endangering a minor isn't included in that. And your ability to feel the zones…'

'You said I was your researcher.' These words came out of my mouth sounding childish and pathetic.

'The board were of the opinion that I should not have taken you,' Dad said. 'That it was too dangerous.'

'It's not *really* that dangerous now, though,' I scoffed.

Dad doesn't reply.

'Is it, Dad?'

Dad closed his mouth tightly.

'Tell me,' I pressed.

'There was an opinion that a sign of the zones' detrimental effect is our belief in your ability.' Dad's voice was flat and neutral, as if he was reporting statistics.

Our belief... 'They think I'm imagining it,' I said. My skin prickled.

'No, no,' Dad said unconvincingly. 'I told them that we minimised risks. That it was also of use to observe the zones' effects on different age groups – the researchers are all in the same age bracket, and mostly male—'

'What do you mean?'

'I argued the case for broader data, and testing others for the ability to feel the boundaries, but they found it ... odd. Even though I said you were proof of the possibilities, not the dangers,' Dad muttered, almost to himself, 'I monitored you so carefully.'

'Monitored,' I repeated.

'It was also a way to make sure you are safe,' Dad said.

I thought of how he would ask me the same question about a place every time we went there. How he took me to the doctor any time I had even the hint of a cold. How he checked my grades and quizzed me about schoolwork and checked my appetite. How he wrote everything down, logged it, checked it. I thought he'd been taking care of me.

I understood. 'I'm your experiment.'

'What? No, of course you aren't.' His voice was loud.

'You took me into the zones so you can see what it's doing to me,' I said.

'And what you are able to do *with* it!' Dad said defensively.

'No, no, no.' It was true, what he was saying, but it *felt* wrong. It felt cold. As if I was another instrument, some other scientific tool he could use.

'We were working together,' Dad said.

'You told them – you made me a reason – and now they think I'm going mad. What's going to happen now? Are they going to come look at me?' I had a sudden panicky terror that they would take me away.

'No,' Dad said. 'Though they made it clear that you are not to go into the zones again. Which I agree with.'

'You think I'm crazy too?'

'I don't, I believe you.' Dad reached a hand to me and I shrugged him away.

'If you stop me then who will look for Mom?' I said, before I could think or stop myself.

Dad's face hollowed out, like something inside him that had been holding him up had collapsed. 'She's *gone*!' His voice was raw with something I had not heard before, anger or desperation. 'That's not what we were doing, Sora! There's no proof, no reason... You have to stop this!'

I flinched. It's what I'd been doing. Even though Dad had never said it, I thought that's what he had been doing too.

The printed kanji were assured and dignified above

my pencil strokes, uncoordinated and awkward. Shame, injustice, awakening. They blurred into scratches and smudges, meaning nothing.

'Sora—'

I was already running away, out of the house, away from rationality and tests and the measurements of science. But I couldn't escape what I knew: that Dad had lied to me, and told others about me, and that when they thought there was something wrong with me he had done nothing but agree. That he had never been searching for Mom. That, for him, time came first and I came second.

玄鳥至

SWALLOWS RETURN

6

After the Shake we stayed in one of the evacuation centres, a high school gym. Despite all the people, in musty clothes and blankets and fear, there was still a gym smell, like sweat and the rubberiness of basketballs. Some people stayed there all day, but most went out searching. Dad wouldn't let me go, even though I argued and begged. When he finally did take me, I wished he hadn't, because I was almost paralysed by the terrible pulling feeling between the desire and terror of finding Mom.

I had nightmares. Everybody did. Maybe we even dreamed the same dream.

There was an obaachan, a friend of my grandparents, who now slept beside us, separated only by centimetres. She had the sort of quiet that formed a bubble around her. If Dad had to go anywhere, even to the bathroom, I held myself tight against panic, until she'd take my hand and let me into that bubble. Her other hand patted my back or reached to stroke my hair, calming and comforting.

There were little shakes after the big one. When they happened, everyone held their breath, and it was as if we were trying to will the ground still with our collective desperation. I cried with as little noise as possible.

'Hush,' the obaachan said. 'It's just the catfish rolling.'

'What catfish?' I asked.

'There's a giant catfish under this island, the namazu. It has lived there for a long, long time, down in the cool mud. Every now and then, the catfish gets restless, or maybe has an itch. And then it twists and turns, but when it does, it moves the land above it. That's when the ground shakes. The catfish is rolling beneath it.'

A story, and still I was angry. 'It breaks everything,' I said. 'I hate it.'

'Long ago, a god pinned it down. Maybe it's become loose. Maybe it's trying to get free. But it will calm down.' Her hand on my hair was gentle. 'It will be still.'

I wanted to tell the police, call the army. I closed my eyes but the anger made my face hot. A story making something abstract alive. A giant catfish like any animal; not evil, not consciously causing harm, but still the cause of it. What would you do with a creature like that? Catch it. Trap it. Put it down like a dog that bites or attacks a child.

The obaachan hushed me. 'Be calm. Be still.' She was speaking to me, to the anger that thrashed beneath my skin, to the catfish.

The official searches ended, but once you begin searching, it's hard to stop.

Dad's fever broke a few days ago and he's sleeping better and eating a little, so it's okay for me to leave the house again. There have been no more strange electric shocks from him. Between that new kind of freakiness and Koki being gone for a week, I'm losing my mind a tiny bit.

So it's good I have a tour today. I don't bother straightening my hair, tying it back instead. I put a mask on – that'll have to do. I'm meeting a woman, Naomi, at a train station. They're always the best places to meet, though the trains here are small and local. At the exit I gaze around, but the few other people are a squatting construction worker drinking a can of coffee, two boys in dirt-streaked baseball gear, and an old lady waiting near the bus stop.

I lean against the wall and send an email. *I'm here.*

A minute later, a woman emerges from the smoking area. She's taller than me, wearing jeans and a white T-shirt that are somehow both plain and stylish. She looks Japanese.

She pauses beside me and murmurs, in English, 'I'm Naomi.'

She continues walking and after a few seconds I follow. She goes briskly down several other streets until we reach a car. She gets in and watches me hesitate before I open the door and slide into the passenger seat.

'Hello, Yuna,' she says in English, with a neutral American accent. She hands me an envelope.

I check the notes inside. 'Have you done this before?'

'I'm very discreet,' she says. 'Here.'

'Compared to home?' I ask.

'To many places,' she answers evenly, but not in an unfriendly way.

She's sharp. I wish I'd straightened my hair.

She starts the car and I give her directions. She drives carefully but faster than I expect.

'You're Japanese?' I ask.

'Yes. Sansei American, to be exact,' she says.

'Interesting. Take the next left,' I say, and wait for her inevitable *where-are-you-from?* in return. It doesn't come, which somehow makes me both relieved and annoyed. 'Park here, then we'll walk.'

She nods and follows me without question, down a barely noticeable trail and then through the fence. I watch her from the corner of my eye as we pass over the boundary. She winces and breathes in sharply, but doesn't say anything.

We walk until we reach a structure almost entirely covered in greenery. I lead Naomi to the place where I've cleared the vegetation, where we could peer inside. The plants and leaves have pressed themselves right up against the walls, rioting against the glass. I point out an almost invisible door. 'This was a greenhouse. Want to go inside?' I ask.

Naomi seems sceptical. 'I don't think I need to. They appear to be coming out towards me.'

'Well, they weren't carnivorous last I checked, but things do change quickly around here.' I haul the door open. The air that rushes out is like the exhalation of a rainforest.

Naomi peers in. 'It's a jungle.'

'Yeah. The plants cracked through the glass.' I shut the door and go to the other side of the glasshouse. I point out strawberries dangling at eye level, plump and red. 'Want to try?' I pluck a few, rinse them from my water bottle, and eat a couple, dropping the green caps on the ground.

Naomi takes the last one from my hand and eats it whole.

Nobody ever takes a strawberry. That's why I bring them here.

'You're surprised,' she says.

'Never seen someone eat the green part.'

'You can't even taste the difference,' she replies. 'And barely feel the texture. Where are we going next?'

She's going to be hard to impress. Maybe this will be more interesting than usual. I take her through the town, letting her absorb the disintegrating cars and curtains fading in windows. She doesn't take photos or say anything pitying, but her eyes darken with sadness. I abandon my usual route.

I lead her to a shop that sold dishes, small furniture, things for a home. There's broken pottery on the floor, shaken by the earthquake, but the pottery still on the shelves is whole, just dusty. Cushions and blankets made from nylon and polyester are falling apart, melting almost, as if they had remembered the oil they had come from. I gesture to the corner with clocks, with hands that have stopped at different times.

'Interesting,' Naomi says. 'I suppose the batteries couldn't have all run out at the same time.'

'In other places, the clocks stopped at pretty much the same time. In the slow zones, there are clocks that still work. Or at least,' I correct myself, 'the hands still move.'

Suddenly, there is a noise that I think at first is an alarm, far away, but I realise it's the pottery tinkling against each other a moment before I feel the earthquake. I move away from the shelves and stand close to the wall, in a spot where there are no shelves above me. By the time I get there, the shaking has stopped. Naomi hasn't moved.

'A small one,' I say. 'You okay?'

Naomi doesn't reply, frozen in fear – until I see that she's watching the clocks.

'I thought I saw some of the hands move,' she says.

'You did, because everything was shaking.'

'Ticking, not trembling,' she says impatiently.

'How many ticks?'

'Four or five.'

'The earthquake lasted about three seconds.'

'And we are in the fast zone,' Naomi observes.

'Did they *all* tick the same amount?' All the clocks are motionless now.

'No. They didn't all tick, either.' Naomi picks up a small bedside clock carefully, turns it over in her hands, leaves fingerprints on the dusty glass.

'The quakes do that, sometimes,' I admit.

Naomi puts the clock down. 'So you know. Why not simply say so?'

'It doesn't always happen. And it freaks people out.'

'I hardly ran screaming,' she says dryly.

'Maybe you were about to. I don't *always* know when people are about to do that.' I go outside, where I lean against the wall of the shop and check my watch. Another half an hour before we leave.

Naomi comes out, brushing her hands together. We watch the dust float away. 'How do you calm them down?' she asks.

'By telling them something will hear them.' I had actually only done this once, but the guy had shut up straight away before asking very quietly what kind of *thing*.

'You've never run screaming yourself?' she asks.

I remember the cattle, the shadows in doorways and windows, the appearances of creatures I had read about in folk tales. 'I'm not really a screamer.'

'Me neither,' she says. 'I'd like to watch these clocks for a little longer.'

'Okay.' I don't want to see their ticking hands any longer. I wander to the back of the shop, where there's storage and a break room.

I pick up a cup with a vaguely psychedelic orange pattern around the rim. It's very 1960s, very Showa, like something my grandparents would have owned for decades. I put it down gently, back into the little circle it had made in the dust of the countertop, and turn to go.

There's a faint scraping noise behind me. I spin around, scanning the window, the corners of the rooms. The ceiling. Nothing moves. But the countertop... There's the clean ring the cup had left in the dust. And there's the cup, somehow at the end of the counter. I stare at it, then sweep my gaze around the room again, but nothing else seems to have moved. The cup is still and innocent in its new place. I pick it up gingerly and turn it upside down. Nothing strange. Another noise. A clink, a rattle, from a drawer. I pick up a chopstick and use it to pull open the drawer, standing as far back as possible and trying not to think of what sorts of things could leap out.

Nothing does. I peer inside, but there's only a few tarnished spoons. I close the drawer firmly. Surely the *things* weren't moving. Was this actually a weird Japanese version of *Beauty and the Beast*? I back out of the room.

Naomi is still in front of the clocks, but now she's writing in a notebook. She flips a page and I catch a glimpse of something that isn't a drawing or notes; it's equations.

She notices me peering before I can guess what she's been working out and shuts the notebook tightly. 'Done.'

There's something cagey about how she tucks the notebook back into her bag and quickly zips it up.

'Let's go,' I say.

'Already? You seem very sure of the time.'

'I am.'

We return the way we came. I can't stop thinking about the cup, even though I really don't know why a piece of kitchenware is so creepy to me. If it was a knife I might have some excuse.

When we get through the fence, I say, 'Let's rest for a few minutes.'

'Mmmm. My head's a bit...' Naomi puts her hand to her temple.

She sits heavily on the ground, then puts her hand to her mouth as if she's going to retch.

'Deep breaths.' I give her a hard sweet from my bag. 'Suck on this.'

She takes it obediently and her face pinches at the taste. 'Sour.'

'Ume. Dunno why, but it always helps me.' I put one in my mouth too, even though I feel fine. I think my body has adjusted the way I imagine flight stewards adjust to jet lag.

Naomi sips some water and begins to look steadier. She checks her watch. 'You were right about the time. Almost to the minute.'

'I told you.'

She stares at me a little too keenly. 'You definitely did.'

Naomi drives back to town more slowly, her face pale. A few blocks from the station, I say, 'I can get out here.'

She stops the car. 'Thank you for a very interesting tour.'

'Glad you enjoyed it.'

We both pause. Usually I don't linger but I want to say something more to Naomi. I just don't know what.

'Be careful,' she says suddenly.

'Of what?'

'The zones. Everything.' She nods at me. 'Goodbye.'

I take the hint and get out of the car. I should have asked her about those equations in her notebook, but her car is already passing me by. She doesn't wave.

At home, I put my browser on incognito mode and search, *cups moving by themselves.* The results are mostly about poltergeists and ghosts. That wasn't the vibe I'd felt, though. I search in Japanese, and after scrolling for a while I find tsukumogami.

Oh, shit. The objects that get possessed after a hundred years. The cup couldn't be a hundred years old, even with time moving faster … could it? Another strange thing to worry about, which was now entirely normal. Would they all begin to move, soon? Maybe everything will come alive, with a new kind of life. Or a very old one.

❧

'I don't understand,' I said. I was fourteen, in Dad's old lab.

'It's somewhat difficult to get your head around at first,' he said.

'Or third, or fourth, or fifth.' Soo-jin smiled at me with a patient kind of pity.

'Let me start with a question. What do you think time *is*?' Dad asked.

Soo-jin rolled her eyes. 'Is that what you think is an easier start?'

'Time is ... clocks and watches.'

'Is a ruler length? Is a thermometer heat?' Dad asked.

'No, okay. That's just how we measure those things. So with time that's day and night – like, maybe the world spinning around. Or ... it's a thing like ... gravity. We can't see it, but it's there?'

Dad nodded. 'Gravity, yes, that's one way we could think about it. It's a "rule" of the universe. An invisible force.'

'Day and night are the first ways people learned to tell the time,' Soo-jin said. 'We know that clocks measure time, but a clock could stop or break and no clock is perfect. Nothing can affect the sun moving across the sky, though, or the stars—'

'But at different times of the year the days are shorter—' I said.

'Absolutely,' Soo-jin agreed. 'The seasons tell time on a bigger scale. Like a day is a second and a season is an hour.'

'However, if the sun froze in the sky, what would the result be? Would time stop too?' Dad asked.

'We would freeze,' I said. 'But ... wait, if the sun is just a way to *tell* time, then we wouldn't? Because if a clock runs out of battery and stops, that doesn't mean that *we* stop.'

'Correct,' Dad said.

'The sun has never frozen, however, so we can't know that for certain. Or if it *has* frozen, then we *did* freeze, and never knew the difference,' Soo-jin says.

That was terrifying.

'You're worried,' Soo-jin said.

'What if we're freezing and have no idea, but somewhere in the universe a billion years passed? Anything could have happened and we wouldn't know...'

'Does time pass differently in other parts of the universe?' Dad said.

'If the planet turns faster or slower,' Soo-jin replied, '*if* the life on that planet measures time in that way.'

'How would we know?' Dad asked.

'Something would have changed,' I said.

'Ah, so *change*.' Dad's eyes lit up. 'Some say time is the measure of motion, which is change.'

'If something doesn't change, then we can't measure time?' I asked.

Soo-jin jumped in. 'But think: what doesn't change in the world we know?'

Nothing. Everything would break eventually, or fall apart. Even rocks, the ocean, the centre of the earth. We were all quiet.

'Who thought of that, that things moving is the measure of time?' I said.

'Aristotle theorised it,' Soo-jin said, 'more than a thousand years ago. It was more of a philosophical idea that a scientific one.'

'So … after Aristotle died, his idea didn't change. Like, his personal idea that we still use now. He couldn't think anything different or change that idea.' Just to be clear, I added, 'Because he's dead.'

Dad and Soo-jin said, 'Hmmmm,' at the same time, and it was a nice harmony.

'Yes,' Dad said thoughtfully. 'That's true.'

'It is?' I was surprised. 'Does that mean I win?'

Soo-jin laughed. 'You're a true philosophical debater.'

'The idea hasn't changed,' Dad continued, 'but the manner in which we interact with it has. People have agreed and disagreed with it since, disproved it and so on, and – who knows? – maybe it will be proven beyond doubt in the future. And what if everybody dies and all record of Aristotle is forgotten? Does that idea even exist then?'

'Yes?' I guessed. I had no idea. 'It still *existed*.'

'It did,' Soo-jin agreed. 'Though imagine everything that we don't know about. That's a lot of things, but we don't know what they are. Each of them, for us, doesn't exist and can't change, and time can pass and we might never know. Can time measure things we don't know if we never know them?'

We all thought again.

'I … don't know,' I admitted finally.

'But now that you don't, you have time to think about it,' Dad said.

'Do *you* know?' I asked.

'Not remotely!' he said cheerfully.

'Neither do I.' Soo-jin didn't sound as happy about it.

'It would be dull if we knew everything, don't you agree?' Dad asked.

'So … when will you actually finish work? That's what I asked you in the first place. I'm hungry,' I said.

'Oh, let's go now. Now is always *now*, that can't be disputed. Soo-jin, will you join us?'

'Oh – yes. Why not?' Soo-jin was pleased to be invited.

We left the lab and walked to a restaurant. I tilted my head to the sky and wondered if time was stopping and starting over and over again, and if I'd ever know.

鴻雁北

WILD GEESE FLY NORTH

7

I'm fidgety right down to my bones and I don't know why. There have been two tremors in the past few days, only small, but maybe the reverberations are trapped inside my skin because I can't stay still. Dad hasn't gone back to the company since he got sick. I don't know what they told him to do or prevented him from doing, but he's been working busily from home instead. He won't tell me anything more about what happened. He says he can't remember. But there have been no more of those jolts from him and I know I should be grateful.

Koki's been gone for three weeks. We're still messaging, but we haven't spoken about how we said goodbye. I want him to bring it up and I also want to totally avoid it. It was a goodbye. It was a thing that happened. I read back over our conversations compulsively and then don't reply to him for hours or days. I don't know whether I want him more or less. I push him and that last afternoon away to think about later, and the thing I like about later is that it sometimes never arrives.

But I need to escape it, at least for a while. I examine my maps and roam through the zones. Once, in the rattling branches of a tree, I see round eyes gazing back at me; something like a bird, something like a man, crimson-beaked. Is it a spirit like a tengu? Have they ever killed a human? I have time to wonder, before it retreats back into the leaves.

I wonder how time passes for myths and demons. I count the minutes and seconds against the beat of my heart. It's a timepiece that's both inconsistent and reliable, but at this stage I know, at least, how to recognise it when it changes.

After Dad told me I couldn't go to the zones any more, we didn't properly speak for months. He stopped trying to explain what he said I had misunderstood. He left for work before I went to school and came home late. He didn't talk about the research he was doing and I didn't want to ask him. We had hardly anything to talk about.

We broke the silence at Christmas, in a sort of holiday truce. It was better until spring. But the pull of the zones was irresistible, my *need* to start searching again. I wanted to go back and feel the changes of time. I wanted to go there and remember.

'Holidays finally start next week,' I said to Dad over that night's reheated dinner.

'Ah, yes. I suppose you want to do something *fun...*'
He peered at me. 'Is that what you young people call it
these days? *Fun?*'

I patted his hand. 'Don't worry, I'd never force you to
try something new at your age.'

He snorted.

'I was wondering if we could go see how my flower
clock is doing,' I said, as casually as possible. I pushed a
piece of soggy sweet potato tempura around my bowl.

When I eventually raised my eyes, Dad was tapping his
chin impatiently. '*No*, Sora. They're starting to limit even
official field research into the zones. New regulations,'
Dad said.

'I thought field research was *the* most important thing.'

'Adverse effects have started to show.'

'Like what?'

'Equipment isn't holding up very well, which is costly.'
Dad paused. 'It's difficult on researchers too. The work
can be a strain.'

'Has someone been hurt? There's a lot of wild boars
around.'

'Over time...' Dad said. 'Some people's health has
declined. They need to rest. Soo-Jin among them.'

'What!' I exclaimed. 'Is she okay? Is she leaving?'

'She's going to return to her hometown for some R&R.'

'What's that?'

'Rest and recuperation. Soldiers get R&R, during
wars—'

This reference panicked me. 'Dad, what *happened*?'

'People have been experiencing side effects of being in the zone. Such as hallucinations, strange lapses in … judgement.'

I leaned forward. 'They're seeing things. Like what?'

'They have seen things which are not real, which is the definition of a hallucination,' Dad said evenly.

Hope pounded in my chest. 'I thought that's what you guys would *want* to study. I mean, if you're seeing *people* or those other weird things—'

His expression stopped me.

'There are no *people* there,' he said emphatically. 'I've told you. And what other weird things are you referring to?'

There was something carefully casual about how he asked this that reminded me of tests, and of the scientists who thought I was crazy.

'Everyone says there are ghosts,' I said.

'There are phenomena that make people *think* there are ghosts,' he corrected me.

'There's…' I trailed off. If Dad dismissed the possibility of people being in the zones, if he still couldn't believe in ghosts, then there was no way I could even begin to explain what I had seen.

'So they think these people are going mad too.'

'Mad is an archaic word,' Dad said. 'There is an increasing amount of agreement that the zones are simply not safe, and we are not learning enough to protect ourselves there. The research is suffering. There are already so many rumours. You know they're bad for the area. Don't you remember when people didn't want to go to other prefectures because their car license plates said where they were from?'

'I can't drive.'

'You understand me quite well.' His rational-debate tone was gone. There was annoyance in his voice now. 'There are complicated interests at stake. I'm not the one making the decisions. I just want to continue my work. I sense that the research might not be funded for much longer. All these issues are proving difficult to manoeuvre around…'

'*You* keep going into the zones—'

Dad's annoyance turned abruptly to anger. He banged the table with his hand. '*I* will be fine! *You* are never to go in there! Do you understand?'

'Sure,' I muttered.

'Promise me.' Dad took hold of my hand and held it, too tightly. 'Promise.'

'I promise,' I said reluctantly.

Dad was right; the lab closed less than a year later, citing the risks associated with the research. The zones became even more abandoned, even more lost.

Rumours multiplied and mutated into urban myths about what had happened to the scientists – breakdowns, amnesia, death. Everybody knew that Dad was a researcher, and somehow it had got out that I used to go into the zones with him. Parents told their kids to stay away from me, and they did. Even though other kids ventured into zones now and then, it was a game, a dare. People going in again and again, hoping to find something rational or real – that was something different. It was crazy. Only Koki didn't keep his distance.

The researchers' *hallucinations* only gave me more hope that people might somehow still exist in the zones. So I broke my promise to Dad the very next day, and then over and over again.

Dad is in the kitchen, staring into the fridge as though there's a TV in there.

'Hungry?' I ask.

'No, my face is hot.'

I reach to check his forehead and he bats my hand away. 'I'm joking!'

'You're sweaty. Your hair's all damp.'

'I had a *bath*. You didn't tell me I was also suffering from smelliness.'

'I was being polite.'

'I recall you frequently informing me when I'm smelly, in need of a haircut, wearing stupid clothes – what's changed now?'

'When I do that I'm being honest for your own good. This time, I was afraid you'd drown in the bath.' This isn't a lie, even though he seems to have recovered.

'Well, there's the honesty again.' He's grinning.

I feel a burst of hope at this cheerfulness. 'So you *are* hungry?'

'Yes, I am.'

'What do you want me to make?' I'm getting tired of cooking.

Dad closes the fridge door. 'Something's not right.'

'What do you mean?' Usually Dad doesn't notice my moods, or he ignores them.

'I noticed there's no beer,' he says.

Same as usual. 'You shouldn't be drinking.' I rummage in the cupboards to hide my face.

'I always have a post-bath beer. A tradition!'

'I think milk is the tradition. I'll make some kind of noodles.'

'Beer is your ojiichan's tradition, which means you should respect it. Where is he? Out buying some?' Dad says.

'Stop it!' I say, just as I'd said to the shaking ground. 'Ojiichan's dead. You know that.'

Dad leans against the fridge. It rocks slightly under his weight. I resist the urge to take his arm, steady him. I'm too angry. He can't keep doing this, making me work and worry and then act as if it's all fine until he says something like this.

'Drink some water.' I slam the cupboard doors shut and it's as if the noise has a solid shape, because Dad sways backwards, stumbles, almost falls.

I grab his elbow and feel a tiny shock. An instant later it's gone. No, not again. I check my watch, but nothing has happened. Static, I'm sure, I'm sure.

'Ah – a bout of dizziness. I wonder if my blood pressure is low,' Dad says.

'Sit down.' I pull a kitchen chair towards Dad and he sinks into it.

He breathes deeply and something shifts; his eyes focus. 'Runs in my family,' Dad says, suddenly chirpy. 'My father had low blood pressure too. When he was old, every now and then he'd have a swoon.'

'A swoon. How Victorian.' Romantic. Not terrifying at all.

'I mean, he *was* old.' Dad gives his head a shake. 'I'm full of vigour! Fine now!' He stands up.

I jump closer, but he doesn't sway or stumble.

He pats my arm. 'Don't worry. I'll add more salt to my food from now on, get the blood pressure leaping.'

'I can also make you mad,' I offer.

'A kind soul, a generous daughter!' he proclaims. 'I'll go ahead and make you that tea.'

'I didn't say I wanted tea.'

'Really? I sensed you wanted some, then.' Dad fills the kettle.

'Useful spidey sense.' I bring the chair back to the table and sit, watching him.

'I always know which drawer has cutlery too. Put me in any kitchen, I challenge you.' He waves the tea strainer in the air. 'I will find it.'

Dad keeps chattering as the tea seeps. We drink it together and argue about salt curing blood pressure and Dad seems fine, better than usual, even. But I can't lose the feeling of wrongness. Nothing's gone away, nothing's really been cured.

A few months after the Shake, I asked Dad when we were going home to Vancouver. He stared into the distance. I thought he hadn't heard me.

Then he said, 'We'll go home when we find her.'

I was ashamed, because I should have known. I shouldn't even have thought about leaving Mom.

But I asked again when the searches stopped.

Dad said, 'The research I'm doing is very interesting, and perhaps I can find some answers if I continue.'

Of course I couldn't argue with that. Answers were important. Who else could say they were trying to find answers to the Shake?

The third time I asked, Dad just said, 'Do you really want to go home?'

Suddenly, home was hard to imagine. I thought of our house, but it could hardly be our house any more, with so many missing pieces and empty spaces in every room. I said yes anyway, in between those hiccupping sobs that only happen when you've been crying for too long.

'I'm trying – I'm trying...' he said.

'You're being selfish,' I told him.

'I am?' he asked.

Yes! I wanted to shout. For taking me away from my friends, my school, my bedroom, my home – but every reason I could name was *mine*, which meant that I was the more selfish one, really.

'Mom—' *wouldn't have wanted this* was how I thought I would end the sentence. But when I looked at Dad, it was the first time I had seen anguish on a real person, not just an emotion described in a book that I understood the definition of, but not the meaning.

Neither of us could speak or breathe for a while. It might have been hours or days. When we returned to each other, I put my head against his chest and he put his arms around me and we understood that we were not leaving, and I hated it, and there was nothing I could do about it. There was a new kind of rift between us. Mom had been the bridge – no, that wasn't right, because that chasm hadn't been there before she had gone. She was part of the solid earth and green grass and without her, a pit had opened.

We went back to Vancouver once. Everything was as we'd left it. The dishes stacked on the draining board and cushions crumpled on the sofa. In my room the bed was messily made. The plants were still alive, the garden lush and unharvested. I stood in my room and thought that it was the bedroom of a little girl, and I missed her very very much.

Dad told me to pack whatever I wanted to take with me. I filled a box with books. I began to put clothes in a bag, stuffed toys, trinkets that I had collected, but when the bag was full I just stared at it. Dad came in and asked me if that was everything I wanted.

I said, 'I don't want any of it.'

He said, 'Okay.' He went into his office.

In the kitchen, on the fridge, was a calendar and notes, the entire door covered with stickers and pieces of paper about what to remember, dentist appointments and school meetings. Plans for a future that didn't exist any more. I took off each piece of paper and, slowly and deliberately, ripped them to shreds.

After a while, Dad came downstairs. I pretended not to notice that his eyes were red. He pretended not to notice the scraps of paper all about my feet. 'Are you ready to go?' he asked.

I stared at him. From the car, I watched my home recede in the distance and be lost behind other homes and trees as we turned corner after corner.

I said goodbye to my best friend, Sasha. We didn't have much to say to each other. I had missed all the important things that had happened in school. She didn't know what to say to me because when you're twelve you haven't learned all those things that adults say at funerals. We said we would email and Skype. She said she would visit Japan, for sure. I said I would be back, definitely. We hugged each other.

Japan became our home.

Dad gathered up all the theories. The Shake had moved time as if they were tectonic plates and cracks must have opened in between. What if you'd been standing on one when they moved? Would you fall between times? Could you disappear?

Or: if you had been in one of the slow or fast zones, perhaps you'd been flung far into the past or the future, and had become old and died, or become so young that you ceased to exist, that you became a random little bundle of cells once more.

Or: those people ran away and took the opportunity to start new lives.

Or: the change in times had made them lose their memories, and they couldn't remember who they were or where their homes were.

Or: they were somewhere out there still, roaming so deep in one of the slow or fast zones that they couldn't find their way out.

But no amnesiacs have reappeared to search for their memories, and wouldn't one of those people with new lives miss their old one? They could be lost, though; they could be trapped.

And what I believe and Dad doesn't is that maybe they will come back. Maybe she will return. Maybe we just keep missing each other by minutes.

虹始見

FIRST RAINBOWS APPEAR

8

Dad huffs and gets into the driver's seat. He's much better today but I'm still forcing him to go to the doctor. He puts on the mask I hand him. He's annoyed and drives silently, which is fine with me. It's quite peaceful.

'How is your job hunt going?' Dad asks.

So much for peace. 'It's going.'

'Going where?'

'Just … proceeding with no destination yet.'

'Do you have possible destinations you might choose?'

'Sure.'

'Such as?'

I tick them off on my fingers. 'Conbini worker, English tutor, waiter, air steward.'

'What do you want to *be*, Sora?'

'Normal.'

Dad raises his eyebrows and turns into the clinic's parking lot.

'You don't need to come in with me, Sora,' he says.

I ignore this.

The only other person in the waiting room is a very small old lady who's about a hundred years old and almost certainly more robust than I am. Dad's name is called and he goes into the doctor's office. I sit down, avoiding the inquisitive gaze of the old woman, and blindly scroll through my phone until Dad emerges again.

The doctor comes out too. 'Sora-san? May I see you for a moment?'

'Um. Okay.' I follow him into his office.

The doctor asks, 'Have you noticed your father forgetting things recently? Being confused?'

My stomach lurches. 'Yeah.'

'At the moment, it's not so serious, but I suspect it's the onset of memory deterioration. I'd like you to keep an eye on him. Try to take note of how he is. It's helpful if he can have a regular, balanced routine.'

I can't talk for a moment, or think, even though this shouldn't be a surprise. 'Are you going to give him medicine?' I force out.

'Don't worry, please. People can function quite well, for quite a long time, with this. No medicine is needed yet.'

'What did Dad say when you told him this?'

The doctor sits back. 'He didn't welcome the news. I'm telling you because it's important for family to understand and support a person dealing with this.'

'I'll support him.'

'Your father works at the company nearby, yes?' the doctor asks. 'They have a doctor there too, whom I imagine your father is entitled to see. It would be good if he visited that doctor. I'm sure they have more information and experience in this area.'

'Which area? Memory loss?'

The doctor shuffles some papers on his desk. 'Yes, well, the area of their employees.'

I don't really get what he means but I don't want to hear any more. 'Okay. Thanks,' I say.

'Take care,' he says.

Dad doesn't say anything when I get into the car, just starts driving. The silence is so hot and thick that I roll down the window to let some of it out. There are hawks circling overhead, wings wide on warm air rising. The road veers closer to the ocean. Deeper and shallower, how could I know? I'd explore the ocean except I don't like depths. Heights are fine; they have a good view. Depths have none at all.

'I need to make a stop,' Dad says. 'For research purposes.'

We turn into a narrower road that winds between trees and climbs a hill. Near the top, Dad pulls in and parks. He gets out. Neither of us asks if I will come. We walk a little further and then Dad veers off into the grass and trees, following a trail that I would have totally missed. Walking with him along quiet strange paths is so familiar and from what feels like so long ago.

We reach a fence. Almost a whole section has been cut

away, only attached on one end, so it can be pulled open like a gate, which is what Dad does. I bite my tongue at his practised familiarity with it. We carry on until we emerge on a road sprouting weeds from every crack, and as we walk, it comes back to me just before the torii gate comes into view: it's a shrine.

We came here before, when we visited Japan during the New Year when I was – eight, nine? There had been queues of people in the crisp cold, waiting patiently to ask for blessings, to check their fortune, to buy their omamori for safety and luck and success in exams. I remembered it as being big and bright, but the gates have faded now, from vermillion to scarlet. And it's small, the shrine, worn by time, but the inari foxes guarding the gates are still alert and poised. Dad and I pause before the gates and dip our heads before walking through. I feel a tingle as I pass.

'Fast,' I say to Dad.

He nods. 'Walk across the path.'

I cross to the other side and there's a change again. 'Slow.' I inch back to Dad, and there, directly in front of the shrine, is the gap between fast and slow zones.

'The fast and slow zones end right there,' Dad says.

A strip of normal time so thin that it's like standing on a tightrope. I return to Dad. 'Feels weird to stand there. Is it normal time? It's not fast or slow but it feels … different.'

'Of course, the centre of the path to a shrine is always for gods, not for humans,' says a voice.

I whirl around to see a middle-aged man wearing navy work clothes. He's holding a rake. Dad is already turning and smiling and walking towards him.

'Hisakawa-san,' Dad says.

'Long time no see, Campbell-san,' the man – Hisakawa – replies.

'It has.' Dad's voice raises the slightest bit at the end of the sentence, almost a question because, I guess, he can't quite remember.

I bow. 'I'm Sora.'

Hisakawa bows back. 'How nice to meet you. Good to have some visitors. Not so many these days.'

'Because it's in a zone,' I say.

'Indeed it is. As I think you noticed, more than one. A very special place.' Hisakawa is cheerful.

'Is that why you think the middle of the path is normal time? Because it's for the gods?' I ask him.

'It might be so,' Hisakawa replies. 'Though I don't know if the gods follow human time.'

I sense an eye roll from Dad, though he's not actually doing one. He doesn't believe in gods, any of them.

I look at the middle of the path, where Mom had always told me not to walk because, at a shrine, the gods have right of way. I try not to show the shiver flickering down my spine.

Hisakawa glances at Dad earnestly. 'Another scholar of time?'

Dad tilts his head. 'Sora-chan is not a scholar but she is certainly a...' He regards me. 'An explorer.'

I want to smile, but can't. Hisakawa beams with enthusiasm.

'Hisakawa-san is the priest here.'

'It's been in my family for many generations. My great-grandfather, grandmother, my father...'

'I didn't know women could do that!' I say.

'Oh, women can do anything,' Hisakawa says.

I grin at him. 'Do you *live* here?' I ask.

'No, I'm not here too much. Just enough,' Hisakawa says. 'I know not to come in and out too much.' He glances at Dad.

Dad says, 'If you don't mind, I'm going to check...' He takes off quickly.

'Check what?' I call, but Dad's disappeared behind the shrine. Nice. 'Thank you,' I say to Hisakawa, who's smiling at me expectantly.

Better go pay my respects. I dig around in my pocket and pull out a five-yen coin. Lucky. I walk up to the shrine, toss it in the offering box, bow twice, clap twice, bow. *Keep us all safe*, I pray vaguely. *Don't let anything bad happen.*

I walk back and find that Hisakawa has also disappeared. I wander in the direction Dad went, stopping by a tall tree with a shimenawa around its wide base.

'Did you know that the first shrines were simply special trees?'

I jump. Hisakawa has reappeared beside me.

'No... How can you tell that a tree is special?' I ask.

Hisakawa peers up at the tree's crown, metres above us. 'What an excellent question.'

I wait for an answer. He doesn't give me one.

'This is an inari shrine,' he says instead. 'The messengers of the gods. Sacred Japan Post.'

I laugh. He walks to another, much smaller shrine. It's only my height, the fox statues tall as my hand. There are offerings in front of them, actual aburaage tofu on a plate and the One Cup sake that I feel must be required drinking for all the gods of small shrines.

Hisakawa follows my gaze. 'The foxes' favourite. Every morning, it's always gone.'

If there are rats around they must be fat.

'Have you seen the kitsune, Sora-san?' Hisakawa asks suddenly.

'What?'

He looks at me steadily. 'They're very swift, and shy. You might have thought they were some other animal, or...'

He's totally serious, but I shake my head instinctively. I'm too used to never mentioning the darting shapes I've seen, the movements in the corners of deserted places, glimpsed from the edge of my eye.

He nods, satisfied, as if I'd given him a long and coherent answer. 'The gods,' he says, 'are coming back.'

Suddenly I hear Dad muttering, and break Hisakawa's gaze before I have to give a response. I follow the sound of my father discovering something. Behind the shrine there are trees, and Dad, staring at three small boxes on the ground. One in the slow area, one in the fast and one in between.

'What's this?'

Dad says, 'Sand timers. I thought I should check the middle time zone.'

A completely useless answer, as I can clearly see the hourglasses in each box. The sand in one is flowing quickly, in the other flowing just a second or two more slowly, and in the middle—

'It's not moving at all!'

I crouch beside Dad, unable to take my eyes off it. What the hell? The sand is entirely motionless, both top and bottom parts of the hourglass almost perfectly half-full.

'Did you put it in there like that?' I ask. 'You didn't start it with the top part full?'

Dad stares at it without blinking. 'I did.'

'Then how—?'

'I don't know,' Dad says, his voice full of wonder and frustration.

'Balance,' Hisakawa says.

'But I've never seen this before. You really think time could *balance* itself like this?' I ask.

Dad shakes his head reluctantly. 'It's highly unlikely.'

At the same time, Hisakawa says, 'Yes, I believe so.'

'Believe,' Dad repeats, tinged with a hint of scorn. As a scientist, belief is nothing without proof.

Hisakawa does not appear offended. He might be the most calmly happy person I have ever met. 'Buddhists believe time is an illusion. That there is nothing but the present and if you transcend your busy thinking mind, you'll understand that.'

Dad is in no way transcending his thinking mind; he's digging in. 'I'm not a Buddhist,' he says.

'Neither am I,' Hisakawa says. 'But I don't know about the foxes.' He gives me a big wink.

I think he's great.

Dad sighs and takes a lot of photos on his phone, scribbles furiously in his notebook, and stalks off to look at the three fox statues. They're weathered grey stone, right behind the shrine, but in the same line as the hourglass boxes.

'No apparent change,' he declares.

'No. They're too old,' Hisakawa replies.

'Things aren't too old to get older,' I say.

'You're right. But too old to show it,' Hisakawa says.

I know the expression on Dad's face: it means he's going to basically go wild with a marker and whiteboard, or pages and pages of paper, covering them with questions that turn into numbers, words that turn into graphs. 'Thank you, Hisakawa-san. Please let me know if you notice any changes. And if you could note date and time too—'

'I remember,' he replies placidly. Obviously he has received those instructions before.

'Thank you.'

'Good to see you, Sora-san. Keep your eyes open.'

Dad strides off and I jog after him, winding back through the trees, leaving behind the shrine and the sand disobeying time.

Dad never understood how I could feel the changes in time, or trace the boundaries between *now* and *then.*

After living here for seven years, I have a better idea why. In Vancouver, I didn't stand out in any way. I was average at most things: school, sports, friends. I had enough of everything. I went to Japanese school every Saturday, which I threw regular tantrums about, but other kids spoke other languages at home. Every kid was forced to do something by their parents. I wasn't so different.

But here, not on holiday but somewhere that suddenly became my home, I discovered that I was very different, and was better and worse at more things. My Japanese was bad so I became quieter, but it didn't matter because I had fewer people to talk to. I stood out in my class. When an Irish assistant language teacher came to the school, our English teacher said, *Now we have two foreigners here!* I was the other one. And I couldn't claim I wasn't foreign, and I won't claim that I'm not Japanese.

The edge, the in-between, the line between one thing becoming another; it's a place I know. I recognise the feeling of it. If there's somewhere I won't feel it, I haven't found it yet. Maybe I'll become like the sand in an hourglass, but stuck in the middle, helpless and suspended, neither one thing nor another.

Next day I give in and message Koki. *hey. how's university?*
Then I try to distract myself, making lunch, scrolling

through the internet, watching Dad sigh and cough, until Koki replies, hours later.

sorry! it's seriously busy. how's home?

same as always, I reply.

what are you doing? he asks.

now? Is he going to call me or something?

just in general.

I feel disappointed and then I feel stupid. *nothing, also like always.*

you okay?

I stare at the screen. There are a thousand things I could write. I say, *yeah.*

i miss you, Koki writes.

no you don't, I reply. *you shouldn't.*

A pause.

if that's what you want? Koki replies.

I stare at my phone, not sure how I ended up in this conversation. I type and delete, *I miss you too,* and, *go have fun in Tokyo,* and, *you're so annoying.* I don't send any of them.

There's a tap on my door and I fling it open.

Dad's there, taken aback. 'Is something the matter, Sora-chan?'

'No, everything's wonderful. Absolutely fantastic.'

Dad says, 'I see. I'm sorry to disturb you during your happy time, but I wanted to let you know that I'm heading into work for a little while. So—'

'You need to rest.'

Dad avoids my eye and moves towards the front door.

I follow him. 'The doctor talked to me.'

Dad stiffens, but doesn't stop shuffling into his shoes. 'That's a betrayal of patient confidentiality—'

'You know you *are* forgetting stuff, right? That you're confused?'

Dad has his briefcase in his hand, holding it tightly. He gives a short, awful laugh. 'I suppose I'm getting old.'

'You're *not*.' Somehow this is even worse than what the doctor said. Dad isn't old, he's … Dad age. But now I notice the lines around his eyes and his mouth, and is his hair thinner? I want to tell him about the weird jolts of something like electricity from him, but he's never felt them himself. Perhaps he wouldn't believe me; maybe I'm just afraid.

'There's a doctor at the company,' I say, instead. 'Have you gone to them?'

'For my annual check-up, yes.'

'So a year ago.'

'I imagine they would agree that it was the flu, lack of vitamins, that sort of thing,' he says, and is out of the door before I can interrogate him.

I go to my laptop and read about Alzheimer's, dementia, concussion, tumours, vitamin B-12 deficiencies. I search for time zones and illness, time zones and memory loss, jet lag and brain impairments but there's nothing firm, nothing reliable.

I wait a couple of restless hours. Then I get on my bike and head to the company.

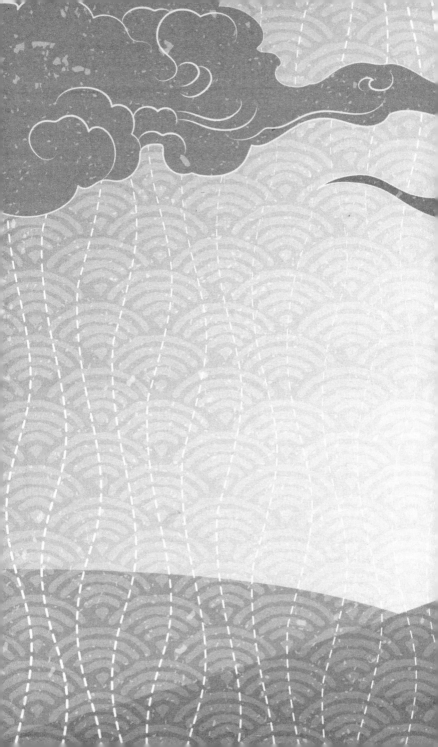

穀雨

RAIN NOURISHES GRAIN

9

The company could have anything within its long, grey, four-storey high walls. It's sleek and anonymous in a way that has money but doesn't show it. I've never been inside, even though Dad has worked here for two years. It's different from the lab he worked in before. This place is a business. I try to smooth down my hair as I enter the sparse lobby and the air-conditioning blows its cool breath over me.

Well, Dad is a dishevelled mess most of the time and they let him in, so why not me? *Because they want him here*, that negative and accurate corner of my brain says. *Because he has a job and knows what he's doing.* No, he doesn't, I tell myself, and then end the mental argument by marching up to the receptionist.

'Hello,' I say.

'How can I help you?' She gives the impression of looking me up and down without actually doing it. It's impressive and I want to learn how to do it.

'My father works here. His name is Campbell. He's sick and I think he needs to see the doctor.' I try to balance worry with calm.

The receptionist is expressionless. She really is good. 'Did your father contact you? Are you to bring him home?'

'No. I thought it was best to inform his department head because my father is very ... dedicated and doesn't want to cause any worry. But I think that his illness *should* be of some concern to the company, due to his research...' I trail off suggestively.

'I see. Allow me to contact Campbell-san—'

'In fact, I would like to speak to the person who leads his department.' I wish I'd found out their name – it would have been a lot more authoritative, instead of sounding like I wanted to complain to a manager about a wrong dinner order.

'That may not be possible. Yamagata-san is very busy.'

'I think it's important Yamagata-san should know this. It's a little...' I trail off again and wait.

'I will see if Yamagata-san is available,' she says, bowing slightly. 'Please, take a seat.'

I back away and sit on one of the smart, uncomfortable chairs, trying not to think of how furious Dad is going to be. The receptionist is speaking and nodding on the phone, her hand covering her mouth. She puts the phone down. She types on her keyboard, eyes fixed steadily on the screen. After exactly ten minutes, she stands and nods her head at me.

When I reach her, she says, 'Please go to the third floor. Yamagata-san's office number is 310.'

'Thank you very much,' I say graciously.

In the lift, I press the number three and try to gather myself because I haven't really thought that I was going to get this far. Yamagata will probably be one of those old guys who always seem to be the bosses, the politicians, the people in charge. I could always resort to crying, or pretending to cry. Or— The lift doors open.

I step out into a clean, plain corridor. It's quiet. Dad's never spoken about his colleagues here, which I haven't really noticed before. 310 is here, the number on a small black plaque on the wall. I knock.

'Yes,' a man's voice says. He doesn't sound elderly. 'Come in.'

I open the door, and there's Yamagata, sitting behind a mahogany desk. He's probably in his early fifties, dressed neatly in a dark suit, with a disorientatingly jaunty tie, patterned green and blue. The tie is so out of place with his serious stare that it takes me a while to notice that Dad is sitting across the desk from him, twisting towards me in outrage.

I hover in the doorway, weighing up the pros and cons of sitting down at the desk or running away.

'Hello, Sora-san. Please, come in. I'm Yamagata.'

'Hello. Thank you for seeing me.' I take a seat and avoid Dad's eyes.

'Ah, your Japanese is very good,' Yamagata says.

'Thank you. So is yours,' I reply.

Dad clears his throat. Yup, this is not a good time for me to get snarky about comments on my Japanese ability.

Yamagata doesn't react. 'I understand that you are concerned for Campbell-san's well-being.'

'I'm fine,' Dad says.

'And I'm glad to hear it.' Yamagata nods at him, then turns back to me. 'Sora-san, I am speaking to you not because I do not trust my employees, but because you suggested that the flu is connected to the nature of your father's work. Which I am somewhat confused about.'

His voice is reasonable and measured, so much so that I can't tell what he's really thinking.

'It wasn't just the *flu*.' Dad's eyes are boring a hole in the side of my face. I speak quickly. 'There are other symptoms, like being confused, forgetting stuff, not knowing what time we're in...' This is when I should say something about the weird jolts, but I've betrayed Dad's trust too much already. And I don't know how I feel about Yamagata yet, or what he would do with the information.

Yamagata gazes from me to Dad. 'Campbell-san, I trust that you are keeping within the limits we have on field research.'

'Of course,' Dad says hastily. The liar.

'Still, it would be wise for you to visit our doctor. Of course, we did recommend that after your previous indisposition.'

If they had, Dad hadn't mentioned it. Not that he would.

Dad nods. 'Yes, of course.'

That was easy.

Yamagata inclines his head. 'Sora-san, I do have some other questions for you. What do you know of your father's research?'

I blink, and now I sense a different kind of danger. 'I … I mean – he works so hard. His hours are long and he's in the zones a lot, outside even when the weather is bad.'

Dad's intense stare makes sense now, because even though he's angry with me, it's not just because I told on him – it's because of the reason I gave. Yamagata must not know that I used to go into the zones with Dad, and I can see why it should stay that way.

I breathe deep and lean forward. 'And … I've heard that there's creepy stuff in the zones.'

'Such as?'

'I heard that there's animals that have sort of *mutated*, and that there're people who didn't evacuate and now they're like zombies.' I widen my eyes. My hands are incredibly sweaty.

'Have you ever gone in, Sora-san?' Yamagata's face is smooth but his eyes have narrowed a fraction.

'No way. They're too freaky. That's why I don't like Dad going there,' I say.

'I can assure you that our research follows all required regulations,' Yamagata says robotically. 'Especially as entry into those zones is tightly monitored by *law*.'

Oh, crap. I know how I feel about Yamagata now.

He's smart, and I don't like him, and I'm afraid of what he can do.

Dad says, 'There's no danger of Sora going in there. She's not the bravest of girls. You may be able to tell by her worries that she's a tad irrational, sometimes.'

I smile at Dad through this treachery. I stare into Yamagata's eyes. 'My mother is dead,' I tell him.

He nods slowly. 'Yes,' he says. 'So is mine.'

There is a heavy silence. I swallow and hope it's audible only to me.

Yamagata's eyes flick between us. 'I'm sure the doctor will be able to see you today. Allow me to ask.' He picks up the phone on his desk, speaks for a minute, and hangs up. 'Luckily, Banno-sensei can see you right now.'

'Yes,' Dad says. 'I'll show Sora-chan out—'

'I think your daughter should stay with you. To assuage her fears.' Yamagata lifts the corners of his mouth.

'Thank you,' I say.

Dad stands and bows and I follow suit. 'I apologise for any trouble. Thank you for your time.'

Yamagata stands too. 'I always have time for matters such as this.'

I follow Dad obediently.

'This way,' is all he says, and we get into the lift, go down a floor, and then through some corridors until we come to a small waiting area. 'Sit and wait,' he tells me. He taps on the nearest door and a doctor opens it and beckons him in.

I sit on the chair and don't move. I have a feeling of being watched and I'm sure I am, because this is the type of place with cameras in corners. I keep my face still, modelling myself after the receptionist, half-expecting somebody to march down the hallway and take me away. I stare out of the window, which overlooks the grounds behind the building. There are sheds, military rows of crops, young conifer trees spaced at intervals from each other. There's more land than I thought, and it stretches into the distance, where a fence glints in the sunshine. On the other side of the fence, the straight lines of growing things continue in a disciplined way.

The door opens and Dad and the doctor emerge.

The doctor beams at me. 'Your father is just fine. Keep an eye on his diet, though. Make sure he's eating – I bet you can cook up some nice dishes for him.'

Is he going to give me a lollipop? 'Thank you. What a relief.'

'I'm sure it is. Take care, now.' He smiles widely at me, and nods at Dad. 'Oh, Campbell-san, Yamagata-san has said that you are free to return home early today, to make sure you get a little extra rest. Very kind of him!'

'Yes,' Dad says stiffly. 'Very kind indeed. Let's go, Sora.'

I follow him silently, past the watchful receptionist and back into the warm air.

'Get in the car,' Dad says.

'I have my bike. I'll cycle back—'

'Put it in the boot.'

I wheel my bike to the car and heave it in. I sit beside Dad.

When we've left the car park and are on the road, I say, 'Dad, I—'

He holds up a hand. 'No, Sora. Don't say a word.'

Mom spoke in Japanese to her plants and trees. I asked her once about the plants that had grown up in Canada – they didn't know Japanese so it was unfair, wasn't it?

Don't be silly, she scolded me. *Plants understand everything.*

So the commands and encouragements she would give those plants were the ones I remembered most from childhood, when other kids might have been told to *eat your dinner* or *wash your hands* or *go to bed*. Instead, I knew *soak in the sunshine* and *reach tall, reach deep, grow strong*. She said them to me, and I guess they applied just as well to a kid as to a tomato plant.

They were the Japanese phrases Dad knew well too. He started learning when I was small, because, *What if you both start making fun of me in Japanese and I don't know it?* he'd said once, in pretend-outrage. Mom said it was fine, we could do that in English if he wanted to be included. He put his arms around her and squeezed her, said she was a bully and they had laughed together, which needed no translation.

We are different people in different languages. In

Japanese, it's hard to be direct or sarcastic. In English, there's so much less nuance and allusion. Even my body changes. Japanese feels like a jungle gym, full of levels and structure that you have to reach through carefully. There are Japanese phrases like *reading the air* and *leaving space* when you speak, because there are things that are left unsaid, that are meant to be silently understood. But when Mom spoke in Japanese, her voice was faster and she made more noises when she listened. In English she would pause more, watch other speakers intently, mispronounce and mix up words in sentences in ways that used to embarrass me. Dad becomes more basic, when in English it sounds like he just ate a dictionary as a snack. Bowing is awkward on him.

I've learned how to listen. How to decipher pauses and gaps between sentences. When Mom was gone, there was a gap. I kept waiting for that pause to be filled, for the silence to end, because it felt like a sentence had been cut short, and I would never know the end of it.

I wish I'd asked Mom if the plants ever replied to her, and if they did, what language they spoke.

Dad is silent when we get home and silently goes into his office and silently stays there all evening. He does the same next day. I don't knock on his door or ask if he's hungry or tell him that he needs to explain things. Some silences feel unbreakable.

I pull myself together the day after and make a decent

dinner. I clatter around the kitchen to make sure Dad can hear me and try to waft the cooking smell down the hall.

'Dad,' I say, outside his study door. 'I made dinner. Come eat.'

He emerges as I'm setting the table. 'Something smells good.'

'Hopefully it tastes good too.' I set down plates of nasu dengaku, fried gobo, salad; bowls of miso soup and rice.

We start eating to fill the silence. Dad is actually eating quite well. But then he might not have eaten since the last time I forced him to. He's thin.

I take a breath. 'Dad, I'm sorry about what I did and … everything.'

Dad swallows. 'I appreciate the apology. It was highly – unprofessional. Strange.' I'd prepared myself for yelling, but he's looking at me as if I'm a serious and totally incomprehensible problem.

'I thought you'd listen to your boss. There's nobody else to talk to you, Dad.' Once I say it, it sounds incredibly sad.

'Your motives were pure. Your methods…' Dad pointedly slurps from his miso soup. 'But I'm fine. I told you the doctor would agree with me, didn't I? And aren't your worries assuaged?'

He had. They weren't. 'Yamagata creeped me out,' I say instead.

'You really shouldn't have mentioned anything about my research. It's confidential.'

'I'm your daughter. It makes sense you'd talk about it to me.'

'Perhaps, but now I assume he knows that you've gone into the zones,' Dad says.

'He's not the police.'

'He's a phone call away.'

I sit up straight. 'You think he'd report me to the police? Seriously?'

'It's the duty of every citizen to report crime.'

'Come *on*. What's his deal?'

Dad sighs. 'He doesn't want the company's work scrutinised. Anything around the zones causes a lot of discussion.'

'What kind of work is he doing?' If anybody could be an evil corporate head, it could be Yamagata.

Dad reads my mind. 'Nothing sinister, Sora.'

'Why does he care about me? Why not just ignore me when I went there?'

'I suppose you alarmed him.'

'That's my effect on men.'

Dad smiles. He says abruptly, 'Found any interesting jobs yet?'

'Meh.'

Dad chews thoughtfully for a minute. 'Maybe a change of scenery would benefit you. You know, you haven't been back to Vancouver in a long time.'

'I should go to *Vancouver*?'

'You could visit people. Maybe if you wanted to get a part-time job there for a little while, it would be good for you. It's hard around here.'

'Yes!' bursts out of my mouth before I can stop it.

Dad smiles. 'We'll need to figure out a clear plan, then. I'm fairly certain that somebody could put you up for a few nights at least...' He names old familiar friends that he and Mom had had, who came to our house for dinner parties or invited us for barbecues. The nostalgia hits me, heavy and enveloping, like sinking into a thick blanket.

'Shall I see if I can contact them?'

I feel dazed. 'That would be great.'

Part of me knows what he's doing – getting me out of the way before I cause more trouble or insist on some kind of medical treatment for him. But another part of my brain argues that he's an adult, it's his choice, and after all the company doctor did say he was fine... And the rest of me? It selfishly says, yes, let's get out of here, let's go back to where we had a normal home.

I say, 'When?'

'We should check flights, but I suppose as soon as you want to.' He pushes himself out of his chair. 'I'll rummage around for emails and phone numbers now.'

'Thank you, Dad.' I grab his hand.

He squeezes. His skin is cool. 'You're welcome. This is a good idea for you, I think.'

We wash the dishes together.

Afterwards, I half-leap to my room and fling open my laptop. I stay up late, going down rabbit holes of job hunts and gigs and places I want to revisit and places I've never been before. I push away worries about Dad. I stare at photos of the mountains and the ocean and all the sky between.

In the morning, I knock on his study door, but he must have gone to work early. Had he managed to get in touch with anybody last night? I push open the door and step into his study, which is not forbidden but is usually such a mess I avoid it. I'm not going to open up his laptop to check but I do peer at his desk in case there's an address book or something.

The walls have always been covered with posters, diagrams, maps, almost incomprehensible notes. I'm pretty sure there are layers, whole strata of knowledge. I see something that I actually do understand, on paper pinned on a cork board. Lines and lines of the same words repeated over and over; not words, exactly, but kanji. I know them because it's the kanji for my name. They are simple: the kanjis for *for ever* and *sky*. It could almost be something preserved from my childhood, from the first time I learned how to write them, practised for hours to get them precise and regular. The writing is uneven and clumsy at the beginning, gradually steadying, as if Dad was learning how to write them all over again. Was he? Had he forgotten?

I read the walls. There is a calendar from three years ago, still stuck on December. The address of our old house, but the house number is wrong; it says sixteen but we were twenty-three. Another list, this time of places I recognise, places we used to go in Vancouver, when there were three of us together: the parks, the restaurants, the museums. Halfway down the list it becomes shaky and unsure. On one sticky note is written, *Where has everyone gone?*

I want to take away the notes or correct them. Everyone leaves notes like this for themselves, don't they? But … Dad's handwriting never looked so unsure of the letters and words they were spelling out. When do your parents start to get old? I thought it wouldn't be until *I* was old. If I somehow had kids, I'd know Dad was old because they'd call him Grandad.

I find a pen and correct the number of our old house. I can see our yellow door, paint flaking around the handle, so clearly. My numbers are deliberate and clear. How long will it take him to notice? I don't know if someone can remember when they started forgetting.

I tear down the sheet with my kanji on it. I rip it up like I'm ripping up the feeling in my heart. When Dad forgets my name I want to know.

葭始生

FIRST REEDS SPROUT

10

After I started primary school, I asked Mom why she had named me Sora.

'Everyone calls me Sarah. Or *Sore*. Why can't I have a normal name?'

'Sora *is* normal.' Mom gave me my very Canadian after-school snack: apple slices spread with peanut butter. She also gave me a Yakult, in honour of Japan and healthy bacteria.

'Nobody else I know is called it.'

'You don't mean normal. You mean common.'

'How's that different?'

Mom thought for a moment. 'The difference is imagination.' She added quickly, 'Do not say that to anybody called Sarah.'

I shook my Yakult bottle fiercely.

Mom sat beside me at the kitchen table. 'You know how to write your name in English and in Japanese, don't you?'

'Yes.' I was proud of that, though it wasn't unique. Some of my new classmates could do this too, in Chinese and Punjabi and Korean.

Mom found a piece of paper and a pencil. 'You can write your name in Japanese, but that's only *one* of the Japanese alphabets.'

'How many are there?' I was horrified.

Mom winced apologetically. 'Three. Four, really.'

'What!'

'But the hardest is the most beautiful and interesting.' Mom drew lines, some straight, some curved, accumulating into two different pieces. 'Your name. This kanji means *for ever and ever and ever*. This one is *sky*.' She tapped it. 'It means *sky* or *space*, like *empty space* by itself too. It's also *sora.*'

'This one is the same as both of these two? Why didn't you just use that one?' It seemed unnecessary.

'You can. But I didn't want to. There are lots of different ways to write your name. Look.' She drew more lines, forming complex dignified characters. 'This is *blue* and *sky*, this is *summer* and *sky*, this is *idea* and *orchid.*'

'What's the idea of an orchid?'

'I don't know. Maybe the soil has the idea of an orchid and then it grows.'

'Did you have an idea of me before I grew?'

'Not really. But when you were born the sky was very clear. No clouds at all! Maybe because you were very small it felt especially big and wide. I saw that the sky doesn't end anywhere. That's when I chose your name.'

'What about Dad? Did he want to choose a name for me too?'

'I don't know. I never asked him.'

I was relieved she hadn't. I had the feeling he would have picked something common.

'Okay, time to learn,' Mom said abruptly. She gave me more paper and counted out the strokes because they had to be in a certain order.

My hand ached by the time Mom proclaimed me good enough.

I stared at my paper crowded with lines. 'My name in English is even more boring now.'

'What?' Mom was exasperated.

'In Japanese there's a story.'

'I think Sora is even better in English. You can think about all the stories it *might* have in Japanese. See?' She gave me another apple slice. 'Imagination.'

I close the tabs, one by one. Summer sublet. Part-time jobs, no experience needed. Free park yoga. Best flight price comparisons. Image search of Vancouver mountains. I stare at the saturated photos and click them closed.

An email dings through. It's Naomi, asking for another tour. My first ever repeat customer. I reply with cost and time, and no pleasantries. I can't bring myself to write anything nice.

I open my closet and raise my face to Mom's photo. 'Why did you—' I begin. 'Where did you go?'

Her face remains the same. One small thing safe from time.

I leave the house. The boundary fence is a welcome sign to me when I reach it, the opposite of what it stands for. *The future* feels like it means nothing here, and neither does *for a while* or *when?* or *how long has this been happening?* or *how long is left?*

The concrete pavements and houses seem to hold the heat of the day, though the sun is paling now. The silhouette of a person appears on a dull grey wall to my left. It stays, unmoving, for several slow seconds before it disappears. I don't stop walking, but I bow quickly as I pass by. A little further on, another: a shadow leans forward in a doorway as if putting a key in the lock. It is there and then gone.

My feet lead me steadily along the uncanny roads, familiar made strange, to Ojiichan's house. I slide open the door and murmur, 'Tadaima.'

I move through the rooms, noiseless on the tatami. I clear the mess on the floor, kneel at the low table and turn on Ojiichan's radio. No sound. I take out the batteries and roll them between my hands to warm them, then replace them. I jump when noise wails from it. It's still tuned to Ojiichan's enka music.

I go upstairs to our old room, where the closet door is open, sweaters and shirts reaching arms out from tumbled piles. I pick up a cardigan of Mom's and can't help but hold the knitted cream wool to my face. It doesn't have her perfume, just the lonely cupboard smell of clothes waiting for their season to come round again. I pull it on and the sun catches a glint at the back of the closet. It's a small hourglass. So Dad *has* been here. I watch the grains of sand falling from top to bottom, slowly, as though they don't want to descend.

I creep downstairs and sit beside the radio again. I know this song, one of Ojiichan's favourites. A man singing about crying, leaving the village, a stone jizo, the distant sky, Tokyo. The music fades, and I pull the cardigan tighter around me.

'Mom?' I whisper. 'Where are you?'

In the hallway I pause, because there's a tingle in the air but no border here. I twist around and a movement makes my heart fly into a gallop before I see that it's my reflection. I walk closer: a mirror has slipped sideways against a bookshelf. The cardigan is a little too big for me, just like it had been for Mom. I turn the mirror to face the wall and leave.

I slide through the fence. The wind sweeps my hair around, and I shiver as the chill skates across the back of my neck. I pull the cardigan closer around me, and beneath my hands there is a tiny buzzing tremble. I take the cardigan off and watch as the hems unravel and holes open like eyes. I clutch it to myself – of course this would happen, it has been years. That little feeling must have been time catching up with it. And then dissolving... I could fix it, though, sew and patch it.

I cycle home, wondering if we even have a needle and thread. Dad is at home when I get in. I put the cardigan in my room before he sees it.

His head pokes out of the kitchen door. 'Hungry?'

I go to him. 'I could eat. Hey, do we have a sewing kit or anything?'

Dad leans against the counter. I'm afraid he's going into a *swoon* and I reach out to steady him.

'I'm fine.' Dad pats my hand, still on his arm.

'My lightning reflexes.' I try to laugh. There is the faintest hum prickling across my palm.

It's like what I felt in the cardigan, as it came apart. It had been taken out of the zone and its time had to change. And Dad...

'Is something the matter?' Dad asks.

I swallow. Dad's body must be readjusting too, shedding minutes and seconds, trying to balance itself.

'Dad. When you leave the zones, what does it feel like?'

He frowns. 'Was that where you were?'

'Tell me!'

Startled, he says, 'That disorientation, that frisson.'

'But *in* you, is there anything?'

'I'm really not sure what you mean.' Dad isn't disapproving any more, only curious.

'Maybe ... it's like an electric shock?' I think of the cardigan. 'Or an unravelling.' I don't know how to explain it.

'Sora, have *you* felt this?' He moves closer to me, concerned.

'No, or I haven't noticed it. But...' I grab one of his hands to show him, but nothing happens.

He gives my hand a little squeeze, bewildered.

'I've felt it before, when I've touched you,' I explain.

'I haven't noticed it... Could it be the dissipation of energy? Like a kind of static?' he says thoughtfully.

'I thought that, but it's different. It's like when time makes something fall apart.'

Dad's face changes. I know what he's remembering. The experiments, the decay, the disintegration.

He steps back. 'Ah. You think that's what's happening?'

'It could be.'

Dad stares down at his hands. It takes me a while to see the alarm spreading across his face.

'I don't know. It's really just a guess,' I say.

'It would make sense, though, wouldn't it,' Dad says softly. 'And in that case...' He turns and heads to his office.

I follow him and watch as he pulls out a notebook and starts scribbling in it. 'What are you going to do?' I ask.

Dad says briefly, 'I'm not sure yet.'

'You're going to go back into the zones, obviously.'

'I'll have to, if this phenomenon occurs after I've been there.'

'That's why you *shouldn't* go back!'

Dad ignores this. 'How to measure...' he mumbles, his pen looping across the page.

'Nobody else can feel time the way I can,' I say. 'Right? You still can't. So how are you going to figure it out?'

Dad's head snaps up. 'You'll have to help me.'

'You want to go back to our *research* together, after what I just told you? Except this time you're the experiment instead of me?'

'I looked after you.' But he won't meet my eyes.

'Not for the right reasons. And not *now*, if you want me to go into the zones with you. I'm not going.'

'You've made that clear.'

'I'm not going to Vancouver.'

Dad's taken aback. 'Why?'

I can't bring myself to answer. I go to my room and slam my door.

Dad is so smart and so stupid, and now I've made it worse. Of course I couldn't tell him something like that and expect him to stop going into the zones, no questions asked. I should have known.

My ojiichan was a quiet man who liked to be surrounded by noise. Obaachan had an aura of good-natured hubbub around her; she told stories and spun gossip and chattered to the food and pots as she made dinner.

When I was ten, she got sick. It happened gradually, Ojiichan said. But we only came to Japan once a year, so when we arrived it didn't feel gradual. Obaachan had changed into an old, confused woman, and her murmurs to herself had become questions. She still told stories, but sometimes she got the endings confused. Now there were happy endings, tragic ones, ones that were so enigmatic that in hindsight they seemed quite literary. I got used to it.

We didn't wait a year until our next visit, just six months. When we got into the house Obaachan looked at me for a long time and held my hand and said, *I missed you.* She asked me once, *Where am I?* and I told her she was at home. Obaachan said, *Yes, I know I'm home, but where is that?*

Dad and I went back home, while Mom stayed longer. She said that too many people would wear Obaachan out, but that she was doing well. So I was surprised when Mom called and talked to Dad and he wiped his eyes. He handed the phone to me and put his hand on my back, so when I started to cry it was easy for him to put one arm around me and stretch the other out to catch the phone when I let it fall.

We didn't go back for the funeral. We went back in the summer, like we always did. I did my best to fill the house with noise so that Ojiichan would feel better. He had a portable radio that he carried around with him, tuned to a station that played a lot of enka. I tried to sing some enka songs, which made him laugh. I did radio taisou with him every morning. We visited Obaachan and poured water over her gravestone.

We went back the next year, and the next, but that was when it all ended. I want to imagine that Ojiichan and Mom were close to each other when the Shake came, that despite whatever terrifying noise was happening, Mom could speak to him and he could hear her. It wasn't until afterwards that I learned the differences of silence and quiet, because I realised Ojiichan's quiet was one that listened. Silence is when nobody is there to hear.

霜止出苗

FROST CEASES AND
SEEDS GERMINATE

11

'That electricity pole is sprouting.' Naomi points to a wooden pole which has been released from its thick wire ropes; near the top, slender twigs have grown and opened leaves. We've started in the fast zone, at her request.

'Yeah … I thought the wood in those poles was completely dead.'

'Are dead things coming back to life?' she says, so mildly that I can't tell if she's serious or not.

Around us, cement is in the process of crumbling into dust, paint fading to shades of grey, birds building nests in deserted kitchens.

'I don't know,' I say.

Naomi raises her eyebrows and I understand that I should have said, *no.* She pulls a plastic thing and a bottle of water from her bag. She squats, places the plastic thing on the ground and then pours the bottle of water into it. The plastic thing is a bottle cut in half, the top half inverted and stuck upside down into the bottom. Water drips through a small puncture in the lid, reaching and passing measurements drawn in black marker.

Well, this is new.

Naomi watches each drop fall, unblinkingly. When the top half is empty, she takes it out and pours the water back into her bottle. She makes notes.

'That's a water clock,' I say.

'It is. Can we go deeper in? Or faster in, I'm not sure how you describe it.'

'You didn't do this last time,' I say.

'No, but now I'd like to do it in a few other places, ideally.'

'Faster?'

'Yes, and then in a slower area.'

'If we keep going in this direction it'll get faster, and then we can swing east and cross into a slow zone. We can get back to your car that way, but from the other direction.' It would take us close to Dad's company, but Yamagata would hardly be roaming around the woods. I might even get a glimpse of the field research that followed required regulations so well.

'That'll work nicely,' Naomi says.

'Why are you doing research?' I ask.

She looks at me sideways. 'To satisfy my own curiosity,' she says sharply.

I shut up, wary as we walk away from the houses down the roads farmers used when there were farmers here. We stop in an unruly apple orchard.

167

Naomi crouches among the fallen apples, eyes on the water clock. 'Fruit grown close to the slow areas is popular. Among some.'

'Right, there's a rumour about slow food, that it'll help you look young. I guess women in Tokyo want it?' I ask.

'Wealthy women. I don't know any personally,' she replies. 'Did I tell you I'm from Tokyo?'

I shake my head. 'Aren't you?'

'I live there.' She stands up. 'Done.'

'Do you want to see another kind of clock?' I find myself asking.

Naomi turns to me with interest. 'Certainly, if you think it's worth showing me.'

Not so far away is a modernist house surrounded by curving high walls, hiding the wide lawn that had made this the perfect place for what I had made a few years ago. Grew, not made; because it measured time with flowers.

I push open the stiff gate and beckon Naomi through. She takes it in silently.

I'd dug two circles and sown them with different seeds, one inside the other, the outer one for daytime and the inner one for night. Now, they've burst their beds. The centre is still there but plants radiate around it, like the spokes of a wheel.

I'd brought Dad when everything was flourishing and flowering and read the time from the blooms that opened and closed. I'd said that Mom would've been able to tell the time perfectly here, and Dad's face had clouded over. He didn't come back after that.

'This is the clock,' Naomi says at last. 'You made this.'

'It wasn't so hard,' I lie. 'I found the idea online and tried it.'

She walks around it, her eyes flicking from the flowers to me. 'Can you read it?'

I study the blooms, the petals opened or closed. 'Two p.m., two-thirty? It's not very accurate.'

'But it's beautiful,' Naomi breathes, and pride blushes through me.

The ground trembles suddenly, and we both freeze, though it's only a passing shiver. I look at the flowers and see that all their blooms have opened, as if it's all their times at once, and then a second later they close, apart from the flowers that say two p.m, almost three.

'Very interesting,' Naomi observes. 'Thank you for showing me this. It's an excellent tour feature.'

'I've never brought a tourist here,' I tell her.

'I'm honoured,' she says.

I shake my head as if it's nothing. We leave, and I close the gate on time, reaching out across the grass and up into the air. We continue on our way quietly. The road soon curves uphill, steep enough for it to be natural for us not to talk.

Naomi puts a hand on her stomach. 'Are we in slow time now?'

'Yeah. We came in around there.' I point to a road sign with a deer warning on it.

We pause at the top of the hill. Below us and to the east is Dad's company. Behind the building are those straight lines of plants and covered semicircular plastic tunnels used for the plants that need more protection. They must have expanded them recently because around the edges of the ordered farm are the jagged remains of cut trees, trunks piled carelessly. The earth left behind is raw and wounded.

'Ugh. Horrible,' I say.

'Not pretty, is it?' Naomi is frowning too.

'It's awful.' I drag my eyes away from the destruction. 'Downhill from here.'

'Good,' Naomi says.

The road swoops gently, and the trees thin out. Through them I can see the military lines of the company's farm. It stretches from here to the back of the company buildings, less than a kilometre away, and ahead of us for another couple of kilometres, surrounded by a low fence. What are they growing? Dad's never talked about the company's fruit and veg.

Naomi notices. 'We're quite close to those buildings.'

'Nobody's around. You can do a check.'

Naomi glances at the buildings and moves further into the undergrowth on the other side of the road. She jots down notes, clearly relieved when it's finished.

I peer at the crops, not a weed in sight. There's more variety than I thought – small sections are corn, maybe, others low bushes. I take a sudden breath, louder than I mean to.

'Is something wrong?' Naomi asks.

'No, no.' I hadn't known that there was a boundary

here. I study the crops again. Interesting that they've been planted so close to two zones.

'Where are you going?' Naomi asks.

'Not far.' I climb over the fence; it's not difficult. They're not trying very hard to keep animals out. Or people. I walk carefully beside the tall stalks – yes, corn. As tall as I am, taller. They're all green and straight. Perfect.

'Come back!' Naomi calls sharply, concern breaking through her even voice.

I turn back and hold up a finger. There's a plastic tunnel ahead of me, and through it I can see low-growing plants, blotches of red. I can't help lifting the flap and sticking my head in. Tomatoes. Their warm round smell fills the air, undercut by a biting chemical scent. The tomatoes are plump and unblemished, all the same size and shape, trained to fit neatly in plastic containers in supermarket rows.

I back out of the tunnel and gulp in the fresher air. Naomi waves at me. I walk parallel to her, until I find the slender boundary into normal time by the hair rising on my arms. There's a gap here in the crops, a margin of a few metres. Then a narrow row. So they know where the borders are, and accurately too.

I turn towards the road and Naomi – who I can't see any more. Her face peers around a tree trunk, pale against the brown and moss-mottled trunk. She's mouthing at me, or whispering, but I can't hear her.

'Hey!'

Oh, *shit.*

I swivel around. There's a man dressed in a navy uniform, a guard or a worker.

'Hi. Excuse me. I—'

'What are you doing here? This is private property!' he yells.

He's jogging towards me and even though it's too late I start to run. His hand closes on my arm in seconds.

'I'm leaving!' I try to pull away but his grip tightens.

'You've broken the law!' He's not messing around.

'It's more of a rule, though – I'm going, okay? I'm sorry!'

'Are you alone?' He looms over me. He's a guard, all right.

'Yeah.' I resist looking behind me. 'I'm by myself.'

He scans around. Naomi must be hiding, because he tugs me forward.

'Where are you taking me?'

'I'm reporting you.'

'To the police? Can you let go of my arm? Please.'

He doesn't reply, doesn't let go, just pulls me towards the main buildings of the company. And I begin to feel afraid.

The guard is silent the whole way, until we reach the wide yard behind the main buildings, where there are smaller sheds and other people. We pass close to a shed as a white-coated, white-booted man comes out. In the instant before he closes the door, I see rows of cages behind him. He sees me and shuts it quickly, but I've seen the little animals in there – rabbits or guinea pigs, small frightened things. The man narrows his eyes at me.

The guard, noticing, says, 'I'm taking her to the office.'

The man nods and watches us go. Further behind him are bigger sheds, and I catch a deep sound and a manure smell; there must be cows or some larger animals somewhere.

The guard opens a back door into the main building, and inside there's the sort of reception that hospitals and police stations have: a person sitting on the other side of a thick plastic barrier with a gap at the bottom. The man on the other side, older and also uniformed, does not seem as if he needs this protection.

'A trespasser,' my guard says.

The other man tuts. 'Bring her inside.'

'In where? You can't keep me here!' I really am frightened now. Would Naomi tell somebody what had happened? The police – but she doesn't even know my real name. And she was trespassing too—

'We won't keep you. We do need to ask you a few questions, however, before we call the police,' the older guard says.

'Just call them now.' I'd rather be in a police station than here.

He doesn't reply, but comes out from behind his plastic-protected desk and then opens another door. Inside there's a table and chairs, bare and plain. The guard, who has never let go of my arm, takes me inside.

'Sit down.'

I sit and twist my backpack off my shoulders and hold it in front of me, like a shield, or a teddy bear.

'Take your mask off,' the older guard says.

I glare and unhook it from my ears. Their eyes widen.

'A foreigner,' the younger guard says.

I don't know whether this will make it easier or worse for me.

'Can you speak Japanese?' the older guard asks, very slowly.

'I've been speaking Japanese the entire time!' I snap. Then I regret not speaking English in the first place. I might have been able to stupid-tourist my way out of it.

The guards mumble and huddle together. I sneak my phone out of my pocket.

In trouble at your company first floor with guards, I type and send.

'Put that away,' one of the guards says sternly.

'You can't stop me from contacting my family.' I have no idea if this is true or not.

'What's your name?' he says.

I want to tell him it's Yuna or Erika or any of the other pseudonyms I use. But that would hardly last long, they'll find out soon and it'll be worse then. For me and for Dad.

'Sora Campbell,' I say reluctantly.

'Campbell,' the guard repeats.

'My father works here,' I whisper.

His eyebrows raise. The guards confer, and the younger one leaves the room.

I close my eyes and wait. It's going to be fine. Dad is going to absolutely lose it, but I can deal with that. Maybe I *will* leave the country.

The door opens and I spin in my chair. 'Dad—'

It's not Dad. It's Yamagata.

'Hello,' he greets me, as if we are in a meeting, or an office. 'I am surprised to see you again so soon.'

I swallow hard. 'Yamagata-san. I apologise.'

He sits down calmly and clasps his hands on the table. 'I'm afraid that you are in some trouble. Especially seeing as we recently spoke about this very issue. I almost feel as though I gave you the idea.'

I have the urge to tell him that I'm an impressionable young person. 'Of course not.'

'No, because you often go into those out-of-bounds areas.'

I don't have to try hard to sound pathetic when I say, 'Sometimes I visit my grandparents' house. I know it's not allowed. But I miss them.'

Yamagata looks at me closely. 'So why did you come *here* today?'

'I ... became interested in the work you do here. I was curious.'

'You couldn't simply ask your father?'

'Dad says that work should stay at work. Especially,' I add, 'after our last meeting.'

'Is your curiosity satisfied?'

'Yes.' This is a lie. 'Well, no.'

'We are researching ways that the unnatural changes in time can be used to benefit people. It's not very interesting but food production is quite clearly a positive. We can also farm animals, not only tomatoes.'

More bones of cattle. Would they become confused too, if they were brought out of the zones? Or would there be slaughterhouses among the shadows and the spirits?

I pull my thoughts away from blood. 'Can people eat that?' I think of the strawberries. 'I mean, a lot of it?'

'There's no evidence otherwise,' Yamagata says evenly. 'So much of that land is useless, overgrown with trees and vegetation and so on. Our work is to get it under control.'

'You *can't* control it,' I say.

'Perhaps harness is a better word. Don't you think it would be better for people to associate the zones with something positive? It would certainly help the people here,' he says.

'Yes,' I agree quietly. He's not wrong; it would.

'I believe your father is outside.' He stands and opens the door.

My dad rushes in. 'Sora! What were you doing?' he yells.

Yamagata holds up a hand. 'Please, Campbell-san.'

Dad clears his throat. 'Excuse me, Yamagata-san. I do not know why my daughter was on company property but it's inexcusable.'

'It's also against the law,' Yamagata says.

'Ah... Are you going to pursue this further?' Dad actually pales.

Yamagata gazes from him to me. 'No.'

Dad and I breathe identical sighs of relief.

'However,' Yamagata continues, 'you may no longer work here.'

'What?' I say loudly.

'Excuse – excuse me?' Dad stutters.

'It's unfortunate, and to be honest, I was considering it before this. Your work is somewhat ... erratic. I must say that I have been concerned with your behaviour of late. Believe me,' Yamagata shifts his eyes to me, 'I do *not* want any employees hurt or damaged.' He seems genuine, then returns to his professional tone. 'It would not reflect well on the company.'

'But you were fine with it, before,' I interrupt bitterly. 'Before it became obvious how bad it was.'

Yamagata glances from me to Dad, with a hint of unease. He raises his voice slightly. '*And* we cannot be associated with an employee whose family is in breach of both our own regulations and legal ones.'

Dad is clearly stunned.

'That's not fair!' I say. 'You can't do that – it's not his fault that I did this. You can get the police to come and arrest me!'

'Sora,' Dad says hoarsely. 'Stop.'

'I don't care. That would be fairer than this!'

'Shut up,' Dad says in English. His voice is hard and cold.

Yamagata waits for silence. 'Sora-san, I am the head of a company that is conducting work in an area that people are still *highly* cautious about. You must understand that I can allow no law-breaking or suspicions. There are many people employed here, all trying to find ways we can benefit from the zones. Do you truly think that is unfair?' He is exasperated. He sounds honest.

I have nothing to say, no argument against this.

Yamagata takes a breath and gathers himself. 'Campbell-san, you will have until the end of the week to finish any work you're currently doing. You will also receive a letter of termination.'

Dad just nods. His face is grey. He doesn't look at me.

My head spins. How is this happening?

'You're only being fair to some,' I say to Yamagata, but my voice is weak and hollow.

'We're going,' Dad says.

Yamagata holds the door open for us.

牡丹華

PEONIES BLOOM

12

In the cold fluorescence of our kitchen light, Dad and I stare at each other. His face is blank.

'I'm sorry,' I say, when I can't stand the thrumming silence any longer.

'I don't understand,' he says hoarsely, 'what you were doing.'

'Nothing, Dad. I was honestly just looking at the stupid corn, I wasn't damaging anything or—'

'Why were you there in the first place?'

I could come clean now and tell him everything. How bad was it, really, bringing people in for a few hours? I was hardly exploiting them with my fees either—

Dad's eyes flick away from me. 'This is my fault, isn't it?'

'What?'

'I brought you into those places so many times.'

'Those times were different. I wanted to go. It was to learn—'

'And what did we learn? Nothing of use or help.'

'That doesn't have anything to do with this.' I expected shouting and anger. I'm not sure what this is.

'No?' He stares at me suddenly and urgently. 'How do you feel?'

'Like crap, obviously!'

'I mean, physically. And mentally.'

'I'm not sick.' But how can I be sure? It had been part of Dad's monitoring of me, and he has proven why, with every missed memory, every illness he suffered. 'I'm fine.' My voice shakes.

'It might be wise for you to take some time away from here. While I... You were talking about going away and I don't know why you changed your mind. Canada, yes. Or you could go to your mother's cousin in Aichi.' His eyes are everywhere but meeting mine.

'You don't want me here.'

'I don't think it's good for you here,' he says weakly.

'But it's always fine for *you*, isn't it? You've chosen this place, the zones, over me again and again.' I'm shouting. 'And you expected me to stay, and I have, and now you just decide I can't!'

'It's my duty to take care of you. I am doing that. In this case, I am putting you out of harm's way.' Dad's voice is so even it sounds dead.

'I've kept myself safe so far.'

'I mean the harm *you* can do.' Dad has no emotion on his face.

'I understand.' It's difficult to speak, as though I'm

instructing somebody else on how to make sounds and form words. I do understand. I'm worse than no use and no help. I'm standing in the way of what has always been the most important thing to him, and that is his work, his research, his quest for answers that don't exist.

'I'll go tomorrow,' I say.

Dad doesn't protest or tell me I'm mistaken. I try to measure how long I'm waiting but I can't keep track of my heartbeat. It might have stopped beating.

'I'll go,' I say again, and I find my way to my bedroom.

I pull Mom's cardigan out of the closet and sink down to the floor with it. I squeeze it into a ball and press my face into worn and fraying wool. What would she say if she was here? But this wouldn't be happening if she *was* here. I grip the cardigan in my fists and have to fight the urge to rip it apart. I can't destroy everything. Soon I'll have nothing left.

When I can unclench my hands I crawl on to my bed. My body is heavy, a piece of machinery I have to concentrate to control. I wish I could disappear into sleep, but my mind is swirling and my eyes won't stay closed. I open my laptop. I'm not going to Aichi, to relatives I barely know. Vancouver seems like a dream now.

A ping announces an email.

Are you safe? I hope so. I didn't get to pay you, so I owe you twice over.
    Please reply when you can.
    Naomi.

It's a different email account to the one she used before, which had been an unremarkable one – *naomi* followed by a bunch of numbers. She must have forgotten to use it because this one isn't anonymous. At the bottom of the email, it reads: *Naomi Nomura, PhD Candidate in Time Sciences.* Below that, the name of a university. Koki's university.

I take a breath and force myself upright. So I'm leaving, then. I'm going to Tokyo.

After Obaachan died and Mom came home, we were upside down with sadness until we righted ourselves. Mom phoned Ojiichan every day and always handed the phone to me so I could report what I'd learned in school. Ojiichan would tell me I was smart, correct my Japanese, or recall a rambling story about his own childhood. I loved Ojiichan. I was tired of this formula. I was ten.

One day I shook my head when Mom beckoned me to the phone.

'I have a ton of maths,' I whispered.

'Two minutes, say hello!' Mom demanded.

I crossed my arms and put my face down into my multiplication and division.

Mom was angry with me even though Ojiichan wasn't. Dad didn't seem to notice. He read work papers at the table during dinner. Mom collected the dishes and I washed them. I was annoyed because I felt guilty.

There was a cry from the living room and then Mom came into the kitchen, a potted plant in her hands. 'Dead,' she said.

The plant had dark green leaves, flowers that were such a bright intense scarlet that they made me blink. But most of them were crumpled and wilted, the leaves dry.

Mom thrust the pot towards Dad. 'You were supposed to water it while I was away.'

Dad frowned. 'I did.'

'You added vinegar to water, like I told you?'

Dad put his pen down. 'Vinegar? I don't recall you telling me that.'

'It needs vinegar. Because the soil isn't right. It can't live in this soil by itself.' Mom's hands were gripping the pot.

'How strange,' Dad said. 'It's a lot of trouble to go to for a flower.'

I thought that Dad was being dumb, not noticing that Mom was angry. But his face was straight and alert and that was when I understood that he was angry too. This was scarier than being shouted at.

'It's not. It's just something a little bit different,' Mom said.

'I was busy with work and I suppose it slipped my mind,' Dad said.

'This is our home. It's your job too.' Mom's voice was tight and even.

'Yes, but I'm not the horticultural expert, am I?'

I knew this was not about the plant but didn't know any more than that.

'You need to be an expert to make dinner? To clean? To take care of family?' Mom asked.

Dad blinked.

'So why do you expect me to do it?' She put the plant down, calmly and deliberately, on top of his papers.

'It's not totally dead,' I said desperately. 'It still has flowers.'

Mom and Dad turned to me with the same motion of surprise. They had forgotten I was there.

'You're right, Sora,' Dad said. 'We'll make it better. Let's do it together.' Dad touched a petal very gently, and Mom softened as if he had put a hand to her cheek. 'Sora, can you come here?'

I joined them, relieved, while Dad cleared the table of his papers.

'Oshietekurete kudasai,' Dad said to Mom, which made her smile.

'You're being polite, so yes, I'll teach you.' She started to talk about the alkaline and acid in a soil and the balance a plant needs to thrive, and how we could provide it.

Dad took notes and I mixed the balance of vinegar and water and poured it into the pot. We watched the soil welcome it in.

'See,' Dad said to Mom, 'it will grow again. It'll be happy.'

'You have to take care of it,' she replied, 'every day.'

Dad promised he would. He hugged her and she leaned her head against his shoulder. I watched them, feeling held too, by their love.

Years later, one evening when Dad had drunk too many beers, he told me that Mom had wanted to move back to Japan.

'I said that Canada was our home. It would have been a lot to uproot you, then. Not only you but all of us.' He looked at me the same way he'd looked at Mom, hoping she would tell him how to make a flower grow.

立夏

SUMMER STARTS

13

I'm the last one off the bus. My feet hit the pavement and it's like I've fallen into a river full of fish. People rush and part around me, just another blockage in the swift current. I dodge into the station entrance and lean against a wall, holding my bag tight. It's evening now, the end of rush hour. The sky is darkening and the buildings are lighting up, a blaring confusion of neon and colour reaching to the sky to fill the space the sun has left. On the other side of the road is JR Shinjuku Station, delivering people and taking them away. They all know where they're going.

I feel I should run through the streets, take a selfie with the colourful backdrop of signs and lights and city. Instead, I squat against the wall. I check my watch. There's a hum of noise I'm not used to: machinery, engines, voices; the sound of a city running. I stare at the people, the unmoving traffic on the wide road. There are signs for other places and then, in the centre, I see a strangely cheery illustration. *Emergency road,* it declares in Japanese and English, *Closed in the event of a major earthquake.* The cartoon is a grinning catfish, blue and yellow, pink lipped mouth stretched wide.

It's hot all of a sudden and I tug Mom's cardigan off and stuff it into my bag. Sweat runs down my face, but when I wipe it away I find that it's tears, that I'm crying.

Shit. I fumble for a towel to dry my cheeks. For a second I hold my face against the cloth, smelling home, and I think about how easy it would be to wait for the next bus and let it take me back.

'Sora?'

I snatch the towel away and stand up so fast my head spins. 'Koki!'

'Lucky,' he says. 'It once took me forty-five minutes to find someone I was meeting here.'

I put my hand against the wall to steady myself.

'Do you feel okay?' His concern is real, but he doesn't touch me.

'Koki,' I say again, just to be sure. 'Tired, that's all. The bus. And – Tokyo.' So I've forgotten how to talk. Nice.

Then we stare at each other. He looks different. It might be his hair. He's not smiling, but he's not angry or annoyed either. His clothes are newer. He's standing a little further away from me than feels normal.

I'm rumpled and stiff and clumsy. I'm wearing loose pants and a T-shirt soft with age and I'm suddenly aware how scruffy I am compared to the people going by in crisp shirts and cute dresses and elegant high heels. I must look like such a country girl. Suddenly I want a job and a haircut and places to commute to in professional clothes.

Koki's face changes. 'Hey.' He steps close to me and touches my arm. 'It's too busy here. Let's go somewhere quiet.'

'Yes, *please*.' Then I'm annoyed at myself, at how easily scared I am, how he must feel sorry for me. 'It's not very nice around here, is it? And I'm tired,' I repeat. 'I'm tired.'

Koki nods and picks up my bag and marches off down the street. I keep as close to him as possible. Even though he wouldn't just keep going, even though we have phones and I could call him, even though I could shout his name and he would hear me, I'm afraid that if I lose sight of him I'll never find him again.

Koki knows where he's going. He leads the way with confidence – no, it's not that he's confident; it's that he's relaxed. This is what's normal for him, now.

He pauses at an intersection. 'Ramen, soba, or curry?'

'Curry,' I say, even though it's warm and I'm not very hungry.

'Thought so.' Koki takes a left, a right, crosses a street, another right.

I repeat the directions to myself. I want to make sure I remember where I am. Where the station is. I need to know how to get home again.

Koki stops in front of a small restaurant, its door already open. The waiter greets us and leads us to a table, brings us cool damp cloths and water. I abandon manners and scrub at my face with the cloth. All the miles of highway feel like they've sunk into my skin.

'How long were you on the bus for?' Koki asks.

'Years,' I say. 'I was born on that bus.'

The waiter comes over.

'Chicken curry, please,' Koki tells him. 'Two.'

'You didn't even ask what I wanted!' I say indignantly.

'What do you want, then?'

'Just vegetables,' I say.

'You've changed.'

Good, I think, before I realise Koki's making fun of me. 'So have you.'

The waiter nods and hurries off, probably thinking that this is a date that can only get worse.

I empty my water glass and pretend I don't care that Koki is watching me. He's about to ask me a question, and I don't want to answer any yet, so I say, boringly, 'Do you eat here a lot?'

'Once. By myself.'

I'm not sure why Koki adds this, and suddenly he looks embarrassed. We fall into quietness until the waiter delivers our curries, which is not that many minutes later. What a kind man. He's probably been watching us and cooked as fast as possible to spare us the awkward silence.

'Itadakimasu,' I say, and spoon up the steaming curry

and rice. It's good, and I swallow it down even though it's hot and I have to huff in that stupid way to cool my mouth down.

'Better than CocoIchi?'

'*Different*,' I echo.

Koki grins and we eat in silence, but a calmer one than before.

'You're not really here just to visit me, are you?' Koki says.

I bite my lip. 'I'm going to do other stuff while I'm here. You don't have to take care of me.' I sound defensive.

Koki is still looking at me expectantly.

'I couldn't stay at home,' I say eventually. 'Everybody was gone and I had nothing to do except drive Dad crazy. He drove me crazy too. I was sort of … in trouble.'

Koki's concerned and then he *really* looks concerned. 'What kind of trouble? What happened?'

I stare down at the table, trying to decide whether I should tell him what actually happened, why Dad told me to go. I meet his eyes. They're wide and alarmed. 'It's not that bad, it's not— Oh. *No.* I'm not *pregnant,* Koki!'

The waiter, coming towards the table with a jug of water, turns smoothly on his heel and goes back into the kitchen.

'Right, good, okay. I— If you had been I would, you know, definitely…' he rambles.

'Yes, yes. Wow, it's like I can see your life flashing before your eyes.'

'I mean ... maybe an alternate life.'

For a second, I get a flash of it too. I pick up the receipt and go to pay.

'Here, let me give you money,' Koki says.

'No, let me get yours, please. Think of it as payment.'

'For what?' Koki looks wary.

'For letting me stay at your place tonight.' I smile hopefully at him.

Koki rolls his eyes. 'Where else would you go, anyway?'

'The park,' I say. 'And I'd hide.'

'That can be the back-up, then. But I'll show you Godzilla first,' Koki says.

This time I don't pretend to be uninterested. I stare all around me, at the skyscrapers, the lights, the people rushing along the street, shopping, entering and leaving restaurants. They're alone and in couples and in groups, and there are tourists, wide-eyed and photo-taking, and I hope I don't look too much like them.

Koki doesn't rush me. He points out buildings, tells me about getting lost, the new sights he's seen. He shows me Godzilla looming over a cinema. He's excited. Maybe it was hard for him when he arrived, but I can see that he loves it now, he's been swept up in the energy of this place, so unlike our quiet town, with its silences and spaces. Home seems far away and full of gaps and Tokyo isn't filled up, it's overflowing.

And not with strange things either. There are no odd eyes following me, no skin tingles as time shifts around my body, no shadows. When we pass side streets or dark houses, there's no emptiness; just a lull, a pause before people return or wake up or come home.

My steps start to drag, and Koki notices.

'Let's go home. It's only a few stops from here to my place,' he says.

We're outside a station, much smaller and more manageable than Shinjuku. Inside, I get a Suica card, which Koki says is much more convenient than buying tickets all the time. We tap through the ticket gate and I feel almost like a resident until I fumble my card back into my purse while everyone else smoothly flips theirs into pockets in their phone covers. We stand by the train door, the seats all taken by people asleep or bent over phones or lost in the sounds of their headphones.

Three stops later, we get off, and ten minutes after that we're outside a four-storey building. We climb the stairs to the third floor and Koki unlocks his door and I follow him in. It's tiny, a kitchen only big enough for one person to stand in and a room with his futon folded in a corner, a low table covered with papers, shelves piled with books.

'It's a bit messy...' Koki hurriedly starts tidying stuff away.

I stand in the doorway. The room is so small that I feel the closeness of him more than before. 'Please don't worry. This is too much trouble for you. I'm sorry, I didn't think...'

'About the size of Tokyo apartments?' Koki sees me looking at the futon. 'Ah. I have two futons. You can have the thin one.'

'Yes, perfect.'

He laughs. 'Sit down. Tea? Bath?' He goes into the kitchen.

I sit on a floor cushion. The view from the window is of electric wires crisscrossing, other buildings with squares of light representing homes, and a brief patch of green in the middle distance.

Koki hands me a mug of green tea, the teabag floating inside.

'Thanks,' I say. 'Do you have class tomorrow?'

'Yeah. *And* my part-time job,' he says.

'Where do you work?'

'A cafe. You should come by tomorrow.'

'Maybe I will. I'll order whatever is the most difficult to make.' I'm splashed by a wave of guilt. 'Seriously, thanks for all this.'

'I've known you for years so I can definitely put up with you for a few days.' He's suddenly anxious. 'It *is* a few days, isn't it?'

'It's a few days.' This is a guess.

When the bath's full he gallantly lets me go first. I wash myself with the shampoo and soap that someone has decided are male scents and then sink into the bath. I only feel how tense and stiff I am when the heat begins to melt it away. I struggle into pyjamas in the bathroom and go back in to Koki, very aware of my damp hair and warm body. He's already laid out the futons.

Koki gestures to them and avoids me. 'Kind of early, but you seem tired. I need to get up early too.'

I tuck myself in. The futon really is thin. I take out my phone. No messages from Dad. I didn't say goodbye to him. How long will it take before he bothers to check if I'm alive? I'll think of it as an experiment.

Koki returns, face pink, wearing a T-shirt and boxers. Now it's my turn to avoid him, but he turns off the light to spare us both. He gets into the futon beside me. We're very close to each other; if I put out my arm, my hand would fall on his chest. The room is faintly lit even through the curtains, the streetlights glow outside the window. I'm used to the deep darkness of the countryside.

Now for the real weirdness. I can feel us both gearing up to say something. We do this at the exact same moment.

He inhales. 'Sora—'

'About—'

I grimace. 'Go ahead—'

'Didn't mean to—'

Silence again.

'I'm sorry for ignoring your messages when you left,' I say.

'I understand if you felt … not good. 'Cause I left straight afterwards. That wasn't right.' He shakes his head against the pillow.

'You had to go. You were going anyway,' I whisper.

'Was that why you wanted to…'

I wonder how he's going to shape the question, but he doesn't finish it. I do it for him. 'Sleep together?'

'Yeah.'

I pause as I try to pull my feelings out and put them

into comprehensible words. 'It wasn't *why*, because I wouldn't have done it if I didn't want to. But if you weren't going, maybe we wouldn't have done it *then*. I wanted to … be with you. I didn't know if we'd be together like that again.' This is the best explanation I can give.

'I see,' Koki says, in a very neutral voice.

I turn on my side to face him, but he stays on his back, staring at the ceiling. Or else his eyes are closed. 'You wanted to too, didn't you?'

'Yeah. But I never knew how you felt about me. In that way. And I'd never asked you to be my girlfriend … I wondered if that was how you were saying goodbye. Or…' He breathes out.

'Or I wanted you not to go?' I guess.

'Maybe. I'm not sure. I suppose I'm still confused.'

'I am too.' His hair is like strokes of ink against the white pillow. 'Of course I like you, Koki.'

'In that way? Enough? Still?' he asks.

I think.

He sits up and leans over. Somehow he knows precisely where my lips are. We stay like that for long seconds, only mouths touching. We move away slowly. It's too dark to see the expression in his eyes. He lies down, and then I do too.

That didn't help me think more clearly at all. I don't know if he's still waiting for my answer or if he's found it. I reach my hand out to his, and he clasps it. Not tightly, but enough so that I know I won't drift away.

蛙始鳴

FROGS START SINGING

14

A heavy *thunk* jumps me awake.

'Sorry.' Koki picks up a book from the floor. 'I'm going to class, so you can sleep. Cereal in the cupboard, key on the table.'

'As good as a hotel. I'll come by when you're finishing work. Where's the cafe?'

He zips his bag up. 'I work in the fast zone.'

For a minute I don't understand what he means. 'You *do*? Is it weird?' I sit up. 'Isn't it just a sightseeing spot?'

He puts his bag over his shoulder. 'You know people live there, don't you?'

'Not many people,' I guess.

'It's *Tokyo*,' Koki says with infuriating condescension.

'If you can live in a zone then it can't be that bad. Hardly a zone at all, I bet.'

'For us, sure. A lot of people have never experienced it.'

'Still, they can't know what it's really like—'

'They're going there so they *can* know,' Koki says abruptly. 'What do you want them to do? Go live *our* lives?' His words settle through the air like dust.

'No,' I say. 'I'll see for myself later, I guess.'

Koki softens. 'You will. I'll see you then, okay?'

I fall back on the pillow. I check my phone. Nothing from Dad. I push him out of my mind angrily. There's no way I'm sleeping now. Time to see Tokyo.

It's a fresh, bright day. I didn't know the sky would be so blue over the city. People are on their way to work, moving towards the station with expressions of concentration and worry and unfocused sleepiness. I avoid the train, walking instead through streets laid at abrupt right angles to each other, past houses and buildings in jumbles of different architecture, designed to fill up the odd shapes of small lots.

I walk until my legs ache, and then I give in and navigate my way to the nearest station, the line I need to get, the right side of the platform. I pretend that I've done this a hundred times before. I watch everybody else and try to make my face as bored and closed as theirs are. When the train arrives I slouch in the corner by the door so I can see more. Buildings flash past, roads, houses and people, always people. The shape of the city grows taller and more crowded as we get closer to the hub of Tokyo.

The fast zone is close to Shibuya. It's a real selling point. *The fastest place in the world just got faster!* is their slogan. There are way faster places further north, up the coast from us. And slower too. Our town is known for it, but not in a good way. I get off at Shibuya station and follow signs obediently until they lead me to the Hachiko exit with the dog statue. Everyone seems to be going there. Must be a great statue.

It's only okay. People are crowding around, almost everyone yelling into phones saying, *Are you here? I'm here. I can't see you.* Everything around it is way more interesting: giant screens, lights beaming down on me, even though it's daytime. The famous crossing is ahead, and as I watch, the green walk sign pings on, and crowds of people are released on to the black and white strips that zebra across the road. Tourists are taking photos and videos, which is probably why it's so frantic, because people are standing in the middle of it all and taking selfies. There are lots of foreigners. It's been a long time since I felt like I didn't stand out on a street.

I know I'm getting close to the fast place because the shops have different kinds of omiyage: a variety of watches that run forward, hands whizzing, T-shirts, hats, socks. There's a big sign explaining what the zone is, warning first-time visitors to be careful and not to stay more than twenty-four hours. People are taking photos beside it.

There's a barrier at the entrance and I hesitate before I pass through. Everyone around me is chatting, laughing, phones out to commemorate this moment. There's a toll booth with a disinterested guard who reels off instructions and cautions in English. I don't bother telling him I can speak Japanese. I nod and he waves me through.

There's only the slightest tingle but on the other side people are wobbling, holding each other for balance. The zone feels less than ten minutes faster for every hour; the least of the zones at home are worse than that. Some shriek and laugh, over-reacting, making faces for photos; a few seem genuinely freaked out. I stare around like everyone else. The street is covered and lined with stalls and shops. It's busy with people, not only foreigners, either, but Japanese people. Most of the country is in normal time, after all.

There are clocks everywhere. The mascot is a cute version of a zorigami, a possessed clock, one of the many household items that become angry and alive if left broken or alone for long enough. I push the memory of the moving teacup out of my mind. The zorigami isn't scary; it's adorable, with big eyes and little arms and legs. It's called Zori-chan and looks like a teddy bear and a watch fell in love and had a baby. The other clocks are running exaggeratedly fast, sometimes beside another clock labelled 'normal time' to highlight it. I don't know how they're supposed to be showing normal time in here, but nobody else seems to question it. Oh, it's strange. I peer into the little shops and restaurants. There's a place selling imagawayaki in the shape of clocks and I buy one and eat it fast, the bean paste inside burning my tongue. It's delicious.

Above the restaurants and shops are signs advertising cram schools, capsule hotels, beauty parlours. The cram schools are popular because you get more study time.

There are shared workspaces where you can rent a desk and do your work or assignments or taxes. The largest is new and shiny, run by a big international company. The people coming in and out are rushing, looking stressed and exhausted even though they are supposed to be cheating time. The hotels are probably filled with businessmen trying to get a few more minutes' rest during their lunch breaks.

I leave the covered shopping street. A movement in an alley catches my eye, but it's only a stray cat with a short tail that darts behind a whirring air-conditioning unit. No, there are no flitting creatures here, no spirits or gods.

I leave the cat to its secret errands and head towards a building that's all glass and metal, proclaiming itself to be the information centre. There are various informative plaques beside photos and videos playing on screens. *Wood could not be used in the construction of the building because it was not known how it would age,* one says. There are before and after photos of the reconstruction. In the before photos, the buildings are broken, slumped, cracked. People are on the streets, dusty and hurt and shocked. It's not that bad, I've seen worse, and then I feel ashamed because I want to tell those photographed people: *you don't know how lucky you are.*

The next section is the science bit, where they try to explain why time got confused after the Shake. There's an animated video of the earth spinning, jumping, then spinning faster. It zooms in on Japan, with little pulsing rings radiating from the centre of the Shake. I peer and think I know which tiny red dot is my town. The video doesn't mention it. There's some quick shots of the really bad stuff, but they hurry away from that. I move on to the after photos, where everything is clean and rebuilt. People smile at each other and at the camera, pleased that their lives have been *rejuvenated* and *revitalised.*

I look at my phone because I can't look at this exhibition any more. Koki's already sent the location of the cafe; it's close by. He won't be finished for a while, but I'm tired and I don't feel like walking around here.

I'm on my way, I message to him.

His cafe is in a towering building, so tall that it has an observation deck. Twentieth floor. I squeeze into a lift with a crowd of people, and my ears pop as we ascend smoothly. The doors open and people separate into those who want coffee and those who want a view. I can see Koki through the glass walls, wearing a white shirt and a navy apron. He brings a tray with coffees to two young women. They peek at their coffees and laugh and clap their hands, take photos of them, and beam at Koki. He gives a little bow and returns to the coffee machine. I go in, smiling vaguely as the guy at the door asks if he can seat me.

'Hey,' I say to Koki.

He jumps and splashes himself with hot water. 'Ah!'

'Ah, sorry!'

'It's okay, I still do that a lot.' He runs his hand under the cold tap.

'Are you making magic coffees or something?' I tilt my head towards the two women at the table. They are very pretty.

'Oh,' he says. 'That's our signature latte. Try it.'

I go to the counter and order. It's almost a thousand yen. Seriously?

Koki notices my wince. 'Everything in this area's more expensive.' He starts foaming the milk. 'You should go on to the deck, it's cool.'

Most of the tables outside are empty. The sky is clear, the light turning a soft sort of yellow that makes the city gentler, blurring the sharp edges of buildings. There's an odd dissonance and it takes me a while to figure out what it is; I can see the city moving in slower motion. There's a moment of vertigo that makes me grip the railing.

Koki comes out and hands me a cup. 'Here.' There's a clock drawn in the foam.

'That's the signature?'

'Yeah. The time signature.'

I laugh but can't help rolling my eyes. 'It's all too much!' I say, louder than I mean to. 'The clocks, the souvenirs – it's like a theme park.'

'It's no different from any kind of attraction in the country. Everything's got mascots and stuff.'

'But this … this is different. A bad thing happened here!'

'It's not bad now.' Koki gestures to the people eating cake.

'You don't think so? All those cram schools? There

are people here who need more time and it's not for good reasons.'

'Sora, you think things have to be one thing or another. There's never any halfway with you.'

He doesn't know how halfway between things I am.

He leans his arms on the barrier. 'I thought it was kinda weird, at first. I still do. But it's sort of ... encouraging. It made me feel better that the Shake didn't make everyone miserable for ever.'

I stare down at the straight wide streets dotted with people and the roads busy with cars. They're going about their lives and I feel a hole in my chest open and the air rush in, making me hollow. I don't want to be jealous of them, but I am, and I don't want to feel empty, but I do.

Koki nudges my shoulder. 'Drink your coffee.'

I take a sip. It's rich and smooth and milky. 'It's good.'

Koki's indignant. 'Don't be so surprised! That took me weeks to get right.'

'Why did you want to work here?'

'The pay is good. They pay by the zone hours too.'

'As they should,' I say. 'I thought you got a scholarship, though.'

'It's not enough. Have to work. Other students have to as well.'

'But not many,' I guess. 'Are they all rich kids?' I ask.

'Richer than us.'

'Not hard,' I say.

'They know I'm the scholarship kid. Because the university brings me out sometimes for functions and photo ops. To show how good they're being, helping the disadvantaged regions. I have to be grateful and thank them again.' Koki's hands are tight on the railing.

'That's horrible,' I say. 'The university isn't doing it out of any goodness, then.'

Koki straightens up. 'I know. But I'm getting an education, aren't I? It'll be worth it.' He's clenching his jaw the way he does when he's determined to get something done. When he's steeling himself.

'You're right,' I say. 'Get as much education as you can and stuff it into your brain.'

He smiles. 'I have to get back to work. My quick break is definitely over.'

I sit down and gaze past the skyscrapers, past Tokyo Tower and the Skytree, and wonder which direction home is in.

After he takes his apron off, Koki leaps into the role of tour guide. He points out an old-fashioned fruit and vegetable shop run by several old ladies who might have been sisters; a particular balcony overflowing with flowers; a group of earnest researchers taking notes.

'There's normal stuff too,' he says. 'Normal life.'

He should know how well people can maintain normality. I nod and agree because he's happy and I don't want to spoil that again. I can laugh here, with him. There's no sense of danger, no emptiness, no spirits.

'What else do you want to do?' Koki asks.

'I don't really have any plans. I wasn't thinking of *Tokyo* exactly, when I decided to come. More about...'

More about escaping Dad and everything that had been screwed up.

'Me?' Koki laughs.

'As if. I wanted to go somewhere different. I can't stay in the inaka for ever.'

'There's so many things you could do. You're *almost* as smart as me,' he says, dodging as I reach to smack him. 'You just need to get out of your comfort zone.'

I don't even know the last time I felt comfortable. I want to say: your mother makes you dinner and makes sure you eat it. Your father remembers your name. But he has no brother to play baseball with, to argue about movies with. What's the point in competing in sorrow?

'Your dad will be okay without you,' Koki says, reading my face, or my mind.

I clear my throat. 'I know what I want to do tomorrow. I'd like to see your university. You're studying science, right?'

'Science, yeah. Because I want to major in *time* science, Sora,' Koki says meaningfully.

I didn't know that, and I should have. 'Take me to a lecture with lots of students. I bet the teacher wouldn't even notice me.'

Koki sighs. 'I'll think about it.'

蚯蚓出

WORMS SURFACE

15

'**C**ome *on*,' Koki says. He grabs my hand, not in a romantic way but in the way a mother hauls along a kid having a tantrum.

'But it's so early,' I weep.

'No, it isn't! And this was your idea, remember?' Koki hustles me on through the station ticket gate, along with other students and workers. 'You can definitely go back to bed.'

'No, no.' It had actually taken a while to persuade Koki. He only agreed because I told him he could totally deny knowing me if anybody figured out I'm not a student.

I wake up properly as we walk through the university gates, along an avenue lined with tall trees and scattered with students. Ahead of us is a red-brick building rising firmly against the faint morning clouds.

'Are we going in there?'

'Don't worry, we're not.'

'I'm not worried.' But the building is intimidating. Maybe people *would* know I don't belong here.

I try to be casual when we enter the lecture hall, though it's excitingly like I imagined, with seats and desks in semicircular rows surrounding a low stage. There are less than a hundred students in the lecture hall, though it could probably hold twice that. They're clumped together, talking and laughing, on their phones, or asleep.

Koki leads me to a row in the middle of the hall, points at the seat at the end of the row, furthest from the lecturer's desk. 'As glamorous as you expected?'

'How could it be glamorous when that guy is drooling on his pencil case? Also, there are literally only three girls here.'

Koki makes a face. 'Yeah, it's not very balanced. Another reason for you to come here.'

'Or *not* to come,' I say.

'You could be a good example.'

'That's the university's job, not mine.'

'No wonder you're unemployed,' he replies.

That shuts me up.

But the lecturer who comes into the hall is a woman. There's a vague murmur.

Koki sits up straight. 'That's not our usual teacher.'

It's Naomi.

I swallow a loud swear word and shout it in my head instead.

'I've seen her around, though, and apparently she's super-smart,' Koki is saying. 'I bet this is going to be an interesting class. Your lucky day.'

'Truly.'

The other students seem to think they're lucky too. Everyone sits attentively and quietens down. There's only one guy still asleep.

Naomi's finished setting up. 'Hello. I'm Nomura. Shirai-sensei is ill, so I'll be teaching you today. He didn't tell me exactly what he was planning for this class, so forgive me if our lesson is somewhat random.' She's speaking almost perfect Japanese.

From the students' reaction, no forgiveness is needed.

Naomi gives no sign that she's creating a stir. Her voice is clear and firm and carries without an echo. 'In fact, our lesson *will* be random because I'm going to talk about entropy today.'

Entropy isn't a word I've heard before in Japanese. I realise, too late, that the whole lecture will probably be like this, full of technical words that I don't know.

'Entropy?' I whisper to Koki.

'Like … disorder. Chaos,' he replies.

Naomi is asking the class if they've studied it before. People half-shrug or half-nod in a way that means they haven't but don't want to look stupid, or else they have but don't want to be asked any questions about it.

Naomi obviously understands, and says, 'Well, then: entropy is how we measure the randomness of a system. We use it mostly in physics and chemistry, but also in cosmology, even in economics. Of course, it exists in our everyday lives, though it's so much a part of living that we don't notice it. Our lives are made much more of entropy than they are of order. For you, as university students, this is certainly the case,' she adds dryly.

There's a cautious titter as everyone understands that it's true but doesn't know whether this is a scolding or a joke.

Naomi begins talking about ice cubes melting and water and steam, then clicks on a presentation that has the kind of equations that I've already mostly forgotten from science class – those sentences of numbers, letters, brackets and symbols. There's a slide with the picture of a jar filled with what looks like ricocheting fireworks.

'In a closed system, chaos can stay the same or can increase. However, it can never get smaller, or calmer.' She clicks to the next slide, the earth inside a glass globe. 'Let's move this to a bigger scale. What if the universe is the same? A closed system. It could answer one of the most interesting problems of science: why can't we go back in time?'

There's a murmur, almost a scoff. The sleeping student has woken up and is blinking rapidly, whether because of grogginess or intellectual confusion I can't tell.

Koki is raising an eyebrow. 'A leap.'

'I thought that's how we get from one idea to another,' I say.

'The arrow of time is so-called because it moves forward in the natural world,' Naomi goes on. 'Once it is released from the bow, it is unable to change direction or fight its momentum. But if the universe is a closed system, then the entropy cannot decrease. It is impossible to return to a time in our system that is exactly the same as it was before; we cannot go back to the past because it existed only then. It cannot be recaptured.'

There's another murmur in the room, but this is more of a shrug, a *so-what*.

But I'm thinking and thinking because even though I understand that, it's also wrong. We can't go back, and yes, the world is chaos, but does a time only exist in the past because of that? We might not be able to physically return to a time, but that's not the only way we can go back. And what about people?

'Aren't people closed systems too? Aren't we made of chaos?'

'*Sora*,' hisses Koki, because I said this louder than I meant to and my questions have landed in a hollow of silence in a pause between Naomi's words.

And now she is looking at me, and her self-control must be incredible because her eyes widen in recognition by only a fraction.

'Sorry.' I resist the instinct to turn to Koki for help. He's fixed his eyes straight ahead, his cheeks flushing.

'Humans are made of chaos *and* order,' Naomi says, and clicks to the next slide, returning to her lecture as smoothly as if my interruption hadn't even happened.

Which isn't the case for everyone else, because I get some glances that range from curious to slightly irritated. Koki studiously takes notes. I watch Naomi, but it's hard to focus on what she's talking about because I'm thinking about the order in people I know.

The projector switches off. The lecture's finished. People

replace notebooks in bags, scrutinise their phones, file from the room. I can't think what Naomi's final words had been.

'It's over,' Koki says. 'You have to go.'

I register the *you* rather than *we* and gather myself. A student is speaking eagerly to Naomi and another hovers behind him.

Outside, I say, 'Sorry, Koki. The thought just came into my head.'

'Well,' he says, 'I guess you think too loud.'

'I don't think at all,' I protest.

'True.' Then he shakes his head and smiles. 'Also a lie.'

I smile back, relieved. 'Thanks for bringing me, Koki. I enjoyed it.'

'It was different, anyway. I'll see you later.'

'See you.'

We go in opposite directions. I walk slowly and count to one hundred before I turn around. Koki's gone. I hurry back to the lecture hall.

竹笋生

Bamboo Shoots Sprout

16

When I get there, Naomi's halfway between the stage and the door. 'There you are,' she says in English. 'Did you enjoy my lecture?'

'Yes.'

'Interesting. I thought you found it inaccurate.'

I check that she's not annoyed. 'No. It was just making me think.'

'Some job satisfaction for me.' She narrows her eyes. 'I didn't expect you to turn up in a lecture.'

'I mean, I was going to try to find you, but this was honestly a coincidence.'

'A coincidence.' She looks at me for a beat too long. Then, 'I owe you your fee. Will you come to my office?'

I guess she wants to talk. 'Sure.'

Naomi's office is more colourful than I expected. There are prints and photos and red and purple flowers lining her window sill. It's smaller than I thought it would be, and shabbier. She settles herself behind the desk and I sit on the other side, back in my student role.

'People *are* order and chaos. But isn't there more chaos than order?' I don't know why this is what comes out of my mouth first.

'We live in a system much bigger than us and we have to obey its rules. But anomalies,' she says, 'exist. Don't they?'

'You *know* they do.'

Naomi looks at me with a hint of amusement. 'So. What happened after you got caught?'

'They asked me questions. I don't know why they're so protective of their little crops.'

'Why were *you* so interested in them?' she asks.

I shrug. 'It just seemed weird. Like ... what are they doing?'

'They're finding ways to make money, I assume. That's generally the explanation.'

'Growing stuff isn't a finding.'

'The method could be. What do you think?' She waits, not as if she's a teacher waiting for the correct answer, but as if she's interested in what I have to say.

'I guess,' I say, 'they can grow faster in some places, which means more money. Slower... It's not true that eating slow food actually makes you age less.' I stop. 'Is it?'

Naomi says, 'Not that I know of. However, that doesn't mean it's untrue and neither does it mean that it couldn't be sold as that.'

'It must be illegal or something.'

'There are all kinds of products that haven't been *proven* to work but are used anyway. Because why not try it, if there's a chance? We buy things out of hope, not proof.'

'So the company really isn't doing anything evil.' My disappointment makes me realise that I'd been counting on them being a sinister corporation. 'They don't even have to market stuff as anti-ageing miracle cures. They can use the land and the time to grow as much as they can. Or raise animals or whatever. I suppose they don't have to be evil to be bad. They can just be capitalist and want to make money.' This is a really dumb revelation.

'That's not really *that* bad, or it certainly isn't considered so by most people. I'm sure it would help the area, which everybody is always in favour of,' Naomi points out.

So in favour of that, they'll ignore how bad it can be for people actually working there until it's too late. The poisoned waters and disappearing creatures and rising temperatures of the earth flash into my brain. It's nothing new.

'My dad works for them.' It almost hurts to correct myself. '*Worked* for them.'

Naomi leans back in her chair. 'Did your interest have anything to do with that?'

'It was my fault.' I stare at my jeans. There's a stain near my left knee.

Her voice becomes gentler. 'I'm sorry that happened, Yuna.'

I forgot about that. 'Sora. My real name is Sora.'

'A true criminal.' Naomi's grinning.

'Professional,' I amend.

'Of course. Well, Sora, why else are you here in Tokyo? Or is this just your professional approach to outstanding payments? Speaking of—' She hands me an envelope.

'Thanks.' I put it in my bag without opening it. 'My friend studies here, in your department. But I didn't know that until after I got here.'

'Another coincidence.'

'Yeah, especially as he's my only friend.' I laugh to make that sound less pathetic. It makes it sound *more* pathetic.

'So you do have an interest in studying time in more detail,' Naomi says.

I hadn't known that I had argued otherwise. 'What were you doing with me in the zones, measuring time with water?'

She blinks as if surprised. 'I wanted to experience it for myself, on a bigger scale than here in Tokyo. And,' she says, 'I wanted to meet you again.'

'What? Why?' I recoil.

'I think that local people have different experiences and ideas about the zones than those who are researching and studying them.'

So I was somebody else's experiment again. My expression must have given away my anger.

Naomi says quickly, 'This isn't my official research, by the way. It's my own curiosity, as I think I told you. I've met others,' she says, 'who take people into the zones.'

'I don't know them.' A while back, I'd fished around

about other tours, but nobody close to me was doing it – or advertising it in any way, at least. I'd thought about messaging the handful of guides I'd found, even considered going undercover to see what they did, but what was the point? It wasn't exactly as if we were competing for Tripadvisor reviews.

'I didn't think you did. But you were knowledgeable in a different way. The flower clock, for instance...'

She's scrutinising me. Maybe I shouldn't be trusting Naomi so much. 'I practised a lot. Maybe the other guides had better things to do.'

'Oh, they were alone in their own ways,' Naomi says crushingly. 'They knew things, of course. Some of them knew a lot about theories – founded and unfounded – and stories about what had happened to the people there.'

I say casually, 'You don't think they might *not* be stories? Isn't there a chance...'

Naomi sighs. 'I'm wary of saying it is an absolute impossibility. Yet as the years go by, it is less and less likely that there are people who have been surviving in the zones.'

'But you don't know for sure,' I mumble. 'You don't know what's in there.'

'The guides were afraid,' Naomi says abruptly. 'Some of them hated the zones, always with good reason. Loved ones lost, homes they couldn't return to. You don't hate them.'

'It's not the zones' fault. They're the result.'

'Ah, you hate the cause.'

Whatever moved the earth, I want to say, was not anything normal. How could it have been, to have caused such terrible, unbelievable damage? A story rolls in my mind. The catfish thrashes in the pit of my stomach.

'It hurts,' I say softly. 'To go into those places, the zones. It's frightening.'

She nods. She stands up and goes to the window, stares out with her back to me. 'You know the relocation centres?'

'Yeah. Where people had to stay while they waited for new places to live.'

'My great-uncle was in one. In a place further north than your home. I visited him several times. It wasn't very comfortable – residents didn't have their own kitchens to cook in and it was all very temporary, even though some people are still living in centres like that now. He wasn't so old, and he wasn't exactly alone ... he had friends. But his wife had died in the Shake and he was in a place that wasn't his home, and he said every day had become the same. Like time had stopped for him.' She raises a hand to her face. 'He died.'

'I'm sorry,' I say. 'I'm so sorry.'

'Yes,' she says.

I can faintly hear voices, students outside or somewhere in the building, talking and laughing, going places.

'My dad's not well,' I say, small and stupid.

'Oh.' She sits down.

'He keeps forgetting when things are. He's not himself. The doctor – one doctor – said he was fine, he just needs rest, but...' I meet Naomi's sympathetic eyes. 'He's a field researcher. In the time zones.'

Naomi makes a sound almost of satisfaction, as though she has found the answer to a difficult equation. 'And *that's* why you came.'

'I didn't think about it that clearly but ... yeah.' I don't feel better, admitting it, that I need help. 'Dad goes into the zones a lot.'

'How much is a lot?'

'A couple times a week, at least.'

'*Every* week?'

'Yeah. I know it's not good. He was the head researcher – the only one really, so there was nobody to stop him. His boss didn't care.' That wasn't exactly true of Yamagata. 'Or didn't care enough,' I amended.

She shakes her head. 'That's negligent. It must be violating some employment laws, if not the actual prohibitions around the zones.'

'Right, 'cause Japan is so good at *not* having people die from overwork.'

Naomi sighs. 'You're not wrong. Have you experienced any adverse side effects?'

'Sometimes I feel sick when I leave a zone. I used to throw up every now and again, but I don't any more. That's all.' But I don't know. There could be effects that I've never noticed, or that I've forgotten. Maybe I had moments like Dad's, and just didn't remember. How would I ever know?

Naomi taps her pen impatiently. 'Go on, tell me. I'm not going to get you into trouble.'

'What about getting yourself into trouble?'

This only makes Naomi more interested.

'So I can sort of sense – physically, I guess – the zones and the borders where time changes.'

Naomi leans forward intently.

'I've taken things out of the zones a couple of times.' I add hurriedly, 'I know I shouldn't do that.'

Naomi shrugs. Guess she meant it when she said no trouble.

'Sometimes there's a feeling when I do that. A tiny bit of ... something, being released. Like electricity. And lately, when I've been around Dad, I've felt that. In normal time, not in the zones. If I touch him, there's something like a shock. Like – like he's releasing time. I don't know.'

Naomi stares at me intensely and unblinking.

'You must have heard of something like this before,' I say. 'Right?'

She shakes her head. 'This is something new. I don't know what this is.'

I slump. I'd thought that she would know, hoped so much that she had researched and proven this. 'People have researched radiation and – other dangerous stuff. So why are the zones any different?'

'I think,' she says, 'that everybody is afraid of time. Your father, how does he experience these jolts?'

'He doesn't. I told him about it, and he was interested – *too* interested. He'll go back into the zones, that's for sure. I shouldn't have said anything.' I'd been so stupid.

'It wouldn't have been right for you not to talk to him about it. He's the person most likely to understand it. Has your father published any papers or anything like that?'

'Oh … yes, actually, years ago. With another researcher he worked with, Kang Soo-jin.' They'd been very happy, and I'd only been able to read one page before I gave up.

Naomi writes this down. 'Can I meet him? Would he be willing to speak to me?'

'I think so,' I reply. 'But you can't say how we met.'

'Of course. I'd like you to see a project I'm working on. Would you be able to come here tomorrow?'

'I have nothing better to do,' I say, as if I don't definitely want to see whatever Naomi is doing.

'In Tokyo?' She raises her eyebrows. 'Whatever you say. Come after lunchtime, that's when my assistant will be there. Meet me at my office.' She glances at her watch. 'I have to go now.'

'Thanks – for talking to me. And everything.' I have an urge to shake her hand or hug her but that would be too weird. She doesn't strike me as the touchy-feely type.

'Thank *you*. This has been very interesting.'

Interesting is a weak word for what it's been, but I just say, 'I'll see you tomorrow.'

I find a cheap chain coffee shop and linger over a terrible coffee, wishing I'd brought a book. I get out my phone to ask Koki when he finishes class, and remember he has to work this evening. I hesitate before calling Dad. I feel a thump of shameful relief when he doesn't answer. I'll try again later.

For now, I know where I want to go. The slow zone.

The guard on duty at the time border is bored-looking. He points to the screen facing me. 'Over sixteen?'

'Yes.'

'Pregnant or in bad health?'

'No.'

'Five hundred yen.' I put a coin on the money tray and he hands me a ticket. 'Time difference in the zone is about five to ten minutes slower for each hour. We recommend you don't stay more than twenty-four hours. Please check the clock regularly.'

'I understand.' I take the ticket and walk through, hearing the guard already repeating his spiel to the person behind me.

A few metres in, I feel the change of zones. Pretty abrupt. Around me, people can clearly feel it as well, but there are far fewer photos being taken and definitely fewer tourists. The buildings are shabbier, paint wearing away, everything more faded. More cheap hotels and internet cafes than in the fast zone, more conbinis with seating areas. Instead of cute themed cafes, there are chain restaurants – the kind with crappy food that never close, where it's okay to nap if you order something every couple of hours. The people around me seem worried and tired and wear rumpled clothes. They're not here to get more work done or bring their teenagers to expensive tutoring lessons. They're here so they don't have to be in the normal world for as long. Later, it'll probably be the people who miss their last trains and want to hurry time up until the lines start running. They want normal time to pass, and that always seems to be in the early morning, the hours leading up to dawn. Those are the hardest hours to live through. You could stay in here for what feels like an hour and leave the zone to find the sun already rising.

I've done it myself. To make a night go faster when I couldn't sleep and need to see the dawn or when Dad was working late and I didn't want to be alone. I walk slowly down the streets, deeper in. There are empty lots here, vacant buildings. It reminds me of home.

I see a small cafe, rundown like everywhere else, but with a warmer yellow light that reminds me of something. A bedroom lamp when I was small, or a nightlight. I push the door open and a bell tinkles like it wants to go to sleep.

'Welcome, come on in,' a woman says from behind the counter.

I sit at a table by the window. 'Hot coffee, please.'

'Of course,' the woman says.

It's an old-style kissaten, retro 1970s with a lot of dark wood and a smell of cigarette smoke, even though nobody's smoking.

'Here you are.' She puts my coffee on the table. The cup and saucer are delicate, bordered with flowers, the gilt worn away.

'Thank you,' I say. 'The cup is pretty.'

'They were my grandmother's. She opened this cafe and then my parents ran it, and now I do. But it's not busy in this area now. Not since the time changed, you know.'

'I see.' I thought Tokyo people were supposed to be unfriendly.

'It's different in the fast zone.' Her voice is bitter. 'Everybody wants to go there. Having a cafe there – it would always be busy.'

'Would you like to open one there?' I ask.

'The rent is so high. Do you know the phrase *time is money*?'

'Of course.'

'A better thing to say now is *money buys time.*'

All those expensive cram schools and sleek shared offices. 'That's right.'

'It's not new,' the woman says. 'Rich people always have more time than poor people. Time to go on holiday. Time to waste. Time to start again… But if you're poor you spend your time working and doing overtime. You can't afford to take time off or spend it with the people or things you love…' She takes a breath.

On the other side of the window, a man with a scraggly beard walks past, a can of beer dangling loosely from his hand.

The woman opens the door. 'Ryosuke-kun! You'll have a sandwich, won't you?'

The man stops, and I'm not sure whether he's drunk or confused. 'What about omurice?'

'That's not a sandwich!' She beckons him in anyway, pointing at his beer. 'No outside food or drinks, you know that.'

He hands it over reluctantly, shuffles to a table in the back and sits down as if his whole body is stiff. The woman brings him a glass of water and disappears into the kitchen, behind the bar.

He gazes at the glass of water, then lifts it to his mouth and drinks. His hand trembles. 'Thank you.'

I understand what it is that's strange about his speech – it's not that he's speaking slowly, exactly, but more that his speech has been slowed down, like a recording played at .75 speed.

I sip my coffee, which is now lukewarm. The old man has a cup and saucer in front of him. He's not drinking. He's examining the pattern around the lip of the cup, what looks like little blue flowers.

'Forget-me-nots,' he says to me in English.

'I won't,' I say, and then turn my face away, understanding that he means the flowers, that he's not requesting anything of me.

I'm saved by the woman emerging from the kitchen. 'Here's your sandwich.' The omurice looks good, a plump yellow semicircle, painted with a perfect streak of ketchup.

The old man smiles, a smile that opens up wide and calm. He claps his hands and picks up a fork.

The woman nods. 'Go ahead.'

He eats, his eyes closing with pleasure.

The woman returns to me and I pretend I haven't been watching. 'Don't worry,' she says. 'He's okay.'

'Oh. Good. Is he ... a regular?'

'He's my brother,' she says. 'He's not really that drunk.'

I nod, glancing at him again. It's time working on him, and something like despair.

'Do you want more coffee? Cake?' she asks.

I shake my head. 'Thank you very much. But I should go. Can I have the bill, please?'

She prints a receipt and brings it to me on another pretty saucer. I put the money on it.

'Thank you very much.' I stand up awkwardly.

'Take care.' She offers me a smile.

Behind her, her brother smiles at me as well, and I see their family in both of their faces.

I wander through the zone for a while longer – about an hour normal time. I catch myself looking for lingering shadows but I see none; every shadow has its person. It's different here, not slow enough, not lonely enough.

At the exit a different guard checks my ticket and waves me through. The times ebb and flow around me and I walk, letting myself adjust to the new buoyancy, the different drag on my body.

I walk to the Skytree because it's the easiest thing to aim for, rising smug and silvery above the other buildings.

The Skytree and time. Dad told me about it not so long ago; that time moves more slowly at the top of the Skytree. It's because of gravity and Einstein, or something like that. I hadn't listened, because so what? People built the tower, and the time could actually be explained. It still isn't interesting enough for me to pay for. It's also the furthest thing from a tree, all dead metal and slick hard lines. A real tree wouldn't pierce the sky like that; it would open out to it. It would give more than it took.

My phone lights up. Koki.

are you dead?

undead, I reply.

do you need brains or blood?

i'm still Japanese, I write. *i need rice.*

you'll have to scavenge some yourself cause i have to stay in the library and do assignments

no problem, I reply.

I eat ramen and then get on the train. Even though it's three-quarters full, it's almost totally silent with people muffling themselves up with headphones and eyes fixed on their phones. Everybody is transporting themselves somewhere else further than where this train line leads, to their friends, to the opinions of photos of strangers, to news about Japan and the world, into books and manga and shows. I gaze out of the window at the lights and buildings, blurred into broad strokes of bright paint.

小満

THE EARTH GROWS LUSH

17

I wake up with the smell of coffee in my nose. I blink myself to daylight.

'Morning,' Koki says.

'Mmmmmhmmmm.'

'You were passed out when I got home last night.'

I sit up. 'I didn't even hear you get back. Was it late?'

'Not that late.' His eyes move away from mine. 'Coffee?' he asks. 'I don't have any time for latte art, though.'

'I can make it myself if you need to go.'

Koki looks at his phone. 'Ah … that might be better. I have to cram for a test before class.'

'Sure, that's fine.' I'm too drowsy and stupid to have a conversation, or ask what Koki was actually doing last night, or talk about what I'd seen yesterday.

'I'll see you later,' he says.

'Good luck with your test. Don't fail.'

'Valuable advice.' He waves and leaves.

My legs hurt. I walked miles yesterday. I get up and shower and make coffee and find my least crumpled clothes. I'll eat somewhere on the way. Then I'll go to Naomi, and hope she has some answers.

◀

'Are you all right?' Naomi asks.

I straighten up in her office chair. 'Uh, yeah, I'm fine. Why?' I wish there was a mirror to check my face in.

'You seem tired. Or stressed. What's going on?'

'I don't know what's going on.' Absolutely not a lie.

She raises an eyebrow. 'I see. Well, I don't know much either.'

'I went to the slow zone yesterday,' I say.

'Did you. How was it?'

'Different from the fast zones… Sad.'

'Yes. It is.' She goes to her window sill, where pots are lined up and labelled. She picks up one and puts it on the desk. It's a seedling, a tentative tendril of green emerging from the soil. She gestures from it to the other pots. 'Here is an experiment.'

'They all seem the same so far.' Growing, fresh and eagerly green. I make a guess. 'Did you take the seeds from one of the zones?'

'I took water. From the stream.'

'So that versus Tokyo tap water?'

'I took water from another stream in the same area, and the minerals and softness and so on are practically the same.'

'Not the same as *exactly*.' It's so like something Dad would say that I hear his voice in my head.

'We both know that that's not the point.' She pushes the seedling towards me. 'Take this.'

'Why?'

'Could you plant it in a fast time zone – one that you're not going to get caught going into? Somewhere that's about … fifteen minutes faster per hour. Then monitor it – but not too often. I don't want you going into the zones to check it every day or anything like that. I'm just curious. Nothing to write about or publish.' She finds a crumpled paper bag, puts the pot into it, and hands it to me with both hands, like a gift. Which it is.

'They fare much better together, so I hope this little one is okay alone.'

It takes me a second to understand she's speaking about the seedling. 'Trees like company?'

'*Need* more than *like*. In the studies done with trees and time zones, the trees grow more steadily together, at a more uniform rate – did you know that?'

I shake my head.

'A single plant in a pot is more affected by differences in time than several plants in one. Trees are better than bushes, bushes better than flowers. Cut flowers can hardly withstand faster time at all.'

I've never been in a house within a zone that's had a bouquet of flowers, so I can't prove or disprove that.

Naomi half-turns to her plants. 'It might be because of how trees in particular can communicate—'

'What?'

She nods. 'In the woods trees can signal to each other

if there's danger, or a disease, share their sugar and water if one of them is dying. It's chemicals, the root network – I don't know the specifics, but it's been proven.'

'They can talk to each other,' I say.

'*Talk* may be an exaggeration,' she cuts in. 'But they can send and receive information of a sort and regulate and support each other. In ways other organisms can't.'

Not even people. 'I should have known that.' Did Mom know about this? Had she told me?

'Sora,' Naomi says.

I pull my eyes away from the seedling.

'Come with me.' Naomi opens the door. 'Don't forget your plant.'

Up a flight of stairs, and through an unmarked door. I know a lab when I see one: computers, charts on the walls, tables with logbooks and vague instruments. Sunlight streams in through the tall windows. A black girl sitting in front of one of the computers swivels on her chair. She's around my age, with long braids and round glasses.

'Sensei!' She notices me. 'Oh, and hello.'

'This is Sora,' Naomi says. 'And this is Maya. One of my best students.'

Maya comes over to us. 'No, no, I'm not.' She flaps her hand in front of her face in a very Japanese way. She switches to English. 'Nice to meet you.'

'I can speak Japanese.' I suddenly feel shy.

'We all can, but I'm a little more comfortable in English,' Naomi says.

'Are you hafu?' Maya asks, smiling.

'Yeah, and Canadian.'

'Me too!' she says. 'Well, the Japanese part.'

'Wow!' I say, and then wince inwardly. I'm sure it's not uncommon for people to be surprised that she's also Japanese, and I should not be one of them.

If Maya notices this she ignores it, which, I realise miserably, she is probably used to doing.

'Okinawa and Chicago, if you want to get specific. Nice to meet a fellow hafu!' She raises a hand, and it takes me an embarrassingly long time to see she's waiting for me to do the same. I lift my hand and she high-fives me enthusiastically.

'Is there a female equivalent for "fellow"?' Maya asks Naomi, who's inspecting one of the tables.

'Not that I'm aware of,' Naomi replies absently.

Maya shakes her head, and her long braids swing in a disappointed way. 'The patriarchy,' she laments.

'What's the latest data?' Naomi asks.

Maya begins listing numbers and recounting details as Naomi nods and asks equally obscure questions. I wander around, not trying to decipher any of the information but soaking up the general feel of a place where people focus on specific and strange things. There's a large screen on the wall, webs of wires spun across floors and desks. There are goldfish in a tank. A rattle, and in a cage beside it, a pair of dark glinting eyes watch me. It's a sleek brown and white rat, which sits up on its hind legs and rests a front paw on the bars.

'Don't feed him, he's too chonky already,' Maya calls. 'Is he your pet?'

'He's an assistant,' Naomi says.

The cages of small frightened creatures in the shed behind the company... Had they been called assistants too?

Maya's eyes stay on me. 'We don't hurt him. Don't worry.'

'Sora,' Naomi says.

I go to the table they're standing in front of. It's covered with wires, different-sized batteries, various tools. There's a metal cube, plain except for wiring looping out of the back, some round dial faces with needles still or quivering slightly. Attached to it by a thin cable is a sort of narrow belt with a disc made of matte, dark grey metal.

'New game console?' I ask.

Maya laughs. Naomi frowns. They both say, 'No.'

'It's our clock. A biological clock,' Maya explains.

'It was a joke, but the name has stuck. Put it on,' Naomi says. 'Stand at the top of the table. It won't hurt you,' she adds, when I don't move.

'No lie,' Maya chips in. 'There isn't even an electric shock.'

I hadn't thought of anything like that until she said it, and now all I can think of is getting electrocuted. I pick it up tentatively. Maya applauds.

'How do I put it on?' I ask.

'Like a watch,' Naomi says.

Maya is way more helpful. She comes over and wraps the belt around my left arm, keeping the round disc on the inside of my wrist. 'Not too tight?'

'It's good. Thanks.' I touch the disc. It's smooth and heavy and cool, not metal but stone.

Maya rejoins Naomi at the end of the table, where the cube is.

'What is this?'

Naomi peers at one of the dials. 'I'll tell you in a little while. Can you tell me when a minute has passed? Relax. Breathe.'

'Watch the fish,' Maya instructs.

There are three of them, glimmers of metallic orange and yellow darting and turning against the grey pebbles and green aquarium plants. People used to pan for gold. Did anyone ever discover a goldfish that way?

'That's a minute,' I say absently, imagining a goldfish rush.

'Thank you,' Naomi says behind me. 'Can you watch this and tell me again when a minute is up?'

The screen on the wall turns on and begins to play a dramatic fight scene from some movie. Two women on the edge of a cliff spin, punch and kick at each other savagely and fluidly. They are extremely cool, and I make a note to find out what this movie is. One woman teeters on the edge of the cliff, while far below, waves smash against rock and—

'That's a minute!' I call.

The screen immediately turns off.

'Aw, come *on*, don't stop it there!' I twist around and Maya wags a remote control at me.

'It's a cliffhanger,' she says.

I sigh and roll my eyes.

'Relax and watch the fish again,' Naomi commands, and I do as I'm told until my tension ebbs away. 'Now watch the disc,' Naomi says.

Red digits are flashing on it, even though I hadn't noticed a screen.

'Can you read the numbers?' Naomi asks.

'They're so fast.' But even as I say that, I concentrate and tune in to the rhythm of the numbers. '306, 307, 308, 309,' I read. I keep going until Naomi tells me to stop.

'Good,' she says. 'You can take it off.'

I unwrap it and join them to stare at the cube. There are two small clock faces, one silvery and new, chunky and modern. The other is a tarnished brassy colour, with roman numerals and delicate hands. They are like non-identical twins. A panel is steadily flashing red digits like the ones I've just read. The other dials I don't understand.

'What do you think this is?' Naomi asks me.

I glance back at the disc, which is grey stone once more. 'You're checking at what speed people can read the numbers.'

'Correct.'

I'm vaguely reminded of some other experiment Dad has told me about. 'Isn't this about the brain? Cognitive whatever?'

Maya and Naomi exchange a glance; surprised from Maya, approving from Naomi. They nod.

'Cognitive perception,' Naomi says. 'We can also adjust the speed of the numbers, which allows us to more accurately find the pace at which people are able to discern them.'

I watch the clocks, check my own watch, put fingers on my pulse. I point at the modern clock. 'So this tells time. The other is the individual time? The one you adjust to find how time runs for me?'

'Yes, that's right.' Naomi looks at me like a teacher does when you're the first in the class to solve a maths problem. 'How does time run for you?'

I stare at the clocks. 'Fast. That's three seconds on a minute, maybe... I bet it's faster than yours.'

'It is, actually.'

'And faster than Maya's?'

Naomi gestures to Maya, to the top of the table and straps herself up. Her gaze shifts to the aquarium, softens and unfocuses. Her eyes move to the disc on her wrist.

'300, 306, 311, um, 317, 325,' She is definitely reading slower than I did, and skipping numbers as if she can't keep up.

Naomi fiddles with the dials and taps one of them, and I remember what I'm supposed to be watching. The clocks are almost the same; the individual time is just a fraction faster.

'Thank you,' Naomi says, and Maya returns to us.

'Mine is way faster. I'm guessing that's not normal,' I say.

'It's—' Maya begins.

'How many times have you been in the fast zones?' Naomi interrupts.

I can't even count that. 'Um. Many. But I've also been in the slow zones a lot.'

'Hold up, where are you from?' Maya asks.

'North-east.' I watch understanding dawn on her.

'Which zone do you think you've spent more time in, if you had to choose?' Naomi continues.

Where my customers want to be taken, where my flower clock is, where I feel further from *now*. 'Fast zones.'

Naomi nods; confirming her deduction. 'If your father were to hold this, how do you think the clock might run?' she asks quietly.

I think of him. He seems so distant. 'It would run slowly, and it'd be much slower than mine is fast.'

Maya says, 'Everyone's a bit different.'

'Almost everybody and everything is a little faster or slower,' Naomi clarifies, 'and that's not even people who've been exposed to different time zones. In various situations too: fear, pain, or trauma, our perceptions change. But you knew exactly when a minute was up when you were calm *and* when you were excited which is … unusual.'

I glance at Maya, whose expression says, *It's really weird.*

'I'm good at telling the time. You knew that already,' I say shortly.

'Indeed,' is all that Naomi, unnervingly, replies.

I swivel towards the fish tank. 'You said every*thing* ... what things?' I ask. 'Only people can do the number reading.'

'We have different methods for animals and plants. They're all able to tell time in their own ways and vertebrates and invertebrates can learn and understand time intervals—'

'—with treats,' Maya cuts in, waving at the rat and revealing why he was both an assistant and chonky.

'With reward systems,' Naomi rephrases. 'It's harder to measure how their perception of time changes in different situations, or for different individuals. In general, though, small animals perceive time more slowly than large animals.'

My fingers reach for my wrist. 'Their hearts beat faster.'

Naomi nods. 'Oh, Sora, what did your father say when you spoke to him?'

'Yeah... He was busy yesterday,' I lie, 'but I'll talk to him today. What if someone has been in the fast and slow zones the same amount?' I add quickly.

'Perhaps it would run at the same time, or perhaps it would stop. Nothing is exactly on time. Even in Japan,' Naomi adds wryly.

Belatedly, I ask, 'How does this work, exactly?'

'I'll explain it to you properly, but not right now. You're familiar with Heidegger's theory of time?' Naomi asks.

'Maybe?'

Naomi turns to Maya. 'I'll test you, then.'

Maya tugs one of her braids. 'We are time. Humans. *We* know what has happened before, and that's how the past exists. We can imagine the future, so that's how the future exists. We live now, so we hold all three together.'

'He was a philosopher, right? Not a scientist.' This is something Dad would say.

'We need ideas first.' Naomi sounds disapproving.

I need an explanation. Instead I say, 'Wait, this is all about how people and animals see time, but the zones aren't something that we all feel differently. They're real *places*, not stuff in our brains.'

'Yes... But what if a whole place can perceive time, and exert that perception on people?' Naomi's tone is different from the one she used to answer my questions. She sounds tentative, as though she is unsure whether to say this aloud.

This question settles into me. It's so strange, an idea I've never heard or considered before. It couldn't be possible, but the zones shouldn't be possible either. The memory of the shrieking earth shuddered through me; yes, the Shake had been fear, and trauma, and pain but...

A bell chimes class to a close.

'Ah. I must go,' Naomi says, breaking a silence I hadn't even heard.

I try to pull my thoughts together. 'You said you've tested plants and trees? How do you measure them? They don't even have a heartbeat.'

'Trees do,' Naomi corrects me, 'in a way. But it only beats once a year. Now I've got to run. Maya, you're here for the rest of the day, aren't you?'

'Yup.'

'Good. Sora, I'd like to find out more about how you can measure time so accurately. Can you come back? Perhaps ... the day after tomorrow?'

My life as an experiment continues. I open my mouth to refuse, but catch Maya beaming at me. 'Sure,' I say.

Naomi nods and goes to the door.

'Once a year.' I can't help asking. 'But when?'

'In springtime,' Naomi says. Then she's gone.

'You can sit down.' Maya pulls out a chair for me.

I collapse into it.

'Nomura-sensei is intense. Scarily intelligent, obviously, and actually quite funny. But mostly intense.' Maya sits down too. 'How do you know her?'

'Through work.'

Maya taps her chin with a finger. 'I'm guessing it was with the time zones. And not the Tokyo ones, either.'

I make a non-committal noise.

'No matter what kind of vague hum you make, you seem to know a lot.'

'How long have you been working here?' I ask, to move the focus off me.

'I'm in my second year. This whole thing is a project class I persuaded Nomura-sensei to let me join.'

'It's interesting.'

'And incredibly hard to understand and sometimes

boring. I really enjoy it. But,' Maya puts her hands up, 'do *not* ask me to explain the bio clock, because I'll do it wrong. Also, it gets hard to measure time when that's *all* you're trying to do. The idea of a second or a minute changes. Now I'm like: where was the second spent? A minute for who? So, yeah, interesting and worth questioning reality over.'

'So you think time is about feeling?' An ally.

'Yeah – at least partly.'

'Naomi – I mean, Nomura-sensei – doesn't seem to think the same.'

'She says she doesn't. But it shouldn't be excluded.' Maya goes to the rat's cage. 'Do you want to say hey?' She's already opening the cage door. The rat scurries to her eagerly and she scoops him up and cradles him in her arms. She sits close to me, the rat on her lap. Her hands are dark and soothing on his smooth fur.

I reach my hand out and the rat sniffs. His nose twitches and his bright eyes judge me. 'I think you're right ... but we can't measure anything then, if it's about *individual* truth. Anyway, isn't this philosophy, not science?'

'I study that too, but I'm not as good at it.' She dumps the rat in my lap. 'His name is Mochi.'

He is a brick. 'Daifuku Mochi?'

'He is a big beautiful boy and I love him.'

I can't say I've ever loved rats, but Mochi is inquisitive and gentle. He scrambles up my arm, sits on my shoulder, and sniffs the inside of my ear.

Maya leans back in her chair. 'The first scientists were called natural philosophers, you know.'

'I always felt like science and philosophy were opposites. Like, science wants answers and philosophy doesn't have answers, and it's a fight between them.' I think of Soo-jin and Aristotle and Hisakawa and Buddhism. 'But now I'm seeing they're kind of on the same side.' I pat Mochi, who seems to have immediately begun napping on my shoulder.

'They both ask a lot of questions, though, so they start in a similar place. They just end in kind of different ones. And maybe they aren't even that different. Who knows? I got a C in my last test so you really shouldn't listen to me.'

'I like listening to you,' I say.

A smile shines across Maya's face. 'That's nice to hear.'

I lower my eyes and shrug. This wakes Mochi, who squeaks indignantly. 'Sorry!' He climbs on to my head. 'Get down!'

'No, he's comfy! Let him chill.' Maya's laughing. 'He suits you.'

'Okay, okay.' Mochi is a warm weight, his feet tickling my scalp. 'But only 'cause hats don't usually look good on me.'

Maya grins. 'So you're coming to study here?'

'Huh? No.' I almost shake my head before I remember Mochi.

'Oh, where are you studying?'

'Nowhere. I'm taking a year out. To work. But my – friend, Koki, he studies here and he brought me to a lecture...'

'Friend,' Maya repeats. 'Or boyfriend?'

'Not boyfriend,' I say quickly.

'Funny, I came here cause of a ... friend,' Maya says. Then, 'Well. She was a not-friend. You know?' Maya puts a faint stress on *she*.

It takes me a second to get it. Maya studiously stares at Daifuku, then glances at me out of the corner of her eye. She's waiting for my reaction.

You're a lesbian, that's cool, does not feel like the right thing to say, so I settle for, 'She's your ex?'

Maya bursts out laughing. 'Wow, do you sound hopeful?'

'No, I don't, I mean, I'm not!' My face is incredibly warm. Maybe I have a fever. Maybe I'm dying of embarrassment.

'Relax, please, don't make me feel bad for making fun of you,' Maya says.

'You can make fun of me, it's fine. I'll join in. I'm good at it.'

'Now I *do* feel bad!'

'Told you I was good.'

'I never doubted you,' she says reassuringly. 'Yeah, she's my ex. But she was my first girlfriend. I think people only stay with their first-whatever in, like, shoujo manga and rom-coms.'

'In rom-coms you *do* end up with your first love. Especially if you're a career woman and then return to your small hometown at the holidays and bump into your teenage crush.'

'Right, or your car breaks down and your crush rescues you.'

'Or you fall in the snow and they help you up, yeah. So maybe you'll get back together in about ten years.'

'Damn, I've got a lot of time to kill.'

I'm suddenly aware of how close we are to each other, and of how steady Maya's eye contact is. I blink and say hurriedly, 'Anyway, Nomura-sensei just thought I'd be interested in all this.'

Maya sits up. 'And are you?'

'Definitely.'

'Interested enough to study it?'

I pause. 'That doesn't mean I *can*.'

'You can,' Maya says with absolute, unfounded confidence. 'Nomura-sensei would help you, I bet. She helped me – usually a second-year student wouldn't get near this kind of work, but she actually listened when I talked.'

'The teachers here don't usually?'

'They mostly do, but less to women, less to a "foreign" woman, less to a black *girl*.' The way she stresses the last word makes me think that she's quoting somebody. 'I've got to fight all the time. You do too.'

It's true. I nod, and this time I do forget Mochi, who squawks and scrabbles at my head. 'Ouch!'

Maya gets up and disentangles Mochi from my hair. 'You bold baby. Sleep in your own bed.' She replaces him in the cage, and he glares at us, betrayed.

I run my fingers through my hair. 'I think I should go. Thanks for talking to me.'

'Of course! Wait—' Maya gets her phone out. 'You have the Line app?'

'Yeah.' I pull my phone out and we share QR codes. 'Thanks.'

She hugs me. She must feel me stiffen, because she begins to let go, until I hug her back. She's warm. It's nice. I relax against her, maybe for a bit too long.

'Anyway.' I grab my bag.

'Is this yours?' Maya holds up my seedling gift.

I take it. 'Naomi gave it to me. An experiment, she said. But it doesn't make much sense to me.'

'At least you'll have something that contributes to the world, even if it doesn't contribute to science,' Maya says.

'Did you know that trees talk to each other?' I ask suddenly.

Maya nods. 'I've heard that. They have a sort of network underground, right?'

A question occurs. 'Have you ever measured the time of trees?'

'Yup, but not a lot. Their time is *real* slow, different level.'

'That's interesting...' I shake myself before I get sucked into asking more questions.

'I'd better go.'

'Bye. See you soon?'

I smile. 'Yeah,' I say. 'Soon.'

蚕起食桑

SILKWORMS START
FEASTING ON MULBERRY LEAVES

18

I walk back to Koki's apartment, thinking and thinking and coming up with no clear thoughts at all.

'At last!'

I jump.

'Are you surprised to find me in what is actually my own home?' Koki leans against the doorway.

'I wasn't paying attention...'

'Especially not to your phone.'

I fish out my phone. I hold it up triumphantly. 'Died. Sorry.'

'Good thing you got back before I also died. I'm hungry. There's a place close by that does five-hundred-yen pizza.'

'Perfect. My favourite topping right now is cheap.'

Koki must be starving because he half-jogs to the restaurant, which is cheerful and busy. We order and my stomach immediately begins growling.

Koki hears it. 'You're hungry too.'

'I guess I am. How were classes? Study? Work?'

Koki stretches his arms. 'All fine. But I'm worn out. You look worn out as well.'

'I had an interesting day.'

Koki narrows his eyes. 'What did you do?'

'Why are you so suspicious?'

'You did *something*, didn't you?'

The pizza arrives. We become completely silent.

'Pizza,' Koki briefly comments.

I don't reply because my mouth is full. The pizzas are quarters before we calm down enough to talk again.

'Okay, so what did you do?' Koki says, sitting back in his chair.

'I visited one of your labs. By invitation,' I add. 'The one with the – bio clock?'

'What?' Koki's slightly stunned. 'You saw it?'

'You haven't?' It's clear he hasn't.

'I'm in first year so we don't do any of that stuff. How the hell did you get to?'

'It's kind of a long story—'

'No skipping.' Koki leans forward. 'Tell me everything."

'Remember when I said I was in trouble that was *not* pregnancy?'

I have to go back to the trips into the time zones with Naomi and begin from there. I skim over Dad's sickness and leave out the strangest parts. Koki eats his pizza, watching me as if I'm a movie screen.

'...and now I kind of want a pet rat,' I conclude.

'Huh. Of course,' Koki says. 'Nomura-sensei is terrifying and weird. No wonder she likes you.'

'I don't know if she does.'

'I don't know anyone who's been personally given a tour of the labs and I'm *on* the course.'

'I didn't ask her to, Koki. Anyway, I thought you wanted me to enrol here.'

He relaxes. 'I do. I just didn't think it would be like this. I guess you did get her out of a lot of trouble – would've been bad if she was caught sneaking around in illegal areas. She definitely owes you.'

I hadn't thought about it like that. Would she have been as nice if we'd both been caught near the company's little farm?

Koki wipes a streak of sauce with his pizza crust. 'Good to know some second-year students can get in on those projects. I might try and do that next year.'

Maybe I shouldn't have told him. So much for my discretion.

'Don't say I told you all this, okay? Just 'cause...'

'I won't.'

A whole new layer of worry settles into my stomach.

'You made friends fast,' Koki says.

'I dunno if we're friends yet. It's just ... she's hafu too. We have that in common. And it's kind of a big thing.'

'Yeah. Nobody else was hafu in our high school.' Koki says this as if he's just realised it.

'In junior high school there was Rin Shimizu. Remember him?'

'He was hafu?'

'His mother was Thai.'

'Didn't know that.'

'I don't think he liked to talk about it. He said in middle school everyone called him a foreigner and he didn't want it to be like that any more.'

'Where did he go?' Koki asks.

'Can't remember. Away.'

'Get working on making Maya into a real friend, then.'

'Hmmm. How should I manipulate her into that?' I'm only half-joking. Maybe even just a quarter joking.

'Find her online. Then figure out what she likes and say you like that stuff too.'

'That's creepy.'

'You're the one who said *manipulate*!'

I roll my eyes, but immediately open Instagram and type in Maya's name. It doesn't take long to find her. Koki leans over my shoulder as I scroll through her photos. There she is with some friends, some photos of food and cherry blossoms, a glowingly blue sea that must be Okinawa.

'She's cute, isn't she?' Koki says.

'She's beautiful.'

'Oh, look—' Koki points to a photo.

It's Maya with a very pretty Japanese girl. They are holding hands and smiling. They have rainbows painted on their cheeks. Beneath it, she's written, *Happy Pride!!!* in English and Japanese.

'Oh, she likes *girls*,' Koki says.

'Yeah. She told me.'

'Really? You didn't say!'

'It's her business,' I reply, feeling suddenly defensive.

'Maybe she likes you, Sora.'

'Why would she like *me*? She's being nice,' I say. 'And I'm...' I find I don't know how to finish that sentence.

Koki's giving me a funny look.

'What?' I ask.

'It was only a joke.'

'Right,' I mumble. 'Still.'

'You're being weird,' he says.

'You're being insensitive.'

We both huff at each other. Koki pointedly takes out his phone and starts scrolling. I go back to Maya's account. She couldn't *like* me. That would be awkward. And impossible. And.

'Wanna go home?' Koki asks. He always gets over his annoyance faster than me.

We stop in a conbini on the way back and get cans of chu-hi. The checkout guy doesn't even raise his head as I tap the screen to say I'm over twenty. We walk and drink and it's good and fun again. The air is warm and weighty on my skin. The narrow roads and telephone wires lead to countless different places, connect millions of people. It could all be okay.

Back at Koki's, we giggle and finish our last can, bump into each other as we spread out the futons. In the freedom of darkness and tipsiness, we find each other. Koki tugs and I roll into his futon. It's soothing to kiss him, softening the tension that's been building between us and which has become layered with so many things.

But we slow, then stop. For a moment there is quiet between us, a silence filled with words that reminds me of the first time we met.

'I think this isn't... Not right now,' I whisper.

'I know. Yeah, I know.' His voice is as soft as petals.

'Can we just go to sleep?' I say.

'Of course. Whatever you want.' He disentangles himself from me gently.

What do I want, though? I don't move back to my own futon, because it's comforting to have somebody close.

Through a gap in the curtains, the sun lights up the four o'clock flowers I gave Koki what seems like years before.

Koki turns over. 'Are you awake?'

'I am now.'

We lie there for a while. I try to shake out my feelings and examine them, but they're a jumbled mess.

I squint at the clock. It's six a.m. 'Do you have class today?'

'Yeah. But not 'til second period.'

I close my eyes, ready to go back to sleep. 'Do you ever have a day off?'

'Do you ever have a day *on*?'

I open my eyes again. 'Excuse me, yes, I do! But right now I'm on a city break.'

'What are you going to do today, then? Be teacher's pet again?' Koki asks.

'I'm not Naomi's *pet*.' I smack his arm softly.

He laughs. 'You want an A for a class you're not even in. I don't know if that makes you a good student or a bad one.'

'I have questions, that's all!'

Koki sits up. 'So do I. That's why I came here.'

'What do you want to find answers for?' I'm curious. Somehow we haven't really discussed this.

'When I was a kid I used to think I could … solve the zones. Put them all back together.' He rubs a hand across his face. 'Stupid.'

'You're not the only one who thought that. Thinks that.'

He glances at me. 'You still think that?'

'No. I mean … not really,' I say. 'But there's so much we don't know. We know hardly anything.'

'It's all too big. I mean – it's *time*. What could we change? Who would it—' He shuts his mouth tight.

Who would it bring back? That's what he wants to say. 'Koki, have you ever seen things in the zones?'

'Ghosts?' He shakes his head.

'Shadows,' I mumble.

He lets out a breath. 'No,' he says finally.

'What have you seen, then?'

'Nothing real, Sora! There's nothing there. Nothing left.' Koki gets up suddenly, stands before me with hands empty and open.

'That's not true. It's our home, our families—'

'It's different for you,' he says.

'*How*?' I snap.

'You're not like us. You could go back to your *real* home.'

Koki's words settle on me. There's no heat of the anger that I would usually feel. I'm cold. 'I am Japanese,' I whisper, 'and it is my home. Maybe it's not real but I don't have anywhere else to go.'

Koki sits down beside me. 'I shouldn't have said that.'

'But you thought it.' I can see from his face that I'm right. It doesn't matter that he's ashamed.

'You could have chosen to leave. I never could,' he says.

I'm shaking my head. 'I had no choice. There was nothing I could do.'

Mom asking me to help her air out the futons. Saying no. Going to the supermarket instead. And then—

'Nothing I could have done,' I say.

Koki takes my hand. He's silent, but his breathing is uneven. I put my arms around him.

'I don't know why we're arguing about this now.' His voice is hoarse.

'Because it's what we always do.'

He nods against me, relaxing a little. We keep holding on to each other, even though I know we're letting go.

紅花栄

SAFFLOWERS FLOURISH

19

I wake when Koki disentangles himself from me gently. 'We fell asleep again. I've gotta go,' he whispers. He tucks the blanket around me.

'Bye,' I murmur. I hide my face in the pillow until he leaves, because I don't know what my expression will be if I look at him.

I doze until my hunger forces me out of bed. I make coffee and toast and wonder what I should do today. Maybe something fun, not connected to science or time zones. Shopping. Sitting in a nice cafe. After that I run out of ideas.

Something is sticking in my mind from yesterday, about trees and time, and suddenly I have the urge to be in a forest. Not Yoyogi, where they are spaced out from each other, but somewhere quiet and natural. I get my phone to search for Tokyo trees and notice that Maya had sent me an emoji of a bear waving, after we added each other as friends.

As if my fingers are possessed, I type: *hey, do you know of a forest in Tokyo?* and press send.

and good morning!! I add.

Then I stare at my phone, wondering if my message is strange, and if Maya will think I'm obsessed with trees.

morning! not sure if it's a forest but Meiji Jingu has a lot of trees. it's more forest-y than other places.

cool, thank you! i'll check it out. i like trees!

not in a weird way!!!! I add.

Maya replies with the most inscrutable emoji, the laughing-crying one.

Then she messages, *i can take you there if you want? you're a tokyo newbie and i have some time.*

really? that would be great, I reply. *if you're sure.*

yeah, course.

We arrange a station and a time to meet, and suddenly I feel hopeful about today.

So hopeful that I call Dad again, determined to be cheerful and friendly. His phone rings and rings. He's usually up by now. I have a shower and get changed. I call him again. No answer. I fix my hair and put on some make-up and wonder if my face is okay. I call him again. Nothing.

An uneasiness unrolls itself in me, as if it's been sleeping since the last time I'd seen his tired, confused face. He went out and forgot his phone. He's probably fine. But that anxiety is fully awake now and twisting like a snake.

I begin to call him again but see the time. I'll have to jog to catch the train. I zip my bag, checking Google

Maps with my other hand, and fling myself out of the door. My uneasiness slithers after me.

I distract myself by watching the news snippets playing on the mini TV above the train door. Floods, bombings, oil spills. I close my eyes until it's my stop. Maya is already at the station exit, her braids in a tall bun, deft and intricate. When she catches sight of me she waves hugely.

'Hello!' she calls, and the energy in her voice makes me feel a little better.

'Hi! Sorry, were you waiting long?'

'No, got here a minute before you. How are you?' she asks.

'I'm okay,' I say.

Maya pauses. 'Are you?'

I try to inject some enthusiasm into my voice. 'Yeah, I'm fine. A bit tired, that's all.'

'You're still down for this?' Maya asks.

'Definitely! A walk will wake me up.'

'Good. Let's go!'

Maya marches off, and I trot to keep pace. She points to some shops and buildings, asks me if I've been there or know that. I feel dumb saying no to everything, but Maya says things like *don't bother going* and *try it sometime!* and tells me funny stories.

By the time we reach Meiji Jingu I don't have to make myself be cheerful.

'Here we are,' Maya says.

The torii gates that lead to Meiji Jingu are massive and made of silvery wood. The avenue beyond them is wide and scattered with people. As we step through the traffic, noise dims, the air softens and lightens. The trees on either side are tall and serene. I inhale and exhale.

'Meiji Jingu is the most diverse piece of woodland in Japan. Maybe that's why I feel at home here.' Maya has lowered her voice.

'Was that the kind of wood they wanted to make?' I speak as quietly as she does.

'Almost all of Tokyo was burned down during the war, including the shrine. When they were rebuilding it, prefectures from all over Japan sent their trees – that's why it's so diverse. It was a whole new forest, sent to grow together.'

We stroll along peacefully. I wonder if any of the trees are homesick.

'That's lovely. I thought it was older.' I gaze around, looking deeper into the trees, feeling for a zone and finding a kind of stillness in time instead. Or the most gradual kind of movement. Here there could be spirits. 'It feels older. I can feel a different kind of time – or as if the things that live here are moving slowly. I mean, not things, but—' I stop talking abruptly, hoping Maya won't ask me about *things*.

She glances at me sideways. 'That's normal for forests, isn't it? I don't know what things you're talking about but … in Okinawa, we have little red-haired demon children who live in the banyan trees.' She grins. 'They're not really children or demons. Kijimuna. They're their own thing. They don't eat people, just fish – the left eyes of fish only, they're very picky.'

'Why the left eye?' I ask, as if that's a rational question.

'I've never asked them,' Maya says, deadpan.

'Have you seen them?'

'When I was a kid, sure, I saw them all the time. What have you seen?' Her question catches me off guard.

'I've seen—' Koki turning away from me, telling me what's not real. Ryosuke in the cafe, speaking too slowly, Dad unsure of when he is. My uneasiness returns forcefully, slick and writhing. I'm afraid I'm going mad.

'Not them,' I manage to say. 'But I've never been to Okinawa.'

Maya laughs and looks relieved when I join in half-heartedly, either because she's nervous about her comedic skills, or because it suddenly seems I'm on the edge of breakdown. It's probably the latter.

'Do you want to talk about anything?' Maya asks me, sounding concerned.

I open and shut my mouth.

'It's totally fine if you don't want to,' she says.

'I do, I just – I just don't know where to start. It's … a lot.'

Maya watches me. 'Try me. I'm listening.'

I meet her steady eyes, then stare ahead at the next set of torii gates. 'The short version is that my dad isn't well and it's connected to the time zones. His memory's going and that makes sense, really, it does. But there are other things ... and nobody seems to know how to help him. I thought Naomi would know, and she said she'd help but—'

Maya puts her hand on my arm. 'Hey, Nomura-sensei is a genius, but she doesn't know everything. Now I get why she was asking about him the other day. If she's going to help, that's great.'

We pass under the torii gates. 'You think she will?'

'If she said she would, then, yeah,' Maya says firmly. 'She'll probably become obsessed with it and your dad will be forced to recover just so she'll leave him alone.'

'I mean, that's what I'd do if I were him,' I say.

'Trust Nomura. Even asking for help can be pretty tough, and you've already done that.' Her voice is soft and reassuring, and it feels like it's been a hundred years since someone spoke to me like that.

I can't tell her that I left him, that he's not answering his phone and that I'm afraid. But that dread has stilled a little bit. I say, 'Thanks. You're good at calming people down.'

She half-smiles, shifts her gaze to the shrine that we have almost reached. 'You know PTSD?'

'A bit. It's when someone's had something traumatic happen to them and they can't get over it. Or recover from it – if that's a better way to say it?'

'Basically. It can affect the brain in a certain way. Sometimes the memory of that trauma keeps happening, as if it's on a loop. You can get stuck.' She turns to me. 'I've only been in the Tokyo time zones, but the slow zone gave me that feeling, in particular.'

'We can get stuck in time, and time can get stuck in us,' I say thoughtfully.

Maya shrugs. 'It's not exactly a theory but it makes sense to me.'

'Me too.' After a pause, I say, 'You know what PTSD's like, then?'

Maya's eyes become wary. 'Yeah,' she says shortly. 'Maybe I'll tell you some other time.'

'Of course.' I curse myself for being so insensitive.

Through the gate of the shrine, we queue, and then toss coins into the box.

I bow and clap. *Please let Dad be okay. Please let everything be okay*, I pray.

'You want to get an omikuji?' Maya asks.

'I don't think I want to know what my future holds,' I say dubiously.

'I get that. I got the best luck one a year ago and I haven't got an omikuji since. So my luck is still good.'

'Is that how it works?' I've never thought of it like that.

'It's how it works for *me*,' Maya says firmly.

'I'll do that next time,' I reply.

'Good.' She smiles at me. 'Is it okay if we head back? I should do my homework.'

'Of course! Please don't fail anything because of me.'

'Hey, who said I was going to *fail*? Anyway, I wanted to … take a break.' Now Maya seems embarrassed.

Was I making her feel embarrassed? Was that good? Or bad? I silently stress about this until Maya starts to happily complain about some of her classes, which makes me ask her about what she's studying, and we chat easily until we're back at the entrance.

'Are you going back to the station?' she asks.

'I think I'll walk around here for a while,' I say.

We stand there awkwardly.

'I'd better go...' she says.

'Thanks for talking to me,' I blurt. 'I dumped a load of stuff on you and I practically just met you.'

'You don't seem like a stranger, though.' Maya tilts her head.

'I know what you mean,' I say, even though I hadn't known it before she said it.

'I was happy to listen.' She holds my gaze for several heartbeats.

There's a kind of warmth in me, and I step back to hide this confusion and this thrill. 'Thanks again,' I say.

She nods. 'Message me if you need anything. Or whatever.' She waves and then walks away, vanishing into the street of people.

I watch her go, and shake myself into motion again.

I turn back, under the torii gates and along the avenue, but get off the main path as soon as I can. I want to feel the trees crowd around me. I head to what I hope is the deepest part of the woods, following the strange, pressing need to be among leaves and branches. It's so silent that it's hard to recall the noise of people and trains and streets and city.

I put my hands out to the nearest tree, pressing my palms against its rugged bark. I reach to the next mottled trunk, the next smooth with raised knots, the next and the next. I'm a tiny creature to them, a bird or a moth or a mouse flitting from one to the other. I lay my cheek against deeply ridged bark and inhale a distant scent of lemons. I stare up at its branches and frond-like leaves. Hinoki. Cypress. Used for sacred things: shrines, palaces. Baths.

I sit where the trunk meets the ground. Beneath me, there is a mirror image of this tree with roots spreading in the soil like the branches in the air. I lean my head back and rest my hands on the earth. Like the trees, I breathe. No need to count seconds and minutes and worry. In front of me is a fallen branch, wood that's hollowing out and collapsing into decay. Along its length are hopeful saplings, leaves swaying and thin branches wobbling like any baby thing. It's almost as though I can see them stretch and grow; I'd forgotten that forests are not as slow as they seem.

And they're communicating – *talking* – the whole time. What would they be saying about me? Nothing, probably. I'm not important enough to be the topic of any conversation, not even for trees. *Especially* for trees. And what would the language of trees sound like? I listen. Wind rustles leaves, branches creak, bark stretches. I close my eyes. Hair strands of roots absorb minerals, the commerce between insects and birds and animals.

There's a tremble in the ground; are the earthquakes following me? I feel time move a little, which surprises me, but we're not far from the Shibuya fast zone, after all...

...go, no, flow, grow, sow, know, oh oh oh...

I sit up, shake my head to clear it, rub my eyes. Were there whispers? But there's nobody around. My mouth is dry. I fumble at my backpack for my tea, wrench it open, drink. I pause, because the seedling in its paper bag is beside it, forgotten and left in the darkness since yesterday. Despite that, somehow it has grown; its leaves have multiplied, its stem thickened. I stare at it in disbelief. It's somehow outgrown its pot.

I suppose the trees have spoken. I never thought about not understanding the language. I get up with my backpack, and my other, sprouting, bag. My head is all jumbled dreams and memories. I touch each trunk that I pass until I return to the path and people.

I'm dazed by the concrete and streets all over again, but locate a flower shop and convince the man there to sell me a bigger pot with soil. He transplants the teenage sapling, patting it into the soil with his fingers.

'Be good,' he tells it, as if he's speaking to a grandchild. He charges me one hundred yen and waves me away.

Suddenly I'm more tired than I've ever been. I haul myself back to Koki's apartment, unfold the futon, and lay my confused, exhausted body down.

麦秋至

20

I wake to the judder of my phone vibrating on the floor beside me. I rub my eyes and fumble for it and answer.

'Hello?' My voice is raspy with sleep.

'Sora-san?' The woman's voice is familiar, but I can't place it.

'Yes. Who is this?'

'Eiko Fujiwara. Koki's mother.'

I sit up and clear my throat. 'Oh! Is everything all right – is Koki all right?' Images of Koki falling on to a train track or ... could he have called his mother to talk about me? The terror.

'Koki's fine but ... I went to visit your father and he's not at home.'

'Um. Okay?' I have no idea why she needs to call me to say this.

'The front door was open, and I stepped inside because there was no answer to the doorbell. The place is rather – it didn't look as it should.'

'It's untidy?' If she expects me to be a good daughter and do some cleaning, I'll scream.

She pauses. 'It looks more as though it has been … wrecked. It might be a burglary – but the television and computer are still there, so it's a little odd, I thought.'

My hand holding the phone is sweaty.

'I waited for quite a while but I don't know how to get in touch with your father, so I thought it would be best to call you. Perhaps you can call him, or his workplace?'

'I'll call him straight away. He could just be out for a walk, or doing shopping…'

'Of course,' she reassures me.

There's a sick twisting inside me that says, *He could, but he isn't.*

'Fujiwara-san, you know I'm in Tokyo, don't you?'

'I do. I was passing near your home and I thought I would drop by and say hello.' She's quiet for a second. 'I saw him last week and he seemed…' She hesitates. 'Bewildered.'

'That's kind of you to visit him.'

'I apologise if I'm intruding,' she says.

'Not at all. I'll find Dad and he can check if anything's been stolen. I appreciate you telling me,' I say.

'Not at all. I'm sorry to cause you any alarm.'

I thank her until we hang up.

Then I try to breathe evenly. I call Dad's number. I should have called him yesterday. It doesn't even ring, just beeps and goes to voicemail. I try again and again and again. I leave a message.

'Dad, where are you? Fujiwara-san called me and said that it looks like the house has been robbed? Are you okay? What's going on?'

I leave another message. 'And call me back!'

I have to gather myself before I call the company. I go to the toilet, then wash my face.

I speak in my best polite voice, hoping they won't recognise me. 'Hello? I'm sorry to disturb you. I'm wondering whether Campbell-san is there? He is a former employee but perhaps he is in the building for a … meeting.'

A cool voice asks me my name.

'Sora Campbell,' I say wretchedly.

The voice, freezing cold, tells me to wait.

I fix my eyes on a patch of blue showing through the clouds outside.

The voice returns. 'I'm sorry, but he is not here.'

'He hasn't been there recently?'

'I'm afraid not.'

'I see. Thank you.'

The line goes dead. The phone is hot against my face. No, it's my cheeks that are hot.

I get up and open the window. I touch the four o'clock flowers, their red-orange-white petals. Their trumpets begin to blossom open, too quickly, too early. Is it me, speeding time up for them?

I back away.

I pace back and forth in front of the door leading into the building where Koki's lecture hall is. Dad's phone still isn't ringing.

'Hey!' a voice calls.

Maya's standing behind me, her grin deflating when she sees my face. I must look like crap. 'Hi,' I croak.

'Are you okay?' she asks.

I swallow. 'Not really. I just got some bad news – not bad, really. Worrying. It's about my dad.'

Maya's face instantly creases in concern. Her eyes land on my bags. 'Oh, no! So you're going back home?'

'Yeah.'

'Is there anything I can do?' she asks.

There might be nothing *anyone* can do. 'No, but thanks. I'll come back to Tokyo. I don't know when but...'

Maya nods decisively. 'I know you will. When you do, make sure you bring more plants. I like vegetation as your accessory.'

I heave a smile on to my face. 'My signature style. It's the seedling Naomi gave me yesterday.'

Maya crouches down beside the bag. 'It's like ... five times the size.'

The bell chimes, ending class.

'I don't know how it happened,' I say helplessly. 'I took it for a walk and maybe it just liked the fresh air. I wandered around Meiji Jingu more after you left and kinda dozed off under trees.'

Maya's still inspecting the plant. 'You had this with you yesterday?'

'It was in my bag. I'd totally forgotten about it.'

'Is that why you wanted to be near trees?' she asks.

'I was thinking about what we'd talked about the other day.' I stare at the sapling. 'Now I don't have any answers, just a bunch more questions.'

'That's science for you.' Maya straightens up. 'Are you going to see Nomura-sensei?'

'No.' I hadn't thought of contacting Naomi, but there's nothing she could do anyway. 'I'm saying bye to my friend. He knows my dad.'

'Your dad's health – it's got worse?' she asks hesitantly.

'I don't know,' I reply, feeling strangely distant. 'He's missing.'

Maya puts her hand to her mouth. 'That's terrible, I'm sorry.'

I nod. 'I'm going home.'

'Of course. Will you be okay?' she asks.

'Yeah, definitely. Thanks.' I attempt a smile but it makes my face feel brittle, like it could fall apart if I move too much.

'Why don't I come with you?' Maya says suddenly.

'To where? The bus stop?'

'No – *with* you. To look for your dad.'

I'm pretty sure my mouth is actually hanging open as I process this suggestion.

'Sorry, is that too much? I didn't mean to invite myself to your house. You probably have a bunch of people who can help you, anyway,' Maya says in a rush.

I snap out of my daze. 'No, I don't. Just – it won't be … fun.'

Maya looks baffled. 'Sora. Are you seriously worried that *searching for your missing father* won't be a nice holiday?'

'I guess, yeah, I am worried about that while also now seeing that was an extremely bizarre thing to say.'

Maya shakes her head, but she's smiling. 'Don't worry. Hey, how about you go home and see how things are? I can come up tomorrow, if you need me.'

I nod. 'Okay. That makes sense. Dad could already be at home when I get there. I don't want you to waste your time.'

'It wouldn't be a waste,' Maya says firmly. 'I'll be ready tomorrow, just in case. Promise you'll message me?'

'Promise,' I agree, though I can't imagine doing it, or that she would really come.

I spot Koki, walking towards us.

'Your friend.' Maya hugs me suddenly, and squeezes me tight. 'Everything will be okay,' she whispers.

For a dizzying moment I think I might kiss her, but then she lets me go.

'Hello,' says Koki in Japanese.

'Ah, hello,' Maya replies, switching to Japanese too. 'I'm Kinjo Maya.'

'Fujiwara Koki. Nice to meet you,' he says.

'And you. I'm sorry, but I have to go before I'm late for class.' Maya turns to me and smiles. 'Don't forget your promise.'

'I won't. Oh … and I guess tell Nomura-sensei that I've gone? Please?'

'Sure.' She gives me one last concerned glance and then hurries away.

Koki raises his eyebrows at me. 'So your manipulation worked.'

'What? No! I don't know.' I half-fall on to the bench. 'I'm going home.'

'My mom messaged me – what's happening?' Koki asks worriedly.

'Dad's sick, Koki.' I twist the strap of my bag in my hands. 'It's his memory and – I think he's gone missing.' I watch him cycle through worry, alarm and confusion.

'He hasn't been *kidnapped*?' Koki says eventually, and unexpectedly.

'No – I don't think so! He wandered away probably – or he could've gone on a day trip for all I know.'

'He wasn't saying anything unusual the last time you talked to him?'

I stare at the ground. 'Haven't talked to him in a few days.'

'Messaged, whatever,' Koki says impatiently.

I shake my head. 'We had an argument and he told me I should go away, and then I came here. He didn't try to call or message me, either!' I say.

Koki holds his hands up. 'I didn't say anything!'

But I saw his expression.

'Can I help?' he asks.

'You have, already. Thanks for letting me stay with you. I know it's been awkward and last night—'

Koki rubs the back of his neck. 'Yeah.'

My face is burning. 'You're my best friend, Koki. I liked … everything. But we're *friends*, aren't we? I think that's what we're supposed to be.'

Koki gives me a long look, then smiles. 'We are. And, yeah, I think you might be right. Friends, but *always* friends. I like you very much, Sora.'

I feel very mature.

'I should tell you,' Koki begins. He rubs his phone anxiously between his palms.

I'm such a fool. 'Do you … already have a girlfriend?' I half-yell.

'No!' he says. 'Honestly! Just … someone I went on a few dates with. Nothing's really happened.'

My maturity begins to dissolve into something else. 'That's okay.'

'Maybe when you come to Tokyo next you can meet her,' he suggests. 'We can go on a double date.'

I take a deep breath, so I don't tell him how dumb he is. 'I'm not letting you set me up with some loser,' I say instead.

He pokes me. 'Bring your new friend. Maya.'

'That wouldn't be a date. That would be … hanging out. Together. Why are you looking at me like that?' I ask.

He shrugs.

'I'm going,' I say abruptly.

He grabs my hand. 'I'm sorry. Tell me if you need help. Or my mother, she's there and will actually be much more helpful than me.'

'I know.' He's still holding my hand. I lean towards him and put my face against his chest, and he wraps his arms around me. I move when I feel my throat get tight and pull away, but his face is so close to mine that I can't help putting my mouth on his, just for a second. Why do I suddenly want to kiss everyone? I step back fast, and I'm on fire and melting in embarrassment.

Koki's hand squeezes mine, and when I meet his eyes I see that he's biting his lip, hesitating, unsure. I pull my hand out of his, not wanting to feel regret. 'Bye, Koki.'

'Message when you're home,' he says.

'I will.' I gather my bags. When I look at him again, his eyes have cleared.

'Be safe. Take care,' he says.

I walk down that broad avenue, away from him. Everything inside me is moving, trembling, rising, falling. At the university gates, I glance back. Koki raises a hand and waves.

I'll see Koki again, but there's another part of him I won't see. If things had been different... They aren't, though. I lift my hand and wave goodbye.

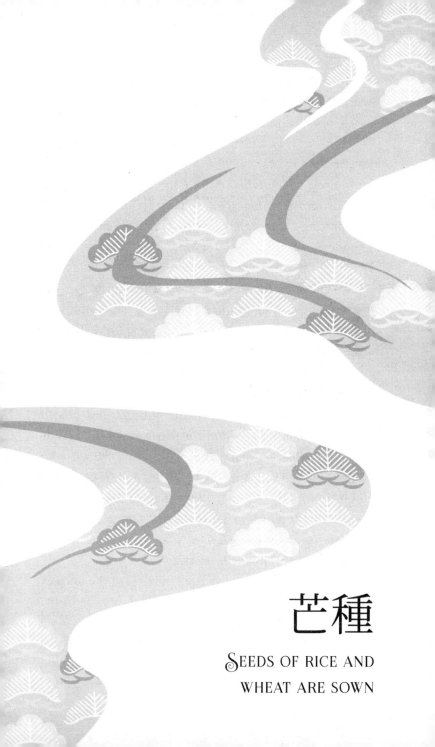

芒種

SEEDS OF RICE AND
WHEAT ARE SOWN

21

The house is worse than I imagined. The hallway's a mess, coats and bags on the floor, *shoes inside.* My school shoes. I put them on the rack by the door.

'Dad?' I already know there's nothing living here.

Except, in the kitchen, a little black beetle with two red spots on its back. I open the window and hold it on the tip of my finger until it flies away. Dad's study has been half-torn apart. His bedroom is strewn with clothes, his bed unmade. My bedroom door is open. My closet is, too. My clothes have been pulled aside, and there's Mom's photo in her makeshift shrine. Dad must have been searching in here, for what I don't know.

'Where is he?' I whisper to her.

I called Dad's phone every ten minutes of the journey from Tokyo to home. Koki's mother said that she hadn't seen him yet, but was asking around. The whole town will know Dad's gone by now, and I don't know if that makes me feel better or worse. I should go to the police, probably, but it seems too soon. He could wander home this evening and I'd have caused a fuss for nothing. I'll start searching myself. I get my bike. I'll begin with the neighbours.

The Uchimuras are closest. I've barely rung the bell when the door flies open.

'Uchimura-san.' I bow.

'Sora-chan – I heard, how terrible, your father—' Her daughter, Risa, had been in my class. She always ignored me.

'You haven't seen him lately? Yesterday or today?'

Uchimura's hands clap themselves on her cheeks. 'No, but I'll call my husband, maybe he has.'

Her husband has an office job that, like all office jobs, I have no understanding of. If he's told, the entire staff he works with will be too. I guess it'll save me from having to do it.

'Thank you,' I say.

'Of course. You'll call us if you hear anything, won't you?' Her anxious eyes follow me as I leave.

I go to the next house, and the next, and both have already heard that Dad is missing. After that, I don't bother. Everybody will have told each other. I half-expect an announcement to come over the loudspeakers.

I cycle away from the houses, towards the ocean. I follow the boundary fence, looking in, watching for movement, but I see nothing for miles and miles. I'd got used to the gaps and absences, the places that used to have people, the spaces that used to be filled by houses. After

Tokyo, I notice them again. It's not exactly emptiness, because I can still see what was there before. I remember.

I should go home. I should keep looking. I should go to the police. I don't know which is the best, which *should* is the right one. I'm thirsty, though, so I let that lead me to the nearest conbini. The air-conditioning blasts over me and the sweat cools on my back. I put my face in the fridge for as long as possible and then buy a cold green tea.

Outside, an old man in loose work trousers is leaning against the bike rail. He's drinking a can of black coffee and mopping his forehead with a handkerchief. I lean beside him and drink. He's watching the sky, the clouds, the birds.

After a while, I say, 'Have you seen my father?'

'Ever?' he says. 'Or recently?'

'Recently.'

He takes a long drink. 'No.'

'He's missing.'

I watch his eyes watch a crow flapping steadily inland. 'Who is he missing?'

'I don't know,' I lie.

He nods. We stay there until we have finished our drinks. Then I get back on my bike.

'People come back,' the old man says.

'Some of them,' I say.

'They still come back.' He raises his face to the sky.

I go to the Fujiwaras.

'Sora!' Koki's mother ushers me inside as I stumble out of my shoes. 'Your father?'

I shake my head. 'I was looking for him but...'

'You should have a drink. Are you hungry?' She hurries me into the kitchen.

'No, I'm not,' I tell her, sinking down at the table.

She blatantly ignores me, pours a glass of cold barley tea, and inspects me. 'You should eat.'

'I ate a ton in Tokyo. Koki knows lots of good restaurants.'

'Does he?' she says doubtfully.

'We went to one place where everything cost three hundred and sixty-five yen.'

She laughs. 'He's a student, then.'

'Truly.' I drink. It's so cold my head aches.

'Even more reason for me to make you dinner.'

'I'd like to go home as soon as I can. In case Dad comes back.'

'I understand. I'll make you something you can take home.'

I surrender and say thank you.

She looks relieved and heads to the fridge, opens cupboard doors. 'Have you spoken to the police?'

'No.'

'I think you should, Sora-chan.'

'Yes,' I say reluctantly. 'I will.'

'I can go with you, if you'd like me to.'

'I should be fine, thank you.'

'All right.'

I listen to the steady, quiet chop of her knife. There's a family photo on the wall that I've never noticed before. Koki's dad is standing straight and his mother looks exactly as she does now but with a slightly different haircut. Koki's short but old enough to not be cute. And his brother. He's a head taller than Koki, a skinny teenager who must have been watching his dad because he's standing very straight too. He looks like Koki but his hair is neater, his mouth is wider – he looks serious but also more innocent, somehow. Koki and I must be older now than he is in this photo.

Fujiwara-san comes back, and I turn away quickly, but she's seen me staring at the photo. Her smile falters and disappears, and her face is open and bare without it. She hands me a bento box.

I take it and stand up awkwardly. 'This is very kind of you.'

She puts her hand on my shoulder, and then leans in and gives me a hug so careful it's almost frightened. I want to put my face against her and cry, but I grit my teeth and hold my breath.

'Once,' she whispers, 'afterwards, he came to the door. His clothes were all wet, and he asked for something dry to wear. I wanted to ask how he had ended up in the water. But I didn't. When I brought him clothes, he was gone.' She takes her arms away. 'Please call me if you need anything. You're not alone, Sora-chan.'

I can only nod.

When I return home, it's as empty and terrible as I left it. I clean the hallways, the kitchen, the living room. I message Koki and tell him his mother's wonderful, that everything's okay for now. I open the bento: three onigiri tucked tidily in a row. I bite into one, and my mouth meets the bitterness of pickled plum. It's so dumb and anime to eat a rice ball and cry that I laugh when tears come to my eyes. I eat another: shiso and dark red-brown miso. After that, I'm full, and slightly better and capable of going to the police. I bring the bento with me, for comfort, to eat if I feel weak again.

The sun sets as I cycle, the sky turning a fretful purple as the sun sinks into the ocean. The police station is cramped, and the two police officers look as though they were expecting me.

'I have to report a missing person,' I say.

I sit down and begin answering their questions. On the walls there are posters of wanted criminals and missing children. Will they make a poster of Dad?

'How long has he been gone for?'

'Three days,' I guess.

They murmur and make notes.

But he could have been gone longer, could be in Hokkaido or Okinawa by now, or in an old bar or on a grey beach.

I answer more questions about Dad, and when they ask about his work I name the company but tell them that he stopped working there recently.

'We will be in contact with you,' they say, 'if we find anything.'

'Will you search for him?' I ask.

They exchange glances. 'We will alert the police network.'

'But you won't actually be *looking* for him?' I say.

'Only in specific circumstances. In this case…'

It's not the right circumstance. I'd had an image of search parties, people with flashlights and walkie-talkies, but in the plainness of the station it retreats into the movies and TV shows it came from.

On the way back home, I realise that Koki's mother had lied to me: I am alone, after all. It's almost too dark to see. I stop and get off my bike to get my light, but I can't find it in my bag and how will I get home?

I slump on the gravel. This road is narrow and quiet. I'm so completely exhausted that I could sleep here. I scrub my hands across my face and see fireworks behind my eyelids, and when I lift them I'm dazzled, because the moon has appeared, radiant and almost full. It illuminates a shrine a few steps down the road, the wood so silvery pale it could be made of moonlight too.

It's long and filled with rows of jizo statutes. Jizo watches over children and travellers, a kind, small god of the everyday. These statues are lined up, three rows deep, as if they're about to have a class photo. Some are dressed in little jackets or kimonos, some faded, some bright, all cheerfully patterned. There are some toys. Sweets and snacks. Flowers.

In the front and centre there is one worn jizo wearing the traditional red cap and bib. He smiles patiently, as if he's the teacher in this classroom. Now I see that the other jizo *are* children – or, at least, are dedicated to them. One for each child lost in the Shake. Eighteen or twenty from this area, taken by the earthquake, or the waves, or by those cracks and breaks in time. I've never stopped here before.

The oldest central jizo has a withered mikan and a One Cup sake beside him. I place the last onigiri in the bento on the shrine.

'O-jizo-sama,' I whisper, 'the onigiri is very delicious. So please help me.'

I bow and leave him to appreciate the rice in peace. The other jizo-children surround him, quietly waiting. The moon is bright enough to bring me home, but once I get there, the loneliness seeps back into my skin.

My phone vibrates. It's a message from Maya.

how are you?

not great, I reply.

I swallow hard.

did you mean it when you said you'd come here?

I send it before I change my mind.

Maya replies straight away.

yes.

'It's only thunder,' Mom said, but that didn't stop me being frightened.

It rattled everything in the house, which wasn't hard because Obaachan and Ojiichan's house was old and traditional and basically made of wood and paper. I was six or seven, the first Japanese rainy season I could remember.

'Hide your bellybutton or Raijin-sama will eat it!' Ojiichan told me.

I started to cry.

'Have you forgotten that used to scare me when I was a kid?' Mom yelled at Ojiichan.

'Ah, so like your okaasan, Sora-chan!' Ojiichan grinned and took one of my hands and placed it over my bellybutton. 'There. Raijin-sama can't see it now.'

'Who's Raijin-sama?' I sobbed.

'Oh, you don't know him? He's the god of thunder. He's the one making all this noise, playing taiko!' Ojiichan stood up, pulled a pretend-angry face and smacked invisible drums. 'Bambambam-BAM!'

Mom laughed and I giggled too.

'You don't think my drumming is good?' Ojiichan drummed on my tummy, which made me laugh harder.

Thunder rolled and rumbled overhead.

'Raijin-sama is better than me, but then again, he has much bigger drums. He won't hurt you. Thunder's good for the rice, you know. You can put up with this noise if it means tasty rice, can't you?' Ojiichan said.

I nodded.

'Good, see, you're very Japanese,' Ojiichan said approvingly.

Mom opened the screen door so that we could watch the rain hurtle to the ground and feel the thunder in the air. She pulled me into her lap. 'Thunder scared me when I was your age. But it's natural, like clouds, or snow, or sunshine. Only bigger.'

'Like earthquakes?' I said, because they also frightened me.

'Earthquakes,' Mom told me, 'are just thunder underground.'

The shiver of the earth wakes me, but when I blink and sit up it's quiet. Maybe I dreamed it. Maybe I'd dreamed everything, and like the worst-written stories, this waking is normality returning.

I reach for my phone and call Dad. The one-note dial tone hums to me, almost soothing now because it never changes. No normality, then. I reply to a message from Koki and tell him I'm fine. I call the police, who sound surprised to hear from me. They have not found my father yet. They will contact me if there is any change. I call Koki's mom.

Do I need anything?

Am I sure?

Do I have someone who will stay with me?

She should know the answer is no, but the pause is so uncomfortable that I say yes to spare both of us. She says I should call my relations in case...

We could both hear all the possible endings for that sentence, so I suppose neither of us feel the need to articulate them into words, when they are swirling about thickly in the air between us, along the length of the buzzing telephone lines.

I tell her I should go and she says yes.

My mouth tastes of iron because my fingers are bleeding from biting my nails. I need to think. Need to be logical. Consistent. Gather information. I go to Dad's study.

I examine the disarray. Books, notes, maps – strata of paper. His laptop is dead, and I don't know his passwords. There are no more repetitions of the kanji of my name. Maybe he never noticed I'd taken away the sheet. There are blank spaces on the wall where maps had been. On the desk, on the floor – they are fragments of maps, sketches of what could be routes, numbers that might be equations.

I have a breakthrough when I find a list of numbers that turn out to be coordinates, and beside each is written, *no signs* or *nothing measurable* or *no difference*. At the bottom is scrawled, *but how can I know?* It's the same thought I had when Naomi asked if I had any side effects. Would I even be able to tell? So Dad is trying to see if he can measure those jolts and slippages in time I've felt, because I'm a fool, because for some reason I thought it would stop him going into the zones. But I've done exactly the opposite.

I try to pull myself together. I reassemble the maps like they're jigsaws. Parts have been ripped away, and when I line them up I see what's been taken: anything that mapped the northern zones, particularly their more western parts. I get my own maps and lay them down to compare them, to find what's missing. It's a place we'd only partly explored, because time got faster and then slower the further we went, and Dad didn't want me to go on. We'd turned back. I haven't returned there since.

So Dad has gone into one of the most dangerous, unknown areas of the slow zone. It's a strange relief, even as my heart hammers. It's at least understandable, something I know. Somewhere I can go.

The doorbell rings.

I answer the door and there, unbelievably, is Maya. She really came.

'Hey,' she says. 'I made it.'

'Hi.' I smile at her.

'Can I ... come in?' she asks.

'Uh, yes, sorry, come in,' I babble, wondering how long I'd been smiling at her like that. 'Do you want some tea or coffee or anything?'

'Coffee would be awesome,' she says, and we go into the kitchen.

'You must be tired. It's still early. You can have a nap if you want,' I offer.

Maya sits at the kitchen table as if she's done it a million times before and it's completely normal to travel halfway across Japan to help a relative stranger search for her missing father. 'I actually sleep really well on overnight buses. No idea why,' she says.

'That's a rare gift,' I say. Then, 'Thank you for coming.'

'I'm glad you asked me ... but sorry you had to,' she says hurriedly.

'He could still walk in any second now,' I say, too cheerfully.

'Of course,' Maya agrees. 'Could anyone give you any info, though? Any clues about where he's gone?'

I shake my head. The kettle boils and I concentrate on making the coffee, wondering if I should tell Maya what I've discovered. I put a mug down in front of her.

'Thanks.' She looks up at me. 'What is it?'

'I found a clue,' I tell her.

'That's good!'

I'm not sure if it is, but I say, 'I'll show you. You can bring your coffee.'

I lead Maya into Dad's study. Her eyes widen as she takes in the chaos of paper and then narrow as she steps closer to the sketches and notes and equations pinned to the walls.

She lets out a long breath. 'Your father studies the zones. That's why you know so much…'

'He's a researcher.' I correct myself. 'He *was*.'

Maya is already at his desk, examining the maps, and when she turns to me I can see that she already knows what the clue is.

'Yeah. I'm pretty sure he's gone into the zones.' I point. 'Here, I think.'

She takes a gulp of coffee. 'Then that's where we're going.'

I blink. 'We?'

'That's why I'm here. To search with you.'

'Not in the zones, though. I didn't think…' But I had,

on some level, because really this is the most predictable thing Dad could have done. 'I didn't think you would search *there* with me. It's dangerous—'

'Even more reason you shouldn't go alone,' Maya interrupts. 'Unless there are other people who will go? Like, oh, the cops?'

'As if.'

'Exactly.'

'But I'm used to the zones,' I protest. 'I know them. Have you even been in any of the zones before?'

'Obviously I have!' Maya shoots back. 'I do research in the Tokyo zones practically every week.'

'These aren't like the Tokyo zones – people can't just go in to sightsee and buy souvenirs!'

'Only when you take them, right?' Maya sips calmly from her mug. 'In which case you're the perfect person to go with.'

I glare at her. 'That's different. I'm going to have to go way further in. You'll get sick.'

Maya glares back. 'I know that can happen, but I've never been sick before.'

'Never?' I ask suspiciously.

'Honestly, not even the first time I went into a zone. Slow *and* fast,' she says.

'These are different,' I say weakly, because I desperately want her to come with me.

'Hey.' Maya's eyes meet mine. 'I'm aware of what the zones can do. I want to help you. And – full disclosure, okay? – I really want to see what it's like in there. I'm studying it, after all. Have you forgotten you met me in a literal lab?' Her voice is annoyed and amused at the same time.

'If we go in, you have to listen to me. You definitely know more science and theories and philosophy but I know more about the actual real zones. You have to be careful.' I hold eye contact until she nods decisively.

'I understand,' she says. 'Now what do we need?'

蟷螂生

PREYING MANTISES HATCH

22

Before we go through the boundary fence I ask Maya to check that we have everything in our bags one more time: food, flashlights, whistles, and other basic survival stuff I hope we won't need. Then I walk a little distance away from her, brace myself, and call the company.

'I *must* speak to Yamagata-san,' I tell the icy voice that answers. 'This is Sora Campbell.'

'I'm afraid that's not—'

'Tell him I'm trespassing nowhere near him.'

There's a pause. A click.

'Hello?'

'Yamagata-san?'

'Why are you calling me?' He's irritated. 'I have already stated that I do not know where your father is.'

'I know you don't. That's why I'm going to find him myself. But I need you to tell me how far north he's gone in his fieldwork.'

'North?' he asks.

'Slow zone. North, north-west.'

'Nobody goes there. Neither should you.'

'But Dad tried to, didn't he?'

'I did not advise him to.'

'You knew.'

'Not beforehand.'

'Is that so?' I asked.

'What do you think of me, Campbell-san? As a manager ordering mindless workers to their deaths?' he snaps.

Mindless worker has never been on Dad's CV. 'No.'

Yamagata breathes out evenly, as if he's calming himself. 'I must warn you not to go there.'

'Is there anything I should know about the area?' I say stubbornly. He's the only person I could think of who might be able to tell me something, and I need all the information I can get.

'It's not safe. You have to pass between different zones. The time is too ... thin.'

'Thin,' I repeat.

'Such as air, in high altitudes. People become ill. Hallucinate. Please—'

His *please* unnerves me. 'How far have people gone?' I persist.

He hesitates. 'There is – was – a village called Nakagawa... It's in a fast zone, and after that the slow zone begins. Perhaps nine or ten kilometres north of there is as far as has been mapped. After that, there is no known safe area for a hundred kilometres. Sora—'

'I appreciate the information,' I say as composedly as I can, and end the call.

I go back to Maya and together we haul our bikes through a gap in the fence. I watch Maya wobble as she settles into the saddle.

'I'm fine,' she says.

'I didn't say a thing.'

'I can see your face, though,' she mutters.

I'm so glad she's here, and so worried.

'Tell me whenever you need a break, okay? Or if you don't feel good. Or if you see anything weird.'

'Weird like what?' Maya asks.

I get on my bike and start cycling so I don't have to answer. The white line on the road is faded but not gone. It spools away from us and I feel the tremble of time unwinding. I scan the road, the roadsides. Dad could be anywhere; he could be having a nap somewhere out of sight and neither of us would ever know I had passed him by.

'Dad? Dad!' I shout.

Maya uses a whistle, blasting sharp, loud bursts.

It's my familiar searching routine, but horribly different, because I never thought I'd have to look for *this* parent. And this time I have more than a tiny hope; I have a terrible, frightening need.

I guess the road Dad would have taken, because it's the most direct route that isn't the highway. He wouldn't have gone along the highway, the boring straight lines fenced away from the houses and gardens and remains of human life.

We stop in the next village, where Maya shakes out her legs and peers in the windows of decaying houses.

'So this is the fast zone,' she murmurs. 'It's quiet.'

'What you expected?' I ask.

'It's more peaceful and less creepy than I imagined.'

'It can be a lot of both, sometimes.'

We wheel our bikes along the handful of cracked streets, still calling and whistling. We disturb swallows nesting in the eaves of an old sento, the character for 'bath' still readable on the cloth sign. I apologise to them and we continue on our way.

The sun sizzles and the air is as heavy as wool. I hope Dad has enough water, and enough sense to find shade. If he has heatstroke on top of everything else… It's a relief when the road bends and opens on to the sea, the air salting my tongue. I hear Maya gasp and turn to see her face shining like another sun as she gazes at the waves.

'As good as Okinawa?'

She grins. 'Not even close. But still beautiful.'

We stop and sit on the sea wall to drink water and stare over the blues of ocean and sky.

'How long has passed in normal time?' Maya stares at her digital watch. 'I think this is broken.'

I check my watch, then the sun, then my pulse. 'About four hours, but in here it's closer to six.'

'How *can* you keep track of time so accurately?' Maya asks. 'When you did those tests in the lab… I've never seen anyone do that before, and I'm pretty sure neither has Nomura-sensei.'

'I don't know,' I say truthfully. 'I've been going into the zones for years. I was around here when the Shake happened, so I remember that feeling when time changed. When everything changed.'

Maya keeps her eyes on me, waiting.

'I think… It's like having a tight *hold* on time. It could break or slip away again at any moment. But if I can keep a grip on it then I'll know if that happens. And I won't get lost…'

'I get it,' Maya says softly. 'You need that control.'

'Except it can't be controlled! So I know it's useless but I can't stop.'

'It's pretty useful at the moment,' Maya points out.

I manage a half-smile. 'I guess so.'

I stand up and pace along the wall, gazing around. I curse myself for not having binoculars. The waves keep a steady beat.

'Dad!' I call. 'Daaaaad!'

Maya whistles, our own call-and-response, but not the one I need.

We go further in and further in, shouting and whistling. We cycle more slowly, and turn on to random minor roads and paths, but always heading to that unsearched place on my map. *Please let us find him soon, please, please,* I chant to myself, in time with my pedals turning.

At the next town we rest on a wobbly bench outside the post office. Maya closes her eyes and leans back against the wall. I feel out the time, fingers on the pulse of my wrist, watching the second hand on my watch tick forward. Still in the fast zone, but time has slowed a fraction. I peer into the postbox beside me and glimpse the edges of a letter or two. I could post them when I got back, and people would receive belated birthday cards and overdue bills… But anything they'd been waiting for or expecting must be long gone by now. They've got over it, no doubt. No need to stir up the past.

I nudge her with my elbow and she startles awake.

'Sorry!' I say.

'It's okay. Didn't mean to doze off.' Maya rubs her eyes.

I look at her closely. 'How tired do you feel?'

'Normal, not-used-to-cycling-for-hours tired,' she replies.

'All right.' I hand her an energy bar. 'You should eat.'

She opens it and munches away while I check the map, which tells me that Nakagawa is about an hour away. And then ten kilometres after that… I get up and stretch and shake out my tired legs and try not to count the hours of daylight we have left.

Maya stands. 'Can we walk for a while?'

I scan for shadows as we go. I half-want one to appear, to see if Maya notices it and what she would do.

Maya pauses by a stagnant fish tank in the window of a restaurant. 'What happened to the fish?'

I recognise this tank. I've been here before, once, years ago.

'They died,' I say.

Maya squints into the murky water. 'The bones dissolved too?'

I don't like that tank. I move away from it.

Maya glances at me, then says, 'Something wrong?'

I shrug uncomfortably. 'I took them out.'

Her face sweetens. 'That was nice of you.' Maya must love animals, even rats and odd fish.

I can't meet her eyes. 'Not really. I put them in the river. But they were saltwater fish. Or...'

'What happened?'

'They – they fell apart. Dissolved.' The memory makes me feel sick even though it happened years ago. The silver of their scales turning red and then showing the white of their thin bones.

Maya obviously thinks so too, because she pulls a grossed-out face. 'That's weird. Is the river far away?'

It's less than a hundred metres. That's why I'd taken the fish; it had seemed such an easy thing to set them free. We stop on the bridge and stare at the river, not far below.

Maya says, 'Freshwater wouldn't dissolve saltwater fish. I'm not a fish expert or anything but it must have been something else.'

'It was pretty nightmarish. I should've let them alone. Or just fed them.'

'They would have died anyway,' Maya says flatly. Her hand on my shoulder is light. 'At least they got out of the tank first.'

'I suppose.' I feel marginally better.

Maya moves her hand from my shoulder and touches my cheek. I stay very still, held in a moment of confused hope, before she lowers her hand.

'We should keep going,' I whisper.

The road to Nakagawa is lined with trees and bamboo, and they swish me onwards with a noise like waves. Maya's whistle begins to sound like birdsong. When a stream joins the road to run beside it, we stop and splash our faces. There's a rustle in the trees, and I blink the water from my eyes to see two deer staring at me tensely from a few metres away. Maya beside me is transfixed, until I back away slowly, and she does the same. The deer don't move until we begin cycling, and then they leap on delicate legs, not away from us but alongside, until the road curves and we wheel in opposite directions.

Nakagawa is as quiet and crumbling as the other villages we've passed, but there's more vegetation than I've seen before. A tomato plant droops over a garden wall, weighed down with small red fruit. I eat one, and when it bursts on my tongue, it's sweeter and tangier than any tomato I've ever tasted. Maya eats one hesitantly, and I watch her expression as she tastes it, laugh as she reaches immediately for another. Lotus flowers are growing in the street gutters. The thatched roof of a shrine has become a flowerbed. The village smells like a garden and I want to lie down in the middle of the street and let fruit fall into my mouth.

But the day is passing and shadows are lengthening, and between the old homes that have become greenhouses I get the sense of being watched, peripheral movements of things that I don't *think* will hurt me, but are following me carefully. I don't know if Maya notices anything, but she draws closer to me. Yamagata said that time can become thin like oxygen, but the air is so rich here it makes my head spin. At the blossoming shrine I hear the trickle of water.

'I'm going to see if the water's okay,' I whisper to Maya, who nods and sits on the ground gratefully. She doesn't ask why I'm whispering.

I bow and step under the narrow, faded red torii gate, and find the basin to wash hands and mouth, where water is falling in a steady stream from a metal spout shaped like a turtle. I wash my hands and rinse out my mouth. The water tastes cool and clean, and after a second of debating how sacrilegious it is, I fill two water bottles. In front of the shrine, flanked by narrow-faced stone foxes, I clap and bow.

'Please help me find Dad,' I whisper. 'And thanks for the water.'

The foxes' tails twitch.

I turn carefully and walk out, the back of my neck prickling. The torii gate has branches like trees; were they there before?

Maya is standing when I get back, her eyes round. 'This place is strange,' she whispers raggedly.

I just nod.

My legs groan as I push down on the pedals of my bike, but I speed up and Maya keeps pace, leaving the village behind as quickly as we can. Once it's behind us we start calling and whistling again. We're on a road shaded by trees when I feel time begin to change.

I wave to Maya frantically. 'Don't cycle so fast! We're going into a slow zone now and it might be intense.'

She braces herself and we cycle leisurely for a handful of metres before we reach an abrupt threshold. My ears pop and I stumble off my bike, stomach heaving. I swallow hard and turn to the sound of Maya groaning, her hand over her eyes.

'Shit,' I say, when I'm sure I won't throw up.

Maya lifts her palm slightly and half-opens an eye. 'Damn, that was a thunderbolt of migraine or something,' she says through gritted teeth.

I pull a hand towel out of my bag and pour water over it, then wring it out and drape it gently around her neck. She shivers and for some reason I shiver too. Maya opens her other dark eye.

'That's better,' she says.

I try to reply but my brain has become entirely devoid of thoughts.

Maya's eyes widen, and her lips part in delight and I'm leaning towards her until I realise her gaze isn't on my face, but on something behind me.

'Look,' she breathes.

I twist around hurriedly and pray that she didn't notice my bizarre swerving around her face. Then I see what Maya is pointing at, because ahead of us is springtime. The road of green trees has become an avenue of cherry blossom, an abundance of pink and white sakura petals like clouds anchored to the earth by root and branch.

Maya and I pull ourselves together and wheel our bikes beneath them, not really speaking but murmuring, *so pretty, so beautiful*, over and over again.

'How?' Maya asks eventually.

'It's the slow zone. It's hanami here,' I tell her.

'So a couple of months behind what's normal.' Maya's expression becomes mixed with wariness, fear. 'I didn't think this could happen.'

'They're telling their own time,' I say.

We reach the end of the avenue and find ourselves on the top of a little hill. The road slopes away from us, through overgrown rice fields and, beyond, a stand of trees comes into focus – perhaps the tallest trees I've seen. The sun is going down now, gilding the air as a final gift, and the reddish trunks of those trees glow like bronze. It's the golden light that makes my eye catch a glint up ahead, metal shining and reflecting the end of the day.

'Dad? Dad!' I yell. 'Maya, can you see that?'

Maya doesn't reply, and then I see that she's not standing beside me any more, but slumped over her bike, breath rasping.

'Maya!'

I put my arm around her shoulders and half-carry her to the nearest tree, where I lower her and let her lean against the trunk. Her eyes are squeezed shut and she's bitten her lip so hard I can see the red swell of blood.

'Tell me what's wrong! Where does it hurt?' My hands shake as I feel her forehead, try to catch the pulse fluttering in her wrists.

'Hurts,' Maya gasps. 'My head, ugh, my whole body.'

'That's okay, that's okay.' I put my water bottle to her lips, hand her a painkiller, stick a cool patch to her forehead, and feel a wrench of fear because I should never have brought her this far in.

I watch Maya anxiously as her breathing steadies and creases of pain on her forehead smooth a little.

She opens her eyes painfully. 'I think it's passing. That was … bad.'

I sag in relief. 'I thought you said you were never sick,' I say, and my voice is chilly.

'Yeah, never before now. Are you *angry* at me or something?' she says in disbelief.

I stand up. 'No,' I say, extremely angrily. 'I should never have let you come because obviously this was going to happen!'

'I feel a lot better now,' Maya protests.

'*Nobody* should come this far in. How could anyone still be here—' I stop. I stare at the sakura to avoid Maya's eyes.

After a moment, Maya says, 'Your dad will be okay. We can find him.'

I'm not just thinking about Dad, now; I'm thinking about Mom.

'I mean, *you're* not sick,' Maya notes. 'But why aren't you?'

'I didn't feel good either, when we crossed into the slow zone,' I remind her.

'For, like, a second,' she says.

I shrug. 'I sort of grew up in the zones.' I pause. 'They feel like home.' I steal a glance at Maya, whose face is drawn and pained and kind.

'You go on,' she says. 'I'm gonna wait here.'

'No way—'

Maya ignores me. 'I don't feel so sick, but there is no way in hell I am getting on a bike. You keep searching and I'll keep whistling.' She reaches a hand to me. I take it. 'We've come this far,' she says, 'and you can go further. You said you saw something, didn't you?'

I turn towards the glint I had seen in the distance. 'Yeah. But ... if something happens...'

I think of the kitsune, the tengu, the other peering spirits. They've never hurt me, though now I wish there was a little jizo to watch over Maya, just in case.

Maya tugs on my hand, hard enough to pull me down so that my face is level to hers. 'Be back before it gets dark, okay? Please?'

She kisses me, quick and light. Her mouth tastes like all the other fruit I've eaten while wandering through the time zones; sweet and heady and unexpected, like secrets, or gifts.

We part, and I take a deep breath and say, 'I'll come back.'

腐草為蛍

ROTTING GRASS
BECOMES FIREFLIES

23

I speed down the hill, the wind welcome on my warm cheeks. I cycle fast, shouting for Dad as my lungs ache and my throat rasps.

I try to count the distance I cover – how many kilometres of broken-down road? I force my eyes forward, because there isn't long before the sun sets. I don't see that glint I'd noticed from the hill until the road rises again, and then a gleam catches my eye.

It's the metal frame of a bike, and beside it is a figure lying, half on the road, half in the lush grassy verge, in the shade of a slender tree.

'*Dad!*'

I pedal furiously, avoiding the deep ruts, so fast that I skid past him, almost tumbling off my bike.

'Dad, Dad!' I shout.

His eyes blink and he raises his head to stare at me blankly. For a moment I think that this is some other man, it's not Dad at all – but then his eyes clear and he seems to recognise me, but the name he says is not mine. It's my mother's.

I falter, but fall to my knees beside him, taking his hands, touching his face, helping him sit up. I expect to feel a shock but there's nothing.

'It's me,' I say. 'I'm not— I'm Sora.'

Dad blinks and scrunches up his face as if I'm a fluorescent light that's just been switched on. 'The results of my research are inconclusive,' he declares hoarsely. 'I can't really make sense of it. Sora.'

When he says my name, my sense of relief is so immense I let myself collapse on the ground beside him. I breathe out. 'What results?'

'Time is going faster and slower...' He looks as though he hasn't slept in days.

'Yeah. How do you feel?'

He pauses and nods. 'Tired.' He has a backpack with him, grubby and crumpled in an almost-empty way. 'The time here is...'

'Slow?' I open my bag for my water bottle and hand it to him.

Dad holds it gently. 'People are frightened by time. Or they want it.'

I open the bottle and hold it to his mouth. 'Drink.'

When the water touches his mouth, he remembers what thirst is and gulps and gulps until it's empty. He catches his breath. 'Those are the results.'

He must be delirious, but at least he's talking. I go along with it because I think that's what you're supposed to do to stop people from losing consciousness. 'What's the inconclusive part?'

'Why.'

'Because I want to know.'

'I mean, that's what's inconclusive. *Why* people are afraid or want to have it. I don't understand.' He shakes his head.

He hasn't even asked how I found him or thanked me. 'Because death,' I say sharply. 'People don't want to die. Isn't that why people do a lot of things?'

His expression is the most perfect example of bewilderment I have ever seen. It could be put in a picture dictionary beside the word.

I scan him for injuries, but I can't see any.

'Why don't people want to die?' he asks. 'That's what I don't understand.'

'What are you trying to say?' My voice is thin and scared.

He stares down at the grass. 'They were all here, before you came.'

'Who?'

'Well, not all. But she was…'

I crouch beside Dad and grab his shoulders. 'Did you see people?' I steady my grip on him. 'Was Mom here?'

Dad stares into my face. 'She's gone now, Sora, she left.'

'Where's she gone?' I ask.

'Some other place. Where there are trees,' he answers hoarsely.

He drops his head and his shoulders shake under my hands.

I stare at the tall beautiful trees in the distance, ready to get on my bike again, but Dad is still shaking. I can feel his bones.

'It's all right, Dad,' I say gently. 'But we need to go home.' I stand, and when he doesn't move I pull him up. I pick up his bag. 'When did you last eat? Or drink?'

'Morning.' He leans on me heavily.

'Which morning?'

'Which?'

'You've been gone for days!' I stop and stand right in front of him. 'Look at me. Dad, you're sick.'

'I can't remember!' he shouts, so suddenly that I stumble backwards.

Then I get angry. 'You didn't make notes?' He always makes notes.

'Yes, I did. Though maybe they were taken... I don't know if they can touch anything, though, not really,' Dad mutters. 'They're only shadows, but where are the rest of them – who casts the shadows?'

Goosebumps run down my neck like a trickle of cold water.

'I don't know, Dad. Are you hungry?' I give him an onigiri before he says anything else. I haul his bike upright while he eats. He's hungry the way he was thirsty.

'Better?' I ask.

'Yes, much.' He's more alert, but he doesn't ask me any questions, not about how long I've been looking for him or if I'm okay, or what has happened since he's been gone.

'Can you walk?' I ask. 'My friend came with me, she's waiting for us.'

'A friend? Yes, yes, I can walk.'

But he's clumsy. I wheel the bikes, one in each hand, fix my eyes on the pink hill and pray that Maya is okay. Maya's whistle shrills, as if she knows what I'm thinking.

She's waiting at the top of the hill, but hesitates for a moment before rushing over. 'It *is* you!' she exclaims. She hugs me.

'Who else would it be?' I say into her shoulder. 'Did you see something?'

'Who is this?' Dad asks.

'This is Maya, she came to help me find you—'

'Maya,' Dad says. 'Maya, I am found.' He sits heavily on the ground.

'I'm so glad,' she says warmly, but shoots me a concerned look.

'How are you doing?' I say in an undertone.

'Okay. I adjusted a bit, I think. Is your dad all right?' she asks quietly.

'He's not great. We need to get out of here.'

She nods decisively. 'Let's get going.'

The three of us walk back to Nakagawa. The sun is setting. Maya and I stumble as we pass back into the fast zone, but Dad doesn't react at all. For some reason this scares me. I set a faster pace.

At the shrine in Nakagawa, I tell Dad to sit as I lean the bikes against a wall. Maya sits down without having to be told.

'I'm going to get water,' I say to Dad. 'Do you have a bottle I can fill?'

'In my bag.'

I open it. Apart from the empty bottle, there's a flashlight, a notebook, folded papers and torn maps.

'Wait here with Maya,' I tell him.

I pass through the torii gate. Everything is still. I fill my bottle, bow and back away.

Dad is sitting on the kerb, looking at the spot where I had been standing while Maya watches him, confused.

Dad's speaking. 'Water is fine, unless there's a nice cold beer, Sora-chan. Some yakitori would go perfectly with it. But if you can't get that, water and imagination will do me fine.' He laughs at his own little dad joke.

'Imagination it is,' I say.

He twists around. 'That was fast, weren't you just here?' He stares back to where I'd been, where he'd been talking to. He doesn't drink from the bottle I hand him. 'Something happened – you were there and then here...'

'You're dehydrated,' I say.

Maya says in my ear, 'I didn't see anything. He's pretty disorientated.'

I go to the spot Dad had been talking to. 'I don't feel anything.'

'It must have disappeared. But why?' I don't know who he's asking, but it's not me.

'You've felt this before?' I ask.

Now he chooses to drink the water. 'It has only begun to happen recently. It comes and goes and I'm—'

'You've never mentioned it,' I say.

'It comes and goes and I'm—' He stops again.

This isn't good. 'We need to go home now. Bikes, everyone.'

Dad gets on and wobbles into balance. Maya flinches as she settles into the saddle. I lead the way, going slower than I want and probably too fast for Dad and Maya. We cycle in silence for about two painful hours, because Dad and Maya can't seem to spare the breath and I don't know what to say.

Dad calls a stop. He's breathing heavily. I give him a protein bar. I should have brought more. He eats it and doesn't question why I'm not having anything. Maya shares an onigiri with me and I want to kiss her again, just for that.

It's pitch dark now, though the moon is round and bright again. We have lights. We'll follow the road. It'll be all right.

When he finishes eating, I say, 'Let's go.'

'What's the hurry?' Dad says. 'We're having a pleasant bike ride, aren't we...'

I honestly can't tell whether he's joking or not. 'You don't seem to care about how long you've been gone for. Do you know how worried I was? You haven't asked a thing about me! Or Maya, who came all the way here to search for you!'

Maya touches my arm, shaking her head.

'You know what the closest thing to *nice* has been so far?' I snap.

Dad's face says he doesn't want to know.

'Finding you still breathing, Dad, that's what.'

Maya winces and looks away, and now having her witness a family fight seems like the worst thing I've subjected her to yet.

Dad gets back on the bike. When it's clear he isn't going to say anything, I sit on my saddle and ram my feet on to the pedals as if they're a punchbag. Eventually, I have to slow down. I'm tired, I'm hungry, and of course I don't feel good. But there's something else happening to me. My head is spinning but my balance is still fine. It feels like things are blurring, and I don't know why because when I raise my hand to my face I can see it well enough, even in the almost-darkness. I'm moving, but something is tugging me back, and for a moment I think I've stopped cycling – but when I check the road beneath my tyres I'm still going forward.

Suddenly Maya is beside me, reaching across the space between our bikes. She grips my shoulder, hard. Both our bikes wobble and I almost fall, jerking my balance back into the saddle. I shake my head, blink.

'Was I was falling asleep or something?' I watch Dad cycle laboriously towards us, and feel a stab of shame. 'I'm sorry you had to see us fighting. And sorry you heard the horrible things I said.'

'It's okay. People in extreme circumstances do out-of-character things.'

'Were *you* in an extreme circumstance earlier?' I blurt out.

'Were *you*?' Maya shoots back.

'No! I mean, yes, about the circumstance but no to the out-of-character!' I say, though it's the first time I've kissed a girl so actually that counted as out-of-character even though it hadn't felt that way.

I can't see her expression well enough to read it, but then she starts to giggle, and I resume living. I want to kiss her again, but Dad is beside us, and it's also when I see something in the distance.

I'm slow enough to recognise what it is that by the time I do, it's too late to slip down a side street or hide in a house.

'What's that?' Dad asks, at almost the exact same moment.

They get nearer; two small vans, headlights like yellow eyes on stalks.

'I think,' I say, with a sinking feeling, 'it's a search party.'

'For—' Dad begins, and then says, 'Oh.'

'I told you that you've been gone for days, didn't I?'

'What did you do?' Dad asks.

'Me? What did *I* do? I reported you missing to the police!'

'That's not the police.'

He's right. It's not.

'You told the company too?'

'What company?' Maya asks.

'My old employer. Well, I suppose they can't fire me again.' Dad gives a short sarcastic laugh.

'You're horrible.' I'm the kind of angry that could make me cry, and that is exactly what I don't want to do.

Dad finally looks at me properly, with some sort of understanding, some kind of sympathy.

'I didn't even know how long you'd been gone. The house was—' My voice is choked.

'Of course you had to call them. I'm not angry at you. I didn't intend for it to sound that way. I'm sorry.' He reaches and touches my shoulder. 'All I mean is … you shouldn't be here. Or me. Or your friend.'

'What's going to happen?' Maya asks.

'They won't harm us, don't worry,' Dad says reassuringly.

The vans speed up. They've seen us. Maya doesn't appear very reassured.

The headlights fix on us and Dad's face is illuminated in the harsh light. I didn't notice before now that his hair has turned entirely grey.

The vans stop and three figures, dressed in baggy white one-pieces, masks and hard hats, get out.

'We found you.' It's Yamagata. He doesn't sound overjoyed.

I want to point out that *I'm* clearly the one who found Dad but I keep my mouth shut.

'And who are *you*?' Yamagata says to Maya.

'An exchange student,' she replies expressionlessly in Japanese, and I have to clamp my mouth shut to stop the giggles.

Dad bows. 'Yamagata-san. I'm sorry.'

I clear my throat. 'Thank you. You didn't have to—'

Yamagata's eyes flick to me. 'I know. Please get into the van, all of you. It's not wise to linger here.'

The driver opens the door of one of the vans and beckons us. The driver of the other van heaves all our bikes inside. We get into the van, Yamagata in the front beside the driver. It's only when we've buckled ourselves in that I'm aware of how Dad stinks of sweat and dirt. I'm glad that I'm between him and Maya. The van starts moving.

Yamagata turns to look at Dad. 'How long have you been in this zone for?'

'Perhaps ... three days?' Dad's obviously guessing.

'And you, Sora-san? I assume this exchange student went in with you, or did you happen to find her here too?'

I check my watch. It's ticking erratically, hands pointing at ten o'clock. 'Thirteen hours,' I say. From the outside, it's probably been about eighteen, even nineteen hours, but I don't want to show how much I know.

Yamagata stares at my watch. 'Is that reliable?'

'It's a good watch,' I say.

He looks at me evenly. 'If you entered the zone after you called me, then you have been here almost thirty-six hours.'

Maya gasps beside me.

'I told you,' Yamagata says coldly, 'that it is dangerous.'

'But you came...'

'The police wouldn't. Cannot. For the same reasons you shouldn't have,' Yamagata answers.

'That's why I *did*.'

'It seems as though you were more capable than the

police, in any case. How did you know where he would be?'

'I had,' I say blandly, 'a dream.'

Yamagata raises his eyebrows, and, as I see in the rearview mirror, so does the driver. I feel Maya tremble beside me, and I'm glad that it's her turn to hide laughter.

'Really.' Yamagata is not asking a question.

'I know I shouldn't have come here, but I was so worried about my father. You understand that, don't you? He's all I have left.' Even though it works well for my plea, I'm embarrassed to find genuine tears gathering in my eyes.

'Of course I understand.' Yamagata sounds entirely unsympathetic. 'Even though Campbell-san is not currently an employee, you still have a connection to the company. Particularly in this context.'

Of course. Too much to think it was out of pure kindness.

'Well, thank you for bringing us home.'

'We are taking your father to a hospital. In fact,' Yamagata's eyes rest on Maya, 'I think all of you should go.'

Dad stiffens. 'I'm fine.'

'It will likely just be for a day or two. You need observation, Campbell-san. Not many people have been so deep in a zone for so long.'

'I'm not an experiment,' Dad replies sharply.

'You need to go.' My voice is hard. If he thinks this is an experiment, fine. He can know how it feels.

Dad turns to me but I stare out of the window. The van is silent. Dad falls asleep almost immediately. I hold Maya's hand until she dozes off. Judging by our speed, we'll be out of the zone in a couple of hours. Things look different from the van. More abandoned, more decaying. Maybe because we're going so fast and it's so dark I can't see any of the small things that make everything more beautiful.

We cross through a boundary fence as the sun begins to rise, and follow familiar roads to a hospital. We park. I pat Dad's shoulder to wake him and then I hiss through my teeth. There's no sudden jolt when I touch him; now there's a steady static hum. I touch Maya's arm but to my relief, there's nothing – only her warmth and slow movement as she wakes.

Yamagata gets out before I can say something. The door slamming startles Dad from sleep.

'We're here already.' His voice is stubbly with tiredness. 'When did we cross the border? I don't remember showing my passport.'

I rub my hand. 'Passport?' I say.

He stares at me, then past me out of the window. He rubs his eyes. 'I was dreaming. Is the hospital really necessary?'

'Dad, you're not well. You've forgotten more than ever before—'

Yamagata is at Dad's window now, gesturing to us.

'No,' Dad murmurs. 'It's more like I'm remembering—'

Yamagata opens the door. 'Come in, please.'

I take Maya's hand again, because she's groggy and quiet and puffy-eyed. The hospital is almost empty. I check the clock in the waiting room. It's nearly six in the morning. Yamagata speaks to the receptionist, who stares at us in alarm. I don't know what Yamagata is telling her, but we're brought to the top floor, to a private room. I sit down and all the tiredness I've ignored falls into my lap.

Yamagata reappears with a doctor, who tells us that they'll be observing us for effects of disorientation, physical sickness, mental alertness.

'I'll go now.' Yamagata bows. He looks tired.

Dad and I bow back.

'Thank you,' I say, and I truly mean it.

'I hope,' he says, 'that I have done something you consider *fair*.'

'Not fair,' I admit, 'but kind.'

Yamagata nods, gives me a look that could have been a warning, and leaves.

Maya's taken into a different room, but I stay with Dad.

The doctor takes Dad's temperature, his blood pressure, shines a bright light into his eyes and checks his reflexes. They seem slow but she doesn't comment. She asks him a series of rapid questions about headaches, stomach cramps, dizziness, which he answers stumblingly.

Then she says, 'Breathe deeply and relax. Please tell me when you think one minute has passed.' She sits calmly in a chair behind him and beckons me to do the same.

Interesting. I watch Dad's back, slumped in exhaustion or weakness. I can see the curve of his spine through his grubby T-shirt. Fifty seconds have passed. The doctor silently checks her watch. I will Dad to say something, but then it's sixty-five seconds, then seventy, eighty, ninety... The doctor is watching him with more attention now.

Finally, finally, at one hundred and ten seconds, Dad speaks. 'Perhaps it's been a minute?' He's unsure.

'Thank you,' the doctor says evenly, and makes a note. She moves in front of him, telling him that they will do some blood tests and give him an IV.

I follow and try to be as composed and neutral as her, but when Dad glances over at me his expression changes with a flash of something that might be despair. Maybe he's mirroring my face. I force a smile.

A nurse comes in and gives Dad hospital pyjamas and points him to the bathroom, and when he returns he's cleaner, and perhaps he's clearer too. He gets into bed and instantly looks like a patient.

'Sora-chan, you should go home,' Dad tells me.

The doctor has reappeared. 'Before you do, I'll check you quickly,' she says.

She hardly waits for me to agree before doing all the tests she had done with Dad, then declares me in decent condition.

'Really?' Because how could I not be becoming like Dad, forgetful and lost in time?

She gives me a long, appraising look. 'The tests show

nothing out of the ordinary.' There was a faint stress on the word *tests*. 'You're young. However, you need to be careful.'

'I know,' I say.

The doctor sighs, as if she can tell that my knowing won't change very much. She turns to Dad and snaps on a pair of rubber gloves. 'I'm going to take a blood sample.'

'Please, Sora-chan. Home. Sleep. I'll call you tomorrow,' Dad says.

All of a sudden I don't want to see Dad getting his blood taken, don't want to see the needle disappearing into his arm or the red filling up the syringe. 'Promise?' I say.

'Promise, promise, promise,' Dad says.

I stand up. 'I'll come right back if you need anything.'

The doctor holds the needle in her hand calmly, waiting for me to go. I pick up my bag and leave. I hear the faintest hiss of breath as the needle slides into skin.

I find Maya in the next room. She's already tucked into bed, much calmer and tidier than Dad.

'I know I was going to stay at yours but this bed is actually pretty comfy,' she says.

I sit in the chair beside the bed. 'I'd choose this too. There's no call button in our guest room.' I don't say that we don't even have a guest room.

'I'm sorry,' I say in a rush, 'and thank you.'

'You're welcome. I wanted to go with you, okay? That was *my* decision, not yours.' Maya wags a finger at me. 'It was an interesting trip, and it ended well, right?'

I nod, but Dad with his grey hair and confusions doesn't feel like a happy ending.

'Nomura-sensei's going to have to let me do more research after this,' Maya says.

'Are you going to tell her?' I say in alarm.

Maya hesitates. 'Yeah, probably not. Well, not everything. I won't say anything about your dad.'

'And me?'

'Oh, she knows about you.' Maya grins.

'She wants me to plant that sapling in one of the zones because she's doing some tests with water. Probably should have brought it with us because I don't want to go back in there for a while.'

'The waters she's using are both from the same stream in one of the zones, but one's upstream and one's downstream. Dunno if there's any difference – which is interesting because I thought the water from deeper in the zone would have some kind of effect.' Maya yawns. 'Like your poor fish from the tank.'

I flinch. She squeezes my hand.

'You said they died because they weren't in the right water... but what if the water's time and the fish's time were just different?' She blinks at me. 'Does that even make sense? I feel like I'm doing an all-nighter to finish an essay and I just got a really great idea or an incredibly dumb one.'

'Don't rely on me to tell the difference! They were both in the same zone, though. But...' I trail off, thinking.

'I'm glad I got to see the zones. They were so strange and gorgeous.' Maya's voice is dreamy. 'When you left and I waited, I kept remembering things. Like there were memories floating through the air.'

'I know,' I whisper. 'That happens to me too.' I lean forward and give her a shy kiss, and her lips curve beneath mine. 'I'm going to let you sleep.'

'Goodnight,' Maya says.

I leave the hospital, my heart beating and hurting with love and fear.

梅子黄

PLUMS TURN YELLOW

24

The sunlight stretches in through my window hopefully. The liquid, looping call of a bird twirls in from outside. I peer at my watch, still on my arm because I fell asleep before I could take it off. Its hands seem sluggish, but when I check it against my alarm clock it's correct. Nine a.m. – did I only sleep for an hour? I squint at my phone and catapult up. I slept for twenty-five. I fumble, searching for the hospital's number and stammering Dad's name when a calm voice answers.

'Sora?'

'Dad! I slept so much longer than I meant to – are you okay?'

Dad sounds tired and amused. 'Don't worry. I only woke up a little while ago.'

I fall back on my pillow. 'My timing was good, then.'

'As always.'

'I'm going to come see you now. Do you need anything?'

'The usual fruit and flowers, I suppose. Oh!' he adds, 'Balloons.'

'I thought balloons were only if you had a baby.'

'How unfair. In that case, pyjamas would be appreciated.'

'How much longer will you be staying there for?'

A pause.

'I'm not certain, but I do know that these hospital pjs are not very comfortable.'

'I'll bring you some of your own.'

'Thank you, Sora-chan. See you soon.'

I consider calling Maya but even after everything that happened I don't know if we're at the phone call stage. Maybe after the next near-death experience we have together?

I message, *good morning. you feeling okay?*

I shower and dress and rummage up breakfast. I send messages to Koki and his mom, telling them that Dad's been found and is recovering. Fujiwara-san responds with a line of relieved emojis, and Koki calls me, but I cancel it and message to say I'll talk later. I add a few hearts to soften it.

No reply from Maya yet, but she's probably still sleeping – it's going to take her longer to recover. Worry twinges through me. But I'll see her soon, right after Dad.

In Dad's room I search for pyjamas with the specific fear that comes from looking through a parent's possessions. Should I really take flowers? I pass the kitchen – the sapling is longing towards the window. I pick it up and take it with me.

When I get to the hospital it's quiet, and nobody asks why I have a small tree with me. Dad's eyes open as I enter the room. He's less pale, more rested, but he's tired. His grey hair has aged him by ten years.

'How do you feel?'

'Sleepy, but that's fine. The body's medicine, sleep.' He seems preoccupied, chatting to me but focused on something else inside his head.

I sit beside him. I'm afraid to touch him. 'I'm sorry I was gone so long.'

'You needed a rest.'

'I mean when I went to Tokyo.'

'I know.'

'Is that why you didn't message me or anything?'

Dad looks down at his hands. There's a tube in his left one, connecting to the IV bag. 'Is it...'

I try another question. 'What were you doing out there?'

'I had to investigate what you told me—'

I wince. Dad doesn't notice.

'I've never noticed those *jolts*, and I went into one of the zones and returned to see if I could feel it then. But there was nothing, so I supposed I had to go further.'

'But, Dad, *that* far in!'

'I didn't mean to. At a certain point, it began to feel different. It would be more accurate to say I was following something,' he says haltingly. 'I had to go on. Deeper in.'

I try to speak gently. 'What were you following?'

'Remember at the shrine, that part in the centre? I thought it was normal time but the sand was suspended. It was between times, really. I brought a sand timer and kept checking it. And there were...' Dad turns his head on the pillow, towards the window. 'As though...people were calling me. But I couldn't find. I could only follow. There was a strange place...' He trails off and then returns to himself, a little. 'Hallucinations, I think. They have been reported before.'

I grip the metal bar on the side of the bed. 'Where were you trying to go?'

'I'm not sure.'

'You had maps in your bag – where is it?'

Dad turns back to me. 'The bedside locker, I think.'

It's there, grimy and scuffed. Dad unzips it and pulls out the ripped maps. He spreads them out and stares at them in horror. I go through them silently. They're of the same northern area, in different scales, but no routes are drawn on them.

'Notebook?' I suggest.

Dad opens it. Inside, it's all wild slashes and loops; I don't know if it's writing or drawing. He shuts it and lies back.

He says faintly, 'Maybe we can examine it more closely later. No doubt you'll be able to make some deductions.'

'No.' I'm suddenly, blindingly, angry.

Dad pats my hand. 'You know I value your insight.'

'My insight, my opinion, my reasons? You don't value them at all!'

'Sora-chan, we used to—'

'I'm not talking about science, Dad! I'm talking about – about life and, I don't know, *us* – things that aren't measured and proven!' I'm shouting.

Dad stares at the shreds of maps, at my face. 'Please explain,' he says softly.

'You answer all my questions when they're about logic or reasoning but you won't talk to me when I ask about...' My hand is on my heart.

He grimaces slightly.

'About things that are lost, and that we can't explain, and have no reasons,' I whisper. 'About Mom.'

Dad shuts his eyes reflexively. 'It's hard.'

'But you're forgetting things. If you don't talk about them, how will you remember? How will *I* remember?'

He avoids my eyes and looks into the bag. I'm about to scream in frustration when he pauses, then pulls out something slender and gleaming.

It's a gold chain with a flat circular pendant. It catches and warms the cold hospital lights, reflects a shine from another life. Dad hands it to me.

I hold it up, marvelling. 'I'd forgotten about this.'

'You had?'

The pendant swings and dangles. 'I don't know how.'

'Your mother wore it all the time.'

Yes. Tucked into her shirt to keep it out of her way when she was gardening. In the summer, it was almost the same colour as the tanned skin on the back of her neck. And on the pendant... I hold it close to see the faint engraving, smoothed by wear.

'It's a salmon,' Dad says. '*The salmon feeds the trees*, that's what she used to say. That's why she stopped eating salmon.'

'She ate every other type of fish.' I rub my sleeve gently over the pendant to clean it.

'She wasn't perfect.' Dad's face says, *But that didn't matter.*

The fish's curved body, wide mouth, whiskers. 'It's not a salmon,' I say. 'It's a catfish.'

'Really? I always thought it was a salmon.'

'Yeah,' I whisper. 'So did I. Where did Mom get this?'

'Her mother gave it to her. A going-away present before she went to Canada.'

A going away. I give the necklace back to Dad.

He takes it and places it carefully over my head. It's light, it weighs almost nothing, it feels like an anchor, a hand steadying me.

'You had this the whole time?' I ask.

Dad nods. 'Why wasn't she wearing it that day? It was in the car, in the glove box. When I found it, I thought, she can't be gone, she loves this necklace. She would never leave it behind. She will—'

She will come back. We sit in silence.

'I thought you'd got rid of everything.'

Dad shakes his head mutely.

'You tried,' I accuse him. 'And you tried to forget.'

'Yes. I wanted to. I couldn't.'

'You *can't* make yourself forget!' I cry.

Dad speaks over me. 'Sora, you have to move on. You can't hold on to everything. That's not good for you, and it's not even possible to do.'

I'm crying so hard he is forced to stop speaking. 'That's

wrong, you're wrong! Of course she couldn't come back if you didn't want to hold on to her! You stopped looking for her!'

Dad gasps. He's shaking his head, his chest rising and falling too fast, his face becoming paler and paler.

'Oh, no. Shhhh.' I hold his shoulders. 'I don't mean that, I'm sorry.' I lay my head on his chest, trying not to put too much weight on him. There's that terrible hum of electricity, of time, within him, that has returned or never went away. His heartbeat gallops and gallops and slows. He strokes my hair. I sit up and wipe my face. We try to smile at each other convincingly, doing a horrible job.

I begin to tell him what I felt, but what good would it do? I touch the necklace. 'Thank you for this,' I say instead.

He clears his throat. Pats my hand. 'And is that for me?'

'Huh?'

'Your friend in the pot.'

'It's handy to have a friend that won't run away from you.' I pass it to him.

He sniffs it. 'Where did you get this?'

'It was a present.'

'More practical than a bunch of roses. Maybe a touch too big for the bedside.'

'Definitely.'

He raises his eyebrows. 'Are you giving this to me or introducing it to me?'

I'd planned to give to him, but I remember Naomi's request. 'Actually, yeah, I was sort of bringing it to say hello.'

'A terrible gift-giver.'

'I'll bring something better tomorrow.'

'I have all the trees out the window, anyway. They're far away but a tad more impressive than your pal. No offence.' Dad points out of the window.

The grove of trees is thick, a rich and confident green. They're not that close; they're simply very tall. 'I've never noticed them before.'

'They grew while you were gone.'

'I wasn't gone that long.' Then I'm struck by such a strong fear that I grab his hand. '*Was* I?'

'No, no!' Dad holds my hand. 'I'm pulling your leg.'

'Bad joke.' I stand up. 'I'll let you rest until you come up with some better ones.'

'You're right, I'm off-form.' His eyelids are drooping. He releases my hand to touch one of the tender leaves. 'A maple. Shouldn't it be turning red now?'

'Not yet. Not for months.'

Dad nods absently. 'Ah, yes, it's only just springtime.'

My heart drops. 'It's almost June.'

Dad stares at the leaves. 'Nozomi.'

'What?'

'Its Japanese name.'

'It's momiji. Maple. Nozomi is…' Is my mother's name.

'I'm getting sleepy, Sora-chan.' Dad hands me the sapling.

'Yeah, you need a nap.'

Dad smiles and nods. I wait until his breathing is even and then I go to talk to the nurse.

He shakes his head. 'No, we won't be discharging him. We need to monitor him because he's still in quite a weakened state.'

Don't say it. Don't say it. Don't say it. I say it. 'Is he going to get better?'

'Your father is making a good recovery since he was admitted,' the nurse says carefully. 'As for the long term, I can't answer. It would be best to speak to the doctor...'

'Can I speak to the doctor tomorrow?' I'll tell her about the jolts, which have now become that horrible vibration in Dad. Whatever good that will do.

The nurse nods. 'Yes, you can.'

'Thank you.'

I go to Maya's room, hoping I don't look like too much of an emotional wreck. I find her dressed and neat, finger tapping on her phone.

'You're up,' I say, shy all of a sudden.

Maya looks at me, smiling. 'Sora! I was messaging you.'

'And here I am. How do you feel today?'

She stands up. 'Way better. I slept a *lot*. My body's still kinda dead, though. How's your dad?'

'He's ... okay.' I change the subject. 'You think you can leave the hospital today, then? We can—' What *could* we do?

Maya shakes her head. 'I'm sorry, that's why I was messaging you. I've got to go back to Tokyo.'

'Already?' I wish that sounded less needy.

'We lost all that time in the zone, so when I woke up I

remembered I have a dumb but important test today. And I was only going to stay one night.'

'Oh, no, I didn't even think about it!'

'It's okay, I'll be able to do the test, but passing it? We shall see.'

I laugh and want to cry.

'I'm sorry I can't stay.' She leans in and kisses me delicately. 'It all turned out okay, didn't it?'

I nod, but I don't know yet. I want to hold her, ask her what this means, what will happen.

'I've got to go. I'll talk to you soon,' she says.

'Good luck with the test,' I force out. 'And thank you.'

She's gone and I'm left in an empty hospital room. Soon Maya will be back in Tokyo, in her normal life far away from me. I shake my head, trying to dislodge this idea, but my thoughts are a chaos of confusion. I put my hand on the little golden fish at my throat. It feels like a promise, but of what I don't know.

'What's wrong?' Mom asked me.

'They laughed at me in class.' I threw my schoolbag on the ground, threw myself on the couch.

'Why?' Mom sat on the arm of the couch and looked down at me in concern.

'We were learning about salmon and had to draw a salmon and I drew this and everyone thought it was dumb.' I was in second grade.

Mom prised the crumpled paper out of my hand and spread it out. She giggled. 'You drew Kirimi-chan?'

'You're laughing too!' I yelled.

'In a good way!' Mom protested. 'I think it's a very good drawing.'

Kirimi-chan was a Japanese character like Hello Kitty. Unlike Hello Kitty, who was a girl that *looked* like a cat, Kirimi-chan was a being that had a salmon fillet for a head. It turned out that the other kids in my class, and also my teacher, were not familiar with this character.

'I'll put it on the fridge,' Mom promised.

'Don't. I need to draw a boring real salmon now. They're ugly.' I kicked my legs and slid on to the floor in protest.

'Maybe they're not the prettiest. I'll help you. Why were you learning about them?' Mom grabbed my arms in her small rough hands and dragged me across the floor.

'All the salmon are coming up the river. The bears eat them and people eat them. That's it. Boring.'

'Hmmm.' Mom sat at her laptop and started typing. 'Oh. Wow.' She fell silent, clicking and tapping, for so long that I tugged at her leg and clambered on to her lap.

'Salmon!' she exclaimed. 'I never knew. They're wonderful.'

I groaned and flopped over her. She read slowly, switching to English. 'The salmon come from the sea and return to the streams and rivers where they were born. On the way, they are caught by bears and humans. Indigenous peoples have relied on salmon for generations as food.

Salmon is honoured because it was the first animal to offer itself to be eaten to help people.'

'Stupid salmon. Why would it do that?' I muttered.

'Because it's kind. It wanted to help humans live. It regrets that now, probably,' Mom said. 'Listen. When bears eat salmon, they leave the remains by the rivers, and then birds eat them, and other animals and then – Sora-chan! – then what's left is absorbed into the soil and then into the *trees*. The salmon help the trees grow!'

'Weird.' I was bored.

'Sora-chan, it's beautiful. I never knew...' Mom was transfixed.

'Can you get a picture of a salmon so I can copy it?' I asked.

'Wait a minute.' She was reading stuff in Japanese that I couldn't follow, staring at photos of trees beside rivers.

'You love trees more than me!' I said dramatically.

'Well,' she said, 'they are quieter.'

I shrieked and she got annoyed and told me to stop it.

'What's the matter?' Dad said from the doorway.

'Oh, you're home,' Mom said. 'We're learning about salmon. They're very important.'

'You're only discovering this now?' Dad set an armful of books down on the kitchen counter. He laughed. 'How long have you been here, Nozomi? The definition of the Pacific Northwest is anywhere a salmon can get to.'

I felt Mom stiffen. 'I'm learning now. Like Sora.'

'Of course Sora's learning. She's a child,' Dad said.

Mom stood up and almost dumped me on to the floor. '*You* help her draw a salmon.'

'I have a lot of work—'

'So do I.' Mom went out into the garden.

I watched Dad follow her and their mouths move as they argued. I drew the salmon by myself.

When I get home I put an enka playlist on, but the house is still too quiet and too empty. The only other living thing is the sapling, which has thickened, grown more branches to hold the air, more leaves to drink it in.

I touch it. 'What's up with you?'

I give it some water and watch it soak into the soil, thinking about Naomi and her experiments.

I hear the earthquake before I feel it; the creak and jingle of wood and glass warning me just before the jerk makes my knees buckle. I grip the sink with one hand, the pot with the other. Another jump, another. They are fierce and hard, up-and-down instead of the side-to-side of most quakes. They stop before I can move under the table.

I look at the clock, at the second hand jumping forward. Then at my watch. It's quickening, but not as fast as the wall clock. It begins to even out. The wall clock doesn't. This is weird. An even bigger disturbance, to make them so clearly different. My watch hand is still clutching the pot, and my eyes are drawn to the sapling's narrow trunk – why? I stare. Move my face closer to be sure. I can see the trunk swelling. My watch is slowing.

My phone blares an alarm, too late. I grab it and turn it off. A six. A short one but bigger than anything else recently. Fear hits me hard and I have to push it down, shove it away. Not now, not with everything.

The second hand of the wall clock settles down. The sapling has paused its growing, or at least it's not visible to my eye. Something tickles at my brain.

I remember what Maya had said, about the water and those poor fish I'd released into it, how their times might have been different. It wasn't about the different zones, exactly; it was the river, the water. Because what do time and distance mean to a river, always in motion? Impossible to step into the same one twice. Can it carry time within it, though? Can it absorb it into itself, and if it does, does time become less? There could be time captured in pebbles, in stones, in soil. I stare at the sapling, unfurling itself. In trees. Not in man-made things, too flimsy and unnatural. Not in animals or humans, too subjective and brief. Dad's body can't absorb and hold time – nobody's can. But he'll fall apart trying.

I think of that tall grove I saw from the window of the hospital, almost glowing with green. The trunks and branches like bronze. Dad said Mom was somewhere where there are trees. And the earth shaking itself more often, more violently, more and more. Seconds and minutes slipping and jumping.

Dad going to pieces and Mom maybe – just maybe – within reach. I have to go.

夏至

SUMMER SOLSTICE

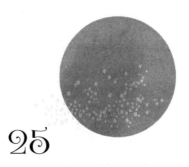

25

At Hisakawa's shrine, I pause by the kitsune. Messengers to the gods, Hisakawa had said, but I have no message to pass on. I gaze at the ancient tree.

'Ah, hello.'

I jump and whirl. Of course it's Hisakawa. He's probably wired directly to the foxes.

'Hello,' I say, as normally as I can. 'I'm just going to...' I gesture vaguely towards the back of the shrine.

He nods thoughtfully. 'Time is shifting again, isn't it? I can feel it. I checked the sand timers, as your father insisted.'

'What are they doing?'

'The middle one was broken.' Hisakawa held up his hand and pinched his thumb and forefinger together. 'Too much pressure. It shattered.'

I don't know how that could have happened, but I shiver thinking of the sea depths where the weight of water will crush.

'The balance is gone?' I ask.

'Perhaps.'

'I have to … check it.'

'There's only now – that's what some say,' Hisakawa continues.

It's the conversation we had the last time I was here. Is he disorientated too?

He goes on, 'Every instant, everything is now, again and again.'

It's like what Dad and Soo-jin told me years ago, about time stopping and starting. But I tell Hisakawa, 'I still don't understand.'

'Neither do I.' He winks.

I have absolutely no idea what he is saying but I can't help smiling.

His face becomes serious. 'Be careful, Sora-san.' His eyes flicker. 'There are many lost and searching things.'

I swallow. 'Dangerous things?'

'Am I dangerous? Are you?' he asks.

'Sometimes,' I whisper.

He nods. 'The kitsune will keep you safe, I think.'

I don't question this. 'Okay. Thanks.'

He raises a hand and watches me go.

I continue until the shrine hides Hisakawa from view, until I come to those three old fox statues. I stand in front of the one in the centre. I shift back and forth until I find it: that strange place between the fast and slow zones. It's not normal time, I can feel that even more clearly now. It's something else. Then I walk along it, balancing as if on a tightrope. It's a struggle with my bike, but I follow the line out of the trees and on to the road, which it miraculously aligns with.

I feel where it's going: north. To that tall grove of trees I'd seen from Dad's hospital window, which was close to where I'd found Dad. He'd said that Mom would be where there were trees. This must be a sign. Here is the path and those trees are the compass. I follow them as directly as I can. It pulls on my body and I abandon myself to it. I don't count my heartbeats or keep track of minutes or hours. Measuring time isn't important any more. Did Dad feel this and try to follow it too?

The sun is strong and high in the sky, no clouds to stop it. My sweat drips on to the sapling's leaves and the dry soil absorbs it. Uh oh. Salt is probably not good for it. I stop and feed it some water, then drink some myself. There isn't much left. The road ahead is empty except for a tidy house with a blue-tiled roof glimmering like a mirage.

When I reach it, I lean my bike against the wall and pick up the sapling. I ease myself in through the front door. It's surprisingly dustless. I slip my shoes off and go down the short corridor and into the kitchen, also clean and tidy. I cross my fingers and turn the kitchen tap and water pours from it like a wish come true. I let it run and gaze out of the window. Somebody used to stand here washing dishes, looking out the same way I am, at children or the birds or their vegetables growing. I hold the sapling under the water and then put my mouth to the stream and drink. I wipe my mouth and pick up the pot.

'You should use a glass,' a voice says, and I almost have a heart attack.

I spin around. 'Hello?'

'Hello.'

It's an old woman's voice, disembodied until I spot her in the next room. She's kneeling, her face in profile. She doesn't turn to me and I'm seized by a fear instilled by ghost stories, that if I get closer I'll see that she has no face at all. It's a trick a tanuki or fox would play.

'Come here.' The fond impatience in her voice moves me with the inexplicable power of a grandma.

My heart still pounds as I leave the kitchen and cross the tatami to the figure kneeling in the engawa, doors open to the sunshine. A wrinkled hand beckons: *come, come*. She keeps her eyes closed and head tilted back as if she's drinking in the sun. She pats the cushion beside her, but I don't sit. After all my searching, I never expected to find somebody so normal and solid and unconcerned.

'Are you ... real?' I ask.

The old woman opens her eyes, which are sharp and bird-bright. 'Are *you* real?'

I shake my head because right now this question is too philosophical to answer. 'I try to be.'

She holds her hand out to me, palm upwards. I hesitate, then lay my hand on hers. Her skin is lined and tough and warm. 'Don't stop trying,' she says.

She is real, and alive. I search her face, but I don't know how to tell if someone has aged naturally or through some uncanny effect of the zones.

'Are you alone? Are there other people here?' I ask.

'Around here there's only me,' she says.

'I'm looking for someone,' I say. 'Maybe you've seen her.'

Her eyes take on a pitying shine. She pats the cushion again. 'Sit.'

I sit, and remember my manners, and bow. 'I hope I didn't startle you. I thought this house was empty.'

The old woman raises her eyebrows in a slightly amused way, as if to say she has never been startled in her life. 'How do you know a house is empty if you don't knock?'

'Sometimes I knock. But nobody's ever answered.'

'Ah. Not for me, either,' she says.

Did she search too? Or does she still? She is so tiny and frail.

'Are you okay? Do you need anything?' I ask her.

She inclines her head towards the garden in front of us. 'I need nothing.'

The trees have vibrant apples, oranges, peaches hanging like decorations from their branches. Tall stalks that I guess are sweet potato, carrots, gobo. There's a wide pond with a stream flowing in and out. The water ripples with sleek movement.

'Koi,' she answers without me asking. 'Not many are so colourful any more. They return to their natural colours in a few generations, you know. Without people there to pick and choose them.'

'I didn't know that.'

'They're not so pretty,' she says, 'but they don't get carried away by birds as often.'

'How long have you been here for?' I ask.

'How long,' she repeats. 'In Japan time is measured in the reign of emperors, but there are no emperors here. It doesn't feel so long to me, but to the fish and the koi and the apple trees – well, I don't know. You understand that, don't you?'

I don't know if I do.

'You seem … healthy,' I say. 'You don't feel sick being so far into the zone?'

'I'm *very* healthy,' she corrects me. 'And I have always lived here.'

'So other people could survive here too – and probably even deeper in, right—'

The old woman interrupts my racing thinking-out-loud. 'Let me see your plant.' Her tone brooks no argument.

I offer the pot to her. She gazes at the sapling closely, her eyes moving from the soil to the tips of its young leaves. She breathes deeply.

I open my mouth to interrogate her more, but before I can, she says, 'What's your name?'

'I forgot, I'm sorry. I'm Sora.' I dip my head and introduce myself.

She stares at me closely, then says, 'Miyuki. What is this tree's name?'

'It's a maple.'

'Yes, but what is its *name*?'

'I … don't know.'

'Bad manners,' she scolds.

'The tree didn't ask me my name, either.'

This earns me a smile. 'The tree is a baby, so you're its senpai. You should take charge. Don't you know that?'

'I never thought of myself as being a senpai to a tree.'

'That's because it's quite rare. However, when it happens you must act properly.'

The old woman's lecturing reminds me of my own obaachan so much that I get an intense rush of memory, of her faded blue house jacket, the sound of her busy voice.

'Sora-chan?' Her eyes search mine. 'Did your mind get called away?'

'Sorry. Please say that one more time.'

'Introduce yourself.'

I'm not sure if she's serious until she nods at me impatiently, as if I'm embarrassing her in front of an important audience. Which, in this situation, is clearly the tree. I release what's left of my dignity. I stand up, bow, and speak my best formal Japanese to introduce myself, and throw in another deep bow. I straighten up to find the old woman tilting the pot back towards me in, what I can't help noticing, is a clearly shallower bow. So much for being senpai.

'Very nice,' Miyuki says approvingly.

'What's the tree's name, though? I still don't know.'

'Keep listening,' she says. 'You'll hear it in the end.'

We both regard the tree until it wobbles in her hands. I reach and cradle the pot with her.

Her eyes blink slowly. She releases the tree to me. 'Now you must return it to the earth. Older sisters need to help their younger siblings grow.'

'If you love something, let it go; if it loves you, it will come back,' I quote from whatever fridge magnet I read that saying on. It doesn't have quite the same ring to it in Japanese.

She gives me an extremely sceptical look. 'Nonsense. A person can leave and still love you. Sometimes people go to places they must stay. Sometimes coming back is not what is right. Don't judge love with a rule like that.'

Her scolding sends a sudden surge of anger through me. 'Do you *have* to stay here?'

Miyuki turns to stare out at the garden. 'Perhaps I could have returned, before... Now I think I cannot leave.'

'So you chose to stay. Because you think you can leave and people will still know you love them?'

Miyuki shakes her head as if it hurts. 'There were no people.'

'That's not true. There are lots of us! You left us. Where are the others?' I demand.

'Which *others* do you want?' she says briskly.

'The ones who are missing. I know they're in the zones, somewhere, and I'm going to find them!' I'm shouting but I don't care. There's only this old woman and the fish and the garden to hear.

Miyuki doesn't flinch. 'What will you do if you find them?'

'Bring them back!'

'Them,' she repeats. 'But you said *someone*, first.'

'My mother,' I say fiercely. 'That's who I'll find and bring back. But there could be other people with her. She looks like me, but her hair is black and straight, her name is Nozomi, she's so strong—'

Miyuki touches my shoulder lightly. 'If I see her, I'll tell her you're searching for her.'

'She'll know that already, I'm sure she will,' I say.

Miyuki nods. 'I don't know what's possible any more. Perhaps you can bring them back. Things have been changing...'

I hear it before I feel it; a creaking and rumbling deep below us. I grab Miyuki's hand and put my hand on the floor with the other, as if I'm going to hold it still. She squeezes my hand, and when the shake stops a few seconds later, she doesn't let me go.

'Excuse me,' I mumble.

'Don't worry.' Her hand gripping mine, strong and kind, feels natural and familiar. 'You remember the story I told you?'

'About the tree?' That was hardly a story but okay.

'That wasn't a story, that was common sense,' she says sternly.

'Right. Um. I don't know, then.'

'Namazu is what the fish under the land is called,' she says. 'A fish with whiskers like a cat. It's large, far larger than anything a human fisherman could catch – or even ten fishermen together, or a hundred. It likes the deep and the dark at the bottom of the ocean, but sometimes it wriggles about, or wants to go to shallower water. Perhaps it wants some company, because there aren't many other creatures way down there. Maybe dragons, but they're arrogant and wouldn't give namazu the time of day.'

A hand on my head, on my back, calming me with words among the noise and chaos of a high school gym filled with frightened people. 'Yes,' I whisper. 'I remember.'

'What's the end of the story, then?'

'The namazu twists and jumps under the islands and makes the ground shake and huge waves smash the land. It breaks and kills everything. It's cruel.'

She sighs. 'Cruel.'

'So then the god of thunder came down from heaven – is that Raijin?' I put a hand on my belly button.

She shakes her head. 'No, it was Kashima-sama. Also called Takemikazuchi. He's also a god of thunder, but a different one. Raijin-sama is his senpai. Rainy season,' she says, 'is busy. Go on.'

'Kashima-sama came down and found a big heavy stone and put it on the fish's head, to hold it down at the bottom of the ocean. But it's not heavy or big enough, and the catfish tries to escape and causes earthquakes and tsunamis.'

'It can't be stopped entirely,' she agrees.

'It should be killed. It deserves to die. The god needs to come back and stop the catfish for ever.' It's a myth, a metaphor. But my free hand is clenching and my face is hot.

'Do the gods still have that power? Some say they have left us or that they don't exist.'

I'm surprised she's saying that. 'Have they?'

She gazes at the garden. 'No, they haven't. They're coming back in some places, as you may know. They have to hide more than before. And if we've pushed them away, can we expect them to come and save us?'

'I thought gods were supposed to be like parents.'

'Some gods are, maybe, in other places. The gods here are different, I think.' She turns to me. 'Besides, you're not a child any more.'

'I feel like one.'

'Me too.' Her wrinkles have been carved from laughter. 'What happens in the end?' she asks again.

'That *was* the end.'

Her hand gently daubs the wetness from my cheek with a handkerchief. 'Was it? I can't remember. It could have been a lifetime ago, an emperor's reign ago.'

Her words are too much like Dad's. She must be mixed up like him, all alone here in this zone. 'I think so.'

'Where are you going now?' she asks.

'Towards the trees, the tall grove, there—' I point.

She releases my hand. 'Take care, Sora-chan. Be careful, very careful. And take your time.' She closes her eyes, raises her face to the sky again.

'Goodbye, Miyuki-san,' I reply.

She murmurs something that I can't hear. I'm outside before I understand it was probably the tree's name.

Then I'm cycling fast but everything feels like a dream.

This strip of time or not-time I'm following has become a bridge, and either side and below me I can sense the waves and rolling tides of time falling against each other, forming whirlpools, twisting into swift treacherous currents.

I feel a sudden drag, a current deeper and fiercer than any other curling around me. It's like the disorientation when I was bringing Dad back, the sense of tipping, spinning, pulling. I close my eyes for a moment because this could be a kind of motion sickness, and focus on pedalling and the wind against my face.

When I open my eyes, I'm somewhere else. Still on a road but instead of fields and trees there are the mountains on one side, the sea on the other. It's twilight. I stop my bike too fast, and half-fall off. This has never happened before. Time has never surged so fast. *Space* has never changed.

I'm hyperventilating. I try to slow my breathing. Maybe it's a dream, maybe I fell asleep. Or passed out. I could be in a coma. Please let me be in a coma. But I can feel the skin of my hand when I pinch myself. My bike handles are firm – I can see the spokes as my wheels turn.

I have an urge to call, *Hello. Is anybody there?* like in a horror movie, but nobody in the zones has ever answered me before. I don't know if I'm even *in* a zone. I should turn back, but behind me I see only fog. I back away; that rolling thick greyness is too much, it would envelop me, lay a blanket of nothing over my body.

Maybe there's another side of this place. Or I'll wake up because dreams this vivid are probably possible, right? Lucid dreaming – that's a thing. That's what this could be. I get back on my bike and cycle on. The road changes from cracked and old to even and newly laid and back again. The mountains on my left are bare and smooth, perhaps stone or scrub. There is snow on one peak, but as I watch it, it seems to melt and be replaced by grey-green grass.

On my right is the ocean, and for the first time in my life I don't want to look at it. I can feel it and hear it, and there's something that's not right. I force my eyes to it and watch; the waves are not regular or rhythmic, they're slow and then fast, ebbing and crashing in a confusion of dim noise, like a song out of beat with itself. And not so far in the distance there's a wave. Hokusai's woodcut is a blue-and-white striped thing, curling elegantly and posing for the picture. This wave is not. It's navy and black and looks like it's bringing the deep cold darkness of the ocean with it. I pedal faster and faster, but when I glance again, the wave has moved only a fraction. I slow down and watch it. It's moving with ominous inevitability; it's dread coming towards me. It's very hard not to scream.

I can't tell how long it will take to reach land. My heartbeat is wild and besides, there is nothing to count. My watch has stopped. I focus on the sapling instead. Its leaves are the brightest thing here, better than a bike light because it's radiating a tiny amount of hope. I keep my eyes on the road. Forward, forward, go on, go on. Time can be measured by change but nothing changes. Even my legs move in a rhythm that doesn't vary, and my stare feels stuck. Panic begins to rise because what if I'm stuck like this, a toy that doesn't wind down?

Then there is something different. A crack in the road, and another, and then more, like tributaries joining a river to form a single large fissure snaking through the tarmac. I have to cycle to the side of it or my tyres will catch. There is a sound. The crack is leading me towards it, and now I drag my eyes up. I skid to a stop. Ahead, there is nothing, just a wide swathe of black.

My eyes adjust. It's *something*: a deep chasm cutting across the road, stretching from the mountains to the sea. The ocean water is pouring into it ceaselessly, waterfalling down and down to the horizon. I inch towards it because my curiosity is stronger than my fear. I lay my bike on its side, careful of the sapling in the basket. I get close enough to peer over, but a wave of dizziness hits me. I sink to my knees and grip the ground to keep myself from tipping over.

I can't see the bottom of the chasm because it recedes into darkness; or perhaps it has no end. I know with certainty that this is not in any zone. This is some other place. If this is in my head, I'm frightened of myself. My eyes get used to the dark as I stare down. Suddenly I can see movement, a swirling restlessness. I lean forward.

I must have lost my depth perception because I can't tell if what I see is far away or within reach of my hand. I catch glimpses of people and places, a kaleidoscope of images and scenes like countless movies projected over each other at once. I feel as if I'm falling among them and through them. Is this true madness? The hallucinations that others have had? Is this what happened to Dad before I found him?

My breath catches because there – and *there* – I can see Mom. There she is, cooking in the kitchen, and there she is walking along our old street. There's Ojiichan turning on his radio, Obaachan sitting at the kotatsu.

'Mom.' My voice is as cracked as the road.

The images swirl on. I am seeing the past.

There's Dad in a hospital bed, Koki at a desk – this is *now*.

Dad's wrinkled face and snow-white hair, our house dusty and empty, our little town changed – could that be the future?

Mom appears again.

'I found you,' I tell her. 'At last. I've been looking for you for years.' Are they even years to her? There is a drag, a pull to the depths. She turns to me, arms wide.

'Mom!' I cry again, louder. 'I'm here now. I came.'

She doesn't reply. Perhaps she can't. I remember what Hisakawa said. *Lost and searching things.*

And I'm one of those things.

The abyss tells me it's true. I think I glimpse a reflection of myself in the swirl of this flotsam and jetsam of what was and what is.

Mom again, the ocean behind, blue and ordinary. As a teenager, she pats earth around some small growing thing. Her and Dad, both young and smiling and kissing. By a river, a child beside her, and they bend to touch the water. Mom points and the child follows her finger, and suddenly I'm *in* that memory, gazing up at branches and the sun patterning the shapes of leaves on my face. Mom's words: *The river and the salmon and the trees, remember?* Of course, of course I remember. *They move, die, grow, keep going...* This is unfamiliar; this I don't know and don't recall her telling me.

With a jerk, I'm back on my hands and knees at the edge of the impossible pit. Back in my body, but I hardly realised that I had fallen out of it. I need to go. I mustn't stay here. This place is not where I should be. As if it heard me, the pull tightens around me, constricts my mind and heart and throat. I can't tell if it's just my mind or my body too, that's dragged back, into a different place, a different memory.

Mom, in the sunshine, spreading out the futons on the roof of Ojiichan's house. I'm beside her, holding the heavy blankets in my arms, and she takes them from me, one by one. When we're done, we stand and look out, the sun warming us, the land peaceful and unmoving.

A car stops in front of the house, and Mom says, 'Your father's back from the supermarket.'

Yes, this is exactly right. I lean against her and she puts her arm around me.

'I have something for you,' she says. She holds out a necklace, twisting and reflecting light into my eyes. A fish, twirling on the end, as though it's been caught on a line.

'But it's yours,' I say.

'Well, we can share it,' Mom says. 'I'd like you to wear it.'

Dad's voice floats up to us, telling us he's brought back lunch.

'We'll come now,' Mom calls back. She puts the necklace over my head. The fish rests on my heart. 'Won't we?' she says.

Yes, I want to say. But I'm looking at the necklace. Wasn't I already given this? By someone else … but that's impossible, because it's Mom's necklace. Who else would have given it to me? The fish winks and trembles in my hand.

I'm remembering something that never happened.

Mom tugs on my hand. 'Come on,' she says.

I tighten my grip on her hand. Dad comes up the stairs and Mom turns to him and they smile at each other, warm with love.

This is a good memory. This is how things could have been. Should have been.

Mom takes both my hands and I squeeze them tight. 'Come with me,' I beg.

She's puzzled. 'I can't.'

'You have to. I found you. I'm here to take you home.' My face is wet.

'This is my home,' Mom whispers. 'Remember?'

I shake my head. 'No. Come on. Come back.'

I feel time sway and bend around me. I struggle to hang on, to stay where I am. But there's a feeling of wrongness. I won't leave her, I won't, I won't. I can stay here, in this alternative moment, in this other, perfect place. I can be happy here.

Even as I think this, the world warps around me. I hold on to Mom, to this moment.

'No, no, no!' I cry.

Dad frowns. Mom is shaking her head at me unhappily. 'My hands,' she says.

I'm clutching her hands so hard that I'm hurting her.

'I'm sorry,' I say, but I don't release my grip.

Dad reaches out, but doesn't touch me.

'Sora,' she says sorrowfully.

I know this isn't really her. She isn't even a memory, just a scrap of wishful thinking, a piece of a dream.

'Sora,' Mom says again.

I have real memories. I know I do, even if nothing seems more real than what I'm seeing and holding right now. I force my fingers to loosen, but I can't stop the sob that rises in me.

Mom smiles and cries. I let go.

I float away, through flashes of images that I shut my eyes to, into darkness. Here is where all the time has gone, pulling memories with it, people, catching them and keeping them. And I'm caught too, I've been caught for a long time. Dad told me I had to move on. That's what he's tried to do. But he did it by forcing the past away, and he's as caught as I am. As others are. We lost so many, and we've become lost, living not-here, not-now, in places less painful than the present. Time holds and suspends me. Everything stops. I can't break free. I'm out of time.

No. No. Some corner of my mind says, *Impossible. I'm still alive.*

There must be time, because I am here. If time is defined by humans, then I can make it what I need. I think of the future. I open myself up to it. I can move forward into it, when I return to Dad, when he gets better, when the cicadas shriek love songs at the height of summer, and Koki might come home for Obon, and then the crisp of a bright autumn, and sakura blooming soft around Maya, and next year, and in ten years, and the world a century later and then and then—

I fall backwards. The necklace swings and falls against my skin, a light touch of golden warmth.

The ground shakes. Above me, the wave. It roars and rolls down.

乃東枯

HEAL-ALL WITHERS

26

When I open my eyes, I'm on my back. There is blue sky, sunlight, my heart thumping and blood rushing in my ears. With a huge effort, I lift my arm. The watch my mother gave me has a crack across its face, but the second hand ticks erratically forward. I sit up. No chasm, no nightmare sea. My mind back in my body, my body on solid earth. It's okay. I'm out of that place, though there are deep cracks around me that weren't there before.

I'm safe, so why am I crying so hard? I clamber up, wrapping my arms around myself. There's my bike, rust blooming on it and grass sprouting through the spokes of the wheels. In the basket is the sapling, surprisingly only a little bigger. I gather it up and hug the pot and try not to let my tears fall into the soil. A movement catches my eye. A flash of white and tall ears. The foxes dart away.

On, I have to go on. I don't want to get sucked back into that place with no time, so frightening and sad and lost.

That chasm. How could it be fixed? Bridges, concrete, walls; they wouldn't work. The ground trembles in yet another quake. That's what broke everything in the first place. If there's some other way to the bottom of the chasm, what would I find there? The catfish? My hands shake. I'd kill it.

I pull my bike up and replace the sapling in the basket and it's only then that I see the road has ended. I can make out the remains of the tarmac, the odd streak of paint that used to mark the centre line, but overtaken by grass, shrubs, young trees. The highway has become a meadow. I set my bike down again. Maybe this is the end. I had found Mom, or something like her, but the current of that other time is still tugging me onwards. I have come so far I can't stop, and if the way back is past the chasm then the only thing I can do is go forward. I hold the sapling and its pot to my chest, and I begin to walk. As I do, I feel myself revive, soothed by these living things. The wind moving leaves is a susurration of soft urgent commands: *go, grow, flow, sow, go*—

Ahead of me hills are rising, their hands laying down to the sea. On their fingers, those colossal trees are growing. They are towering and strong, and must be a variety of many different kinds, because their leaves are not all green, but yellow and red and orange, and some branches bare entirely, even though it's summer. Closer, until I'm among them and walking along the soft ground, dappled by light. There's a busy hush, a quiet coloured in with rustling, birds calling, the sound of growing and dying. The noise of the ocean where it meets the river. The waters mixing. Soil and sand. The air is so rich that I feel almost drunk.

I force myself to keep walking because whatever there is ahead, I haven't reached it yet. The trees get thicker and closer, their roots rising from the ground, and then somehow I have to squeeze through them, step high, hug the sapling close to me, steady myself on rough and smooth bark. I rest for a moment, looking around and above, and I know why the trees are such a range of colours; because they are in spring, summer, autumn, winter. Side by side in different seasons, together the full cycle of a year. And I notice that the line I was following has disappeared. I let myself feel the air and space and time around me. No, not disappeared, but spread out the way a stream joins a lake.

Ahead, there is light, and I climb towards it. The trees end abruptly, and I stumble on to grass as if they'd suddenly opened their arms and dropped me there. The shadows aren't with me any more. The grass is generous and forgiving, the sunlight shushes me. I'm in a wide clearing dotted with little shrines of weathered wood with flowers growing before them, rice stalks bowing their heavy heads to them, and at the centre is water and rock. There are cracks in the ground, dark and jagged among the green softness, all snaking towards one point; the water. Where they reach the water's edge, they disappear under the surface, snakes becoming eels.

The water ripples as if there is something moving

within it, large fish or turtles maybe, though the lake is small enough that it might qualify as a pond. When I get closer I see that it's fed by the river and the stream on the other side rejoins it to go out to sea. There is a stone in the middle, an out-of-place dark cylinder. I have an urge to put my hands on it, but I don't know how deep the water is, if the bottom would be muddy or stony. There might be things living there.

I'm suddenly tired, from my bones outwards. I sit in the grass, peer at the sun, and guess it's around three p.m. My watch is still frozen. It's dangerous to sleep, probably the worst thing to do, but I have to rest. I lie back and it's as if everything around me is humming a lullaby. I blink.

There's a trembling in the ground, a whisper, and when I sit up again the sun is touching the treetops. I almost swear, but here it would feel like blasphemy. Did I fall asleep? Or did time move faster than I've ever seen? I stand. The ground steadies, the water calms, but I can still hear the whisper. There, at the edge of the water, there is a shadow. My heart is shaking.

There's a crackling, a grinding cracking from different points all around me. From the shrines, the worn statues of the foxes, the tanuki, the turtles, the jizo, the little gods so smoothed I can't tell what they are – they're moving, stirring into motion, stretching out the stiffness of their stone joints. They open and close their eyes sleepily. In the trees, things move. In the shade of the branches and tree trunks, there are forms. Other spirits, other creatures.

They are watching me, watching the water. Should I have brought rice and sake for them? Do these gods kill? A round-headed jizo with an apron that must only have distant memories of being red, turns to me. Do they still consider me a child? Jizo gazes at me with the serenity that must come with the calm of being close to the dead. I'm pulled to the water and the shadow. It's like those I have seen before, darkening the places where people had once been. But this one doesn't go away. A person had stood here, walked here, in some different time. And all that's left is this darkness, cast behind them the way my sticks traced circles in sand all those years ago...

I know I'm closer because I've walked, haven't I, but the figure still seems far away. My depth perception is messed up again. Is it on the water, or on the other side of the little lake? The water is close and clear enough for me to see that it's shallow and the bottom is pebble and sand. The fissures go deeper, opening into darkness, and I step around them warily, relieved to feel no tug, no current pulling me down.

A toad watches me with orange horizontal-pupil eyes and says, 'Ge-ro, ge-ro.' He plops into the water, and I watch him scoot over to a rock, no – a turtle, with her stiff neck raised to the sky. I take my shoes off and tuck my socks into them. The water makes me gasp, makes the back of my neck shiver, until the cold eases into a fresh coolness. I roll my trousers up above my knees and wade in. Around my feet, fish dart, scatter and regroup. I glance behind me and two tanuki waddle away from my shoes. I hope their sense of smell isn't too keen, because I've come a long way in those shoes. At least they won't steal them.

I stop in front of the stone. All the cracks in the soil and sand radiate from it, like spokes in a wheel. The stone is almost as tall as I am. If it were a person, I could hold my hands behind their back. It's dark and faintly shiny, and now I can see that it's engraved with kanji so intricate and worn that I can't read them. At least, I think it's kanji. I've seen this type of rock before, in a museum or textbook or something. Igneous rock. Obsidian. Found in places were volcanoes had erupted.

I trace my fingers over a vertical line of kanji, and then from deep beneath my feet comes a rumble, a noise which makes its way through the earth and up my legs. An earthquake, like the one that woke me, and I count ten seconds before it stops. I breathe out. A small one, but still. Two of them, and close together. I wade around the stone carefully and on the other side of it there's a different kind of carving. It's a picture, an engraving. An animal – no, a fish. A giant fish, strange but familiar. Lines sprouting from around the fish's mouth. Whiskers.

'It's a catfish,' I say aloud. '*The* catfish.'

And from somewhere, from inside me, or from the past – they were the same place, weren't they? – a hand, a voice, a story.

In the engraving, there is a tall, wide thing resting on its head, holding it down. I put both my hands on the stone and this time I'm ready for the shaking, and don't move my hands away. It vibrates through the stone, coming from far, far below. How deep is the land of Japan? The shaking came from even deeper than whatever that is.

So. This is what I'm supposed to do, in the dream-logic of this otherworld that I suppose I've given in to. To stop the shaking, to prevent more earthquakes, the stone has to be pushed down farther. The catfish must be pinned deeper into the mud. Will it fix that chasm or only stop it widening?

Am I really strong enough to murder the catfish?

'I can't do this. I'm not a god, or – I'm just—'

The shadow moves towards me. The spirits and little gods are all around, watching me. There are other, fainter shadows lengthening.

I put my arms around the stone, squeeze tight, and push, trying to lean all my weight on it. The ground shakes and shakes, harder and harder, and I count to twenty and it hasn't stopped, and I let go.

'No, no. This isn't good, I shouldn't be doing this,' I say. I'm afraid.

The shadow comes closer to me.

'I can't push it.'

No, I can't.

I put my hand on the engraving, and imagine what it is like, to have something hard and heavy on top of you, holding you down in the dark. A punishment for doing something that is only in your nature, in the way you move and live. How cruel it must be to be held in one place and not allowed to move, alone for years and years and years.

'The poor thing,' I whisper.

I put my arms around the rock again, tight as an embrace. I pull and raise and lift and even as the rumbling begins I don't let go. There's no way I can really move it, raise this thing out of the earth, but if I can loosen it and raise it even the smallest bit—

The shaking changes, as though the ground is pushing *up*, as though something is stretching itself, and I wonder how big this earthquake is, if buildings and people are falling.

The shadows of a thousand lost things put their arms around mine, and we pull and pull. The stone shifts. I don't know how, because whatever – whoever – is helping me can't have more weight or strength than a breeze. Deep beneath us, something is moving, something ancient and tired, but still strong. The stone lifts by a fraction of a millimetre and the earth *leaps* and my feet leave the stones at the bottom of the lake, the toad held mid-hop, the gods around me lifted from the long grass, and kilometres away, buildings and cars and people are thrown into the air. We are held between the earth and the sky, and beneath Japan the catfish has risen too, and is floating between the mud and the stone above it. All of us are weightless in the air and the water.

And time stretches further than I've ever thought it could; a second suspended into the length it takes for me to look at the shadow beside me, to gaze into it and see that it is made of the shadows of many, many people. I can see faces made distant by time, but now in this particular moment, the familiar swim into my focus. I smile and they smile. I cry and they weep. The moment ripples across all the places that have been jarred apart, and for somewhere between a heartbeat and a lifetime, people turn to the air beside them and feel as if somebody they lost has returned to touch them lightly on the shoulder or laugh like they always had or grin in that way of theirs or kiss them the way they had kissed goodnight for decades. Afterwards, people might say that time had stood still, or that the past had come back, or that it had been déjà vu or a forgotten memory returning.

The cracks around my feet ease closed. In that other place, the chasm groans and narrows. And somewhere else, a giant catfish moves because I helped it, and we both feel a burden disappear, a lightness that sings. When that note ends, I sigh, and my feet land on the solid ground at the same time as our hearts beat again.

I close my eyes and when I open them the shadow is moving away. I follow it out of the water.

'I found you,' I say. 'They said you were gone, that you were all lost... But I found you. You can come back.'

The shadow pauses, lengthens and shortens as though the sun has moved across the sky above us.

'Come with me.' Even as I speak I understand that it's impossible. A shadow can't become a person. What I've lost can't be completely found. It can't return. The time for that has passed.

My face is wet as I slide to the ground and watch as it dissolves into the air and evening deepens into night and midnight comes and goes and the sky welcomes the sun back into the dawn and it is morning.

Around me, the gods have returned to their shrines. The fissures in the earth are repairing themselves, flowers already growing where the darkness was. I walk slowly around the edge of the water and back to my shoes. The rubber is cracked and there are puffs of white fluff where my socks had been. I pull it out and the cotton is blown out of my hand by the wind. I put my bare feet into my shoes. I go back the way I came. The last shrine I pass has a jizo wearing a bright red apron, its face clear and freshly carved. I bow to it and its smile doesn't change; and it never will, even after the stone has been worn smooth by the world around it.

I find a good flat rock at the edge of the pond and scrape a clumsy hole in the earth near the jizo, and then shake the sapling gently out of its pot and place it inside. I take a handful of water from the pond and sprinkle it on the soil around it.

'I hope you like your new home,' I tell it.

Its leaves wave merrily in the breeze, and I imagine its roots stretching underground, the way I stretch after sitting at a desk or on an aeroplane for hours. I sit beside it, rest and breathe, and when I raise my head again, a tree has widened and lengthened and embraced the air. It shelters a small jizo, tucked into roots like the crook of an elbow. Its branches hold every season; midwinter bare, fresh and eager as spring, summery green and generous, blazing the way autumn does, or a sunset, or a promise.

The trees, absorbing time the way they absorb light and water. Balancing our air, the spaces we live in and move through. Their trunks swelling to take it in, hold it inside their rings. I don't know if there are enough trees to fix the broken time, to hold what's run away and release what won't leave.

I press my hands against it, then open my arms to hug it, but its trunk is so wide now that my hands can't hold it. Below me are its roots, a reflection of what's above ground, weaving through soil and stones and tiny living things, down into the deep dark. It could keep growing for ever, for as long as people let it, and if it does then perhaps it can anchor the land a little more. Closing cracks and filling gaps. Not a stone pressing down but a tree holding firm.

My cheek to the bark, I close my eyes. I think of Mom. In the sunlight, her arms raised with mine; in the garden, hands deep in soil; in the dusk, her shadow becoming the shadow of trees. If a tree could have a name.

'Nozomi,' I say. 'Goodbye, Mom.'

And I release my arms and gather myself up. A leaf as red and true as a heart flutters down to my feet and I pick it up and put it in my pocket.

Back through the trees, where around me leaves fall and grow. The woods are deeper this time, and I walk for long enough to know I must be lost. I keep going and going until something has changed. I stop and listen, but the birds are still singing and the small creatures are going quietly about their business. I raise my head and see that the leaves are all strong summer green. I walk forward until I'm out of the woods and I can see a road and rooftops not so far away. I head towards them, and when I look back I see nothing but trees stretching much farther than they had before. A forest must have grown as I walked. Up a small hill and I can see the world all around. I hear faintly the sound of the morning chimes, the simple notes that mark the beginning of every day.

菖蒲華

IRISES BLOOM

27

Dad looks like he's sleeping, but before I can creep away, he opens his eyes. 'Good morning.'

'Morning.' I sit in the hard chair beside his bed. 'How do you feel?'

'Good. Much better. I slept well. I'm actually hungry.'

He *does* seem better – his eyes are clearer and his voice is calm.

'I'll get something—'

He waves his hand. 'I'll wait a little longer. I don't think I've been really hungry in a while. I'm enjoying the experience.'

'You haven't eaten much lately.'

'I think that phase is over.'

'Good. Good,' I say.

'The food in Japanese hospitals is better than anywhere else. One of your mother's friends got sick once and insisted on returning to Japan to go to the hospital, you know. She said the Canadian hospital food would undo any good the medicine did.'

'You've never told me that before.'

'We lived in Canada then. I was worried you might need to get your appendix out and demand to be brought to Japan so you could have a nice dinner after the operation.'

I laugh and keep laughing because it's been such a long time since we had a conversation like this, not just because Dad is remembering things but because we are talking like we used to, because he mentioned Mom and because now he is laughing with me.

Then he stops and says, 'Sora? What's wrong?'

I can't stop laughing and that's when I notice I'm crying.

He reaches for my hand and pulls me to him for a hug. 'It's okay.' He rubs my back for a while, then says, 'I wonder if the hospital will make me pancakes.'

That makes me giggle and I sit back and sniffle my tears away.

'Where have you been?' Dad says suddenly.

'At home,' I reply automatically.

'For two whole days?'

I gape at him and don't even know why I'm surprised. 'I was asleep,' I say.

Dad doesn't even take me up on this blatant lie. 'I was sleeping for most of it, which is good because otherwise I would have been extremely concerned. Well, I was a tad worried because of the earthquake.'

'It wasn't that bad, was it?' I hadn't seen any damage on the way to the hospital.

RA KUMAGAI

'I think it was a seven, but it was so quick, it only lasted half a second. A bit strange, really. It felt like...' He looks past me, out the window. 'A release. Do you understand?'

I nod.

'There was a nurse in the room with me, and he grabbed on to my bed, but when it stopped he kept holding on. His eyes were wet... I put one of my hands on his and he let go of the bed and held my hand instead. He wiped his eyes and checked my chart and said I was doing better. I said, so are you. And then he left.' Dad moves his gaze from the window to my face. 'Something happened, didn't it, with time?'

I nod again.

Dad sighs. 'I felt it.'

I hesitate before I say, 'I went in.'

'You did.' There is no question in Dad's voice; there's barely even surprise.

I don't know if I should be bringing this up while he's still recovering in a hospital bed, but I plunge on. 'You said Mom would be where there were trees. So I went to the trees.'

'I said that?' Dad's eyes flicker.

'When I found you in the zone. You told me you'd seen people. Mom,' I whisper.

Dad's forehead creases and he shakes his head slowly, as if he's trying to rouse his brain.

'Did you reach a strange place, where there was a big crack in the road? A scary place. You could've seen someone there,' I say.

'I don't remember that,' Dad says. 'There were so many cracks. A lot of scary places. I didn't mean for you to go searching.'

'I'd been searching for years before that,' I say softly.

Dad puts a hand against my cheek. 'I said that about your mother because … I don't know if there's a heaven. But wherever she is, trees grow.'

Neither of us say anything for a while. Dad wipes his eyes with the sleeve of his pyjamas, and I eventually catch my breath and roughly rub my face dry.

Dad clears his throat. 'I like your hair. Did you do it yourself?'

'Do what?'

Dad reaches out and touches my head. I go to the bathroom to look in the mirror. There's a streak of white in my hair behind my left ear, from the root to the tip. There are goosebumps on my arms suddenly, and I rub my hands over my skin to make them go away.

When I return to Dad, he's yawning.

'Why don't you go ask about the pancakes? I'm sure you can get them to make me some. You're very persuasive.' He closes his eyes. He smiles in my direction and I know he knows I'm smiling back.

I go home. I strip off my clothes and it's only then that I examine my watch. It's cracked and rusted, the strap peeling apart. If the hands are measuring time then I don't know what zone it thinks it's in, because it speeds through hours and then slows to tick one second a minute. I watch it for a while, dazed and lulled. I slowly place it in front of Mom's photograph.

'It's yours, anyway,' I tell her.

I wash and change and eat. I plug my phone in to charge and it comes back to life for the first time in days. There are a bunch of messages from Dad, one from Maya, one from Koki. I check Koki's first, saving Maya's for last, like dessert.

you okay after the earthquake? thought I felt it too but nobody else in Tokyo seemed to, Koki has sent. An emoji of a puzzled bear.

it was only bad for a second. but it was strange, right? what did you feel? I write.

I watch him typing and typing, but when his reply comes it just says, *i don't know.*

What had he deleted? I write, *nothing is weird to me.*

He types for a long time again. *like I heard something in the earthquake.*

A pause, and then he messages again. *maybe words. as if someone had spoken to me. i don't know.*

I want to know what words but I can't ask, at least not this way.

do you feel better? I write instead.

what? he asks.

I'm trying to figure out what to ask instead when he messages again.

yeah. i do.

good, I reply. *i'm glad*

I open Maya's message.

that test was BAD. should have stayed in hospital

getting out of that bed was your first mistake, I reply.

I'll listen to you next time, she writes back.

The *next time* warms me, but fades with her next message.

i'm still kinda tired though. lying down right now so if i don't reply it's because I've passed out.

no worries. sleep! I write.

I clean and tidy. I should prepare something good for Dad tomorrow, make sure there are pancake ingredients for breakfast the day after. And the day after that... I sit at the kitchen table. It's still damp. I watch it dry. Dad will have to rest for as long as I can make him. I go to my room and check my money, pretty depleted after my Tokyo trip.

My days stretch out ahead of me. So much has happened and changed and I know I should feel relieved or even happy, but there is still an emptiness inside me. The future feels formless, dull and heavy like clay I have to wade through, but I don't know what I'm wading towards, or if there's anything on the other side of it.

'Stop it,' I tell myself out loud.

The afternoon is mellow, idling in the last hours before evening and the rush of tired energy bringing people home. In town, I go to the quiet little stores, picking up flour and eggs, fruit and vegetables from the shop on the corner. I buy a bag of mikan. I go to the tiny old place where the obachan has been making tofu for decades. She gives me a candy and tells me to take care.

It's hot, and I get sweaty walking home. I stop at a conbini and rustle around the freezer, and my hand lands on a little plastic container, white rabbits on the label. I haven't eaten mochi ice cream in years. I buy it and walk to a side road and stop at a spot shaded by trees.

I take a mikan and my ice cream and walk a few more steps to the shrine with all its jizo housed inside. I place the mikan in front of it, clap and bow. I sit beside the shrine and open my ice cream, spear it with the little plastic fork, and take a bite. The mochi is chewy but the vanilla inside is melting, making me eat it fast. It's soft and sweet and it's been such a long time since I've eaten it, years and years, sharing it with my mother, one for each of us.

Eating ice cream and crying is probably one the saddest things possible. I eat the other mochi and wipe my nose.

'Sorry, ojizo-sama,' I say. 'I'd have given you one but I think it would make your shrine all sticky.'

Jizo, as always, smiles forgivingly.

A middle-aged man walks briskly past me. I didn't see him coming. He pauses at a jizo at the end of the row, surrounded by models of little cars. He bows.

'Good weather today, eh, Saburo-kun?' He pats it on the hand, seems to ruffle a child's messy hair.

He nods at me, then continues on his way.

Jizo takes care of travellers and children who have died. The land of the dead is a shadowy place, but it doesn't have hard borders. Many can travel. If I hadn't been there, I'd been somewhere close by. And I had returned.

I brush myself off and go home. My mouth tastes of sugar and salt.

半夏生

CROW DIPPER SPROUTS

28

'Today? Excellent, I'm happy to be getting out early,' Dad says enthusiastically. He's dressed and ready to go.

'Yeah, it's good.' Should I leave it at that? I keep going. 'But it's not earlier than planned, Dad.'

'I thought I was supposed to leave on Thursday.'

'It *is* Thursday,' I say.

The doctor beside me says cheerfully, 'Thursday all day today!'

Dad blinks. 'Ah, yes. I'm glad to be going home, in any case.'

I nod.

'I'll just go to the toilet before we go.' Dad leaves the room. His walk is a little stiff.

'It's normal,' the doctor says to me. 'He needs to readjust.'

'Yeah,' I say.

'You should know that your father is much better, but not completely cured. For conditions like this, for memory and deterioration that comes with age, it's not something that can be fixed with medication or any kind of surgery. You have to be patient.' The doctor manages to be kind and warning at the same time.

I like her. 'I know.' I do know, but hearing it delivered like this, a diagnosis, makes it worse.

Dad ambles back. 'Let's go. Thank you very much.' He bows to the doctor.

'See you next month for your check-up,' she says.

'Of course,' Dad says.

'Thank you.' I bow too.

'Take care, both of you,' the doctor says.

We leave the hospital and wait at the bus stop.

'Well, Sora, I hope you're making me lunch,' Dad says.

'I'll make myself lunch. If you're in the vicinity then it's lucky for you.'

The bus trundles to the stop and sighs its doors open.

'Very lucky,' Dad says. He has to hold on to the yellow bar to pull himself on to the bus. 'Very lucky indeed.'

What has happened to luck?

We get home and Dad remains in the vicinity while I make myself lunch, so I'm forced to share.

'Delicious!' Dad says, with his mouth full.

It's good to see him eat and accept a second bowl of rice. His appetite is increasing slowly but steadily.

Dad eats his last grain of rice and claps his hands. 'Gochiso!'

'You're welcome.'

'I don't suppose there's a beer?' Dad says hopefully.

'Nope. It's only lunchtime, anyway.' I'm going to keep Dad away from alcohol for as long as possible. 'Anyway, I don't think you're supposed to mix alcohol with those tablets.'

Dad looks in the paper bag that we got from the pharmacy and inspects the explanatory sheet of the two different types of pills he has to take, morning and night. They're both primarily for memory loss. The closest thing to whatever Dad has, but not the same.

'Any side effects I should know about?' I ask. 'Should I keep an eye out for horrible rashes?'

Dad hands me the paper. 'Rashes always seem to be a symptom, no matter what kind of medicine it is.'

I read the symptoms. Nausea, vomiting, loss of appetite, dizziness, confusion – surely they're supposed to *stop* confusion? 'It says stuff about bowel movements. Please do not tell me if anything weird happens with that, but I'll buy some prunes or something, okay?'

'Are you sure you don't want to be a doctor?'

I snort. 'That opportunity has definitely passed me by.'

'Not necessarily! Lots of universities don't care if you start a year later.'

'I think most of them care about grades, though.'

'Your grades aren't bad.'

'I don't think they're at doctor level.'

'So doctor is perhaps a slight exaggeration in terms of career goals but—'

'Thanks.' I start gathering the dirty plates.

'You don't actually want to be a doctor, do you?'

'No, but...' Shouldn't parents say you can do anything, though? A bit of blind, unfounded confidence would be nice every now and again.

'I'll wash the dishes.' He turns the tap on. 'Where's the washing up liquid?'

It's where it always is. I hand it to him.

'Obviously you can be a doctor, if you want to be.'

'I don't want to be. I'd be a terrible doctor.'

'That's not true. There are a wide range of doctors. You'd be a good medical researcher. Or when somebody's had an accident and they have to do physical therapy so they can walk again? You would be good at that. Encouraging but also intimidating.' Dad delivers these quite depressing reflections of my character in a reassuring tone.

'That's either being an actual researcher or else a personal trainer or something.'

'There you go. Even more career options!'

'Thanks, Dad.' I don't say it sarcastically this time.

'We should talk about universities and degrees you're interested in—'

I watch the water fill the sink up. 'We don't have to. I'm not in a rush. I'm not planning on going anywhere, for a while at least.'

'You don't have to stay here and take care of me.'

'I kind of do.'

Dad looks desperate, standing there in soapy water up to his wrists.

'And that's okay,' I say quickly. 'That's what I want to do.'

'I'll do my best to recover soon. There's time for me to do that, but your last year in high school will go by really fast, before you know it—'

'What?'

'You know how quickly summer comes once you start a new year, and then it seems to be New Year all of a sudden...'

'Dad, I've already graduated. Remember?' I feel sick.

He frowns down at the sink, scrubs the sponge around a plate again and again. 'Ah. How could I forget all those long speeches?'

We nod at each other with relief and fear and love.

A week later, I insist on going with Dad to meet with Yamagata. He sighs and doesn't argue. He's still tired, and has begun to understand that I'm going to take care of him whether he likes it or not.

He doesn't like it.

I sit and wait in the lobby. Yamagata didn't invite me and even I'm not stupid enough to force myself into this meeting.

When Dad returns he says, 'Yamagata wants to talk to you.'

'About what?'

'I don't know.' He sees my face and adds, 'You're not under arrest. Go on.'

I go.

I enter the office and Yamagata and I stare suspiciously at each other before he gestures for me to sit.

'Your father is doing well,' he says. 'I'm glad.'

'Are you?'

He glares at me. 'Yes.'

I relax and glare back. 'Thank you.'

'When you went back into the zone, what did you see?' he asks abruptly.

'Nakagawa was pretty overgrown—'

'I mean,' he interrupts deliberately, 'when you went *back* in.'

I keep my face as still as possible.

'Come now, you're not so shocked, are you? I'm not going to call any authorities about this, if that's what you're concerned about. I'm simply interested.' He spreads his hands, meets my eyes.

'I'm not sure where I ended up. It wasn't as far north as Nakagawa, but further east.'

He opens a drawer and brings out a map, spreads it on his desk.

I lean over it. 'There was a river and a small lake, and then the river flowed into the sea.' I examine the map, but can't see anything that matches it.

'Here?' Yamagata points at a lake.

'That could be the area, but it's too big to be the one I saw. There's no river either.'

'Not now,' he says.

'No.' When would it be what I had seen? The past or the future, or was it like that right now? A forest had grown in the time it had taken me to walk a handful of kilometres, so anything could have happened since then. The stone could be at the bottom of a deep lake now, could have worn away until it was a rock only big enough for a couple of turtles to sun themselves on.

'What happened?' Yamagata watches me closely.

'I don't know, I truly do not.' He's not bad but that doesn't mean I'll ever like him. And I'll *never* tell him about the chasm in the other place. 'But the time is very strange that far in. I don't even know if it's fast or slow because it's so unpredictable. You were right about Nakagawa, what you told me. It was beyond that.'

'Give me an example.'

I had anticipated this. I take my watch out of my pocket, borrowed from Mom's shrine, and lay it on the map. Yamagata stares at it, then picks it up carefully, turning it over in his hands and then watching the hands move for several minutes.

'May I keep this?' he asks.

'Of course not. I don't have much other proof, and you can ignore me if you want to – I don't know – make money and plant cash crops or whatever, but I'm telling you that nobody should go there. Leave it alone. It's not for people, not now.' I hold his gaze until he breaks eye contact.

'Your hair has gone grey,' he says.

'Like my father's.'

Yamagata nods slowly. 'Your father turned down my offer of the reinstatement of his position. But perhaps you should consider employment here in future.'

I raise my eyebrows but he remains serious. I could, maybe I could… 'No. No, thank you.'

'I see. That is all, then.'

'Yes.' I see myself out, but before I close the door behind me, I say, 'Don't cut down the trees. And don't grow them to chop down and sell. Just let them grow.'

I know he'll need explanations and evidence for this, but I'll find it for him, somehow. Naomi might help me. Maybe Maya will too.

'You really don't have to accompany me everywhere, Sora,' Dad says defeatedly.

'Why can't I go for a walk with you? I need exercise as well,' I say. 'Though I don't understand why you're *driving* to go for a walk.'

'Change of scenery.' He's being vague, but in a shady way, not a forgetful one. I think.

After about ten minutes of driving I know exactly where we're going. I shouldn't be surprised. Dad doesn't say anything as he parks the car and we follow the trail off the road and through the boundary fence. We bow silently before the gates of Hisakawa's shrine and walk through on the left side of the path.

I count down silently in my head from ten and when I get to seven, Hisakawa appears from around a corner.

'Hello! Long time, no see,' he says.

'Has it been a long time?' I say.

'Hasn't it?' He grins at me mystifyingly, then turns the grin on Dad. 'Campbell-sensei, it's good to see you.'

'And you, and you.' Dad starts talking about a work break and how he's rethinking some of this research. They ramble off together and go behind the shrine, probably to check on those hourglasses again. I'll let Hisakawa explain the broken one.

I go to the fox shrine and gaze at the statues. 'You did keep me safe,' I whisper. 'I'll bring some tofu next time.'

'Sora!' Dad calls excitedly.

I follow his voice to, predictably, where the hourglasses had been set up. He's crouching and peering at something on the ground while Hisakawa stands beside him, nodding patiently.

'Sora, come see this! Remember the centre hourglass—' Dad starts.

'It shattered, I know,' I say.

'You already know that?' Dad's eyes land on Hisakawa, who blinks back innocently. 'Hmmm. Well, so did I. Or made an educated guess, I suppose. I brought a replacement. And look...' Dad straightens up and beckons me closer.

There are three hourglasses, the ones on the left and right running faster and slower. But the one in the centre—

'It's not frozen,' I say. The sand is falling smoothly from top to bottom. 'It *is* normal time.' I gaze from Dad to Hisakawa. 'How...'

'Yes, *how*!' Dad repeats happily. 'That earthquake.

I wonder if that had anything to do with it – perhaps there's a new kind of equilibrium, or it could be that it shifted time again in a different direction—'

I stop listening. I can feel the fast and slow zones on either side, but they're the slightest bit more even, a fraction more in line with normal time.

I tune back in to Dad to hear him say, 'If I can go in a bit further, I can see the extent of this—'

'You're not going in!'

Dad stops abruptly. Hisakawa's eyes flick to mine.

I take a breath. 'I mean, that's not the type of walk you should be doing, Dad. Right?'

Dad runs a hand through his grey hair. 'No, I suppose not. I'm going to stroll around here, though.'

'Wonderful. Let's go.' I stand shoulder to shoulder with him.

'Sora.' Dad rolls his eyes.

'Shall we?' Hisakawa asks. He's right beside Dad on the other side.

Dad sighs.

We walk around the grounds of the shrine, most of which I haven't seen. We stop when we reach a boundary fence, rusting and vine-covered. There are a cluster of tall gingko trees with fresh shimenawa around them, even though they are on the other side of the fence.

Hisakawa points to the shimenawa. 'I just put them there, actually.'

'How old are these trees?' I ask, then wait for a good cryptic answer.

Hisakawa delivers. 'Do they have an age? They are both young and old.'

I put my hand over my mouth to hide my giggle, then see that he's genuinely thinking.

'They grew very quickly, you see,' Hisakawa says. 'They should be small. But they appear to be decades old. How could that happen? What has made them grow?'

Dad stares up at them. 'They're in the slow zone,' he murmurs, 'so that *is* especially odd, isn't it?'

Hisakawa glances at me. 'The hourglass telling a different time too... There has been a change. I decided to make these trees officially sacred.'

'Good.' I clear my throat. 'Thank you.'

'Thank *you*,' Hisakawa says.

I won't ask what messages the foxes have brought him. I can feel the times more clearly now; the zones aren't reversing or even stopping, but there's an absence of tension. They're not being pushed or stretched. There's no catfish caught beneath them. If there are wounds then perhaps they can heal.

We start walking again. We're not frozen any more. We're like the leaves and foxes and the sand in the hourglasses; moving.

小暑

29

Hi Naomi,

Thanks for the added information about the experiment. I planted the tree. It had grown a lot, I mean a lot. Maybe water from the time zones can put time into trees. But my other theory is: maybe trees could also take time. I mean, actually absorb it. It's related to what you already told me, I'm just thinking about it from a different angle, I guess.

I told my dad about the bio clock but I can't answer any of a million questions he asked me. He definitely wants to visit you. Is that still something you want?

Also, I forgot to say thank you for the money. Thanks for that. And everything.

Sora

Naomi replies rapidly. *It's possible. I haven't considered it. What happened? I know something did, just tell me.*

Below this vaguely threatening demand is a link to the university admissions page.

I scroll through it for a while and close my laptop. So she doesn't know.

My phone lights up. It's Maya. We've been messaging every day, and every time she replies to me I feel giddy.

hey hey! how're you today? and your dad?

I wonder for a second if Naomi and she are coordinating their recruitment attack.

we're fine, I reply. *i mean not GREAT but getting better*

better is good and after good comes GREAT, she writes back.

that's evolution, I answer.

yes, i know that because i crammed it into my head for an exam yesterday, she replies.

'What are you grinning about?' Dad asks.

I whip my head up. 'Huh? I'm not.'

'You most certainly are.' Dad looks pointedly at my phone. 'Is that Koki?'

'No. *No*,' I emphasise.

'Is everything ... amicable with you two?' Dad says nervously.

'It's good. We're friends. Just only that.'

Dad nods. 'I understand. Good. Fine. Who's this, then?'

'It's Maya. You remember her, don't you?'

Dad brightens. 'Yes! Ah, I see.'

'What do you see?' I ask, even though I know.

Dad smiles slowly. 'I see *you*, of course.'

I can't fight the smile spreading across my heated face.

'It's all very interesting,' he says, and wanders off.

'What is?' I call after him.

He turns and I inwardly groan because I've probably induced some sort of lecture on what he thinks is interesting. 'I forgot to tell you – guess who contacted me?'

'Um. Charles Darwin... I mean, his ghost,' I say. Maya's exam is on my mind.

'What? No—'

'Naomi Osaka. A twin you were separated from at birth. Ooh, Keanu Reeves.'

'I don't even know who those people are.'

'You don't know *Keanu Reeves*?'

Dad gives up on the game. 'Soo-jin!'

'*Really?*' This is more exciting than all those people, except perhaps Naomi Osaka.

'She emailed out of the blue, asking how I was. She said she'd heard about the earthquake, or felt it – anyway, she had thought of me. Us.'

Naomi must have got in touch with her. 'How is she? Where is she now? What did she say?'

'She's good. Living in Fukuoka. She said everything's fine, though her work isn't as stimulating as it used to be,' Dad says.

'If Soo-jin thought the zones were only *stimulating* then she's going to be bored by everything else,' I say.

Dad looks away. 'Well, she had to take a break from

that, didn't she?' He perks up. 'She said she would like to come see us.'

'Yes, please!'

'That's what I said,' Dad says enthusiastically.

Of course he's enthusiastic. Dad doesn't really have any friends here. He must be lonely, and I'm ashamed that I've never thought about that before.

'When is she coming?'

'I'll ask her,' Dad says, and rushes off to his study.

I email Naomi.

Hi Naomi,

You found Soo-jin! Can I ask how much you told her about Dad and ... everything?

Naomi once more replies too quickly. She has no concept of leaving a person on read.

I haven't told her anything, primarily because I haven't tracked her down yet.

She includes the link to the university admissions page again.

Could it be a coincidence? Or whatever Soo-jin had felt in the earthquake? Either way, Dad's happy, and so am I.

I turn back to my phone, and Maya.

congrats on the end of your exams

may many As follow.

yes i'm gonna celebrate, she writes back. *actually i'm thinking of going north in a few weeks for a break. have to escape the tokyo heat and okinawa is even hotter.*

it's cooler up here, I write, but my cheeks are warm.

i was thinking that, she replies.

you should come visit, I write.

yeah, she replies. *i will.*

Dad returns from shopping with his arms full of greenery.

'What's this?' I ask.

'Plants! I thought they would brighten up the house. Outside too.' He hands me a pot of sweet-smelling lavender and another of fresh, alert mint.

I breathe deep.

'You showed me that nice little tree when I was in hospital and I recalled how cheerful it was.' Dad brings in several more pots of growing things and begins feeding them water.

I go to my room and return with Mom's photo clutched to my chest.

'Dad...'

'Yes?'

When I don't reply, he turns to me. I hold out the photo. I watch it shiver in my hands. He gazes at it for a long time.

'Can we put Mom's photo out? Please.'

He blinks and raises his eyes to me. 'Sora,' he begins. Stops. 'Yes. Let's do that.'

We clear a shelf in the sitting room and place the photo there.

'Just a moment—' Dad disappears and comes back with a potted plant with soft needle leaves and violet flowers. He puts it beside the photo.

I know that deep, woody fragrance. 'Rosemary,' I say. 'For remembrance.'

'Yes, that's what it's for,' Dad says. 'I almost forgot.'

It's hard to laugh and cry at the same time. Dad hugs me. It's warm and kind, no jolts of static or time. Mom watches us, smiling.

It'll be Obon soon, when the dead come back to visit the living, to check on us, reassure themselves that we are safe and well and good. Then they'll depart again, to wherever they are for the rest of the year.

'I'll remember, Sora,' Dad whispers to me. 'And you will too.'

It will take time. But we have that.

And not so far away, but maybe long ago, or someday in the future, a tree grows. A maple, red as love in autumn; in winter, bare as grief; in spring and summer, it's green, green, green. Time swirls and settles in deep places. Memories leave and return. The ground shivers. The tree won't stop growing, strong and beautiful and holding time within it in circles that won't break.

空

SKY

Deep below the islands of Japan, the catfish moves and the earth trembles beneath our feet. Even the gods can't stop it, banish it, or make it disappear. Like fear or pain, it's always there; but so is release, freedom, joy. We walk on while trees gather the sky in their branches. Beneath land and water, the catfish turns, and rests.

GLOSSARY

The chapter titles of *Catfish Rolling* have been taken from two calendars: the lunar calendar 二十四節気 (24 sekki) and the 七十二候 (72 kō).

The exact dates of the 24 sekki and 72 kō do not match up exactly with the time period of each chapter, though overall they cover the same seasons as the book: from the vernal equinox to midsummer.

The lunar calendar was imported from China, and marks the the lunar cycle and the major turning points of nature. The 72 kō is also Chinese, but was adapted by Shibukawa Shunkai in the Edo period to better reflect the Japanese seasons.

These calendars were used in the past, when people measured time by their environment; the natural world *was* the calendar. Our lives are no longer so closely tied to nature, so few of these phrases remain in the everyday lexicon—though, like in other places in the world, summer is often recognised by the coming of swallows. As climate change worsens, these markers are becoming increasingly confused and disrupted—there are fewer swallows every year.

For the prologue and epilogue, the characters 永 and 空 were used respectively. Together, they are the kanji for Sora's name: 永空.

永
Eternity

春分
Vernal equinox

雀始巣
Sparrows start to nest

桜始開
First cherry blossoms bloom

雷乃発声
Thunder sounds its voice

清明
Sky becomes clear and bright

玄鳥至
Swallows return

鴻雁北
Wild geese fly north

虹始見
First rainbows appear

穀雨
Rain nourishes grain

葭始生
First reeds sprout

霜止出苗
Frost ceases and seeds germinate

牡丹華
Peonies bloom

立夏
Summer starts

蛙始鳴
Frogs start singing

蚯蚓出
Worms surface

竹笋生
Bamboo shoots sprout

小満
The earth grows lush

蚕起食桑
Silkworms start feasting on mulberry leaves

紅花栄
Safflowers flourish

麦秋至
Wheat-harvesting time arrives

芒種
Seeds of rice and wheat are sown

蟷螂生
Praying mantises hatch

腐草為蛍
Rotting grass becomes fireflies

梅子黄
Plums turn yellow

夏至
Summer solstice

乃東枯
Heal-all withers

菖蒲華
Irises bloom

半夏生
Crow dipper sprouts

小暑
Midsummer begins

空
Sky

ACKNOWLEDGEMENTS

Many thanks and much gratitude to:

Angelique Tran Van Sang, insightful and talented agent and, on occasion, rejection cushion.

Alison Lewis, supportive conversation coach and dedicated agent across the pond.

Fiona Kennedy, for her edits and thoughtfulness, and the whole wonderful team at Zephyr.

SCBWI Japan, and most especially Kristin Osani, partner in writing sprints.

We Need Diverse Books and Nicola Yoon, for their valuable mentorship.

Keith Maillard and Madeleine Thien, in whose fiction class this book first took seed, the UBC Creative Writing Department, and all my workshop mates there.

Emily Chou, who zoomed me on Christmas Day to give me her astute feedback.

Tom Morris, literary matchmaker.

Ami-chan (sorry the book made you cry three times), Risako and Kaz for their kanji deep dive, and Cúirt Alt Delete for equal parts entertainment and advice.

My family, for their enduring love and support.

Dabi-chan, patient listener, endless encourager, devoted cat dad.

Clara Kumagai
Tokyo
October 2022

INTERNAL IMAGES: marukopum/Shutterstock.com
ADDITIONALLY: (all Shutterstock.com) Flying sparrow: Graphic Ape; Swallows: Johnny Dream; Geese: Ihnatovich Maryia; Grain shoots: Kalinin Ilya; Reeds: steshs; Germinating seeds: Kovalov Anatolii; Frost: Yojo; Frogs: Reinke Fox; Lilypads: KaliaZen; Safflowers: cuttlefish84; Wheat: Olga Illi; Fireflies: display intermaya; Heal-all: Stella choi; Iris: Anna Chelnokova

Zephyr is an imprint of Head of Zeus.
At Zephyr we are proud to publish
books you can read and re-read
time and time again because they tell
a brilliant story and because they
entertain you.

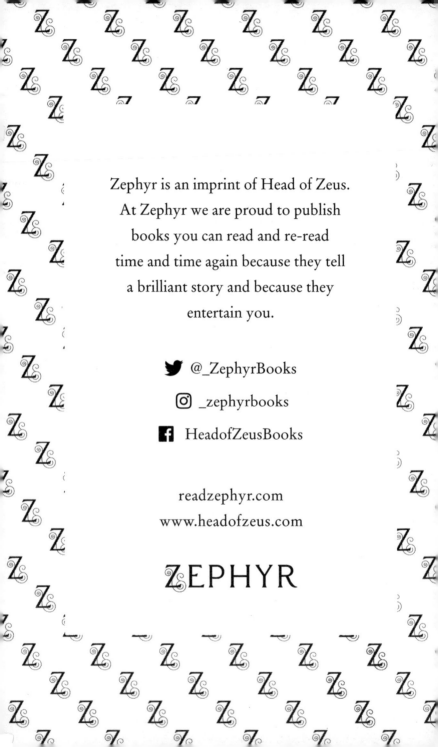 @_ZephyrBooks

_zephyrbooks

HeadofZeusBooks

readzephyr.com
www.headofzeus.com

ZEPHYR